PEOPLE LIKE US

ALSO BY JASON MOTT

Hell of a Book

The Crossing

The Wonder of All Things

The Returned

The First

We Call This Thing Between Us Love

Hide Behind Me

PEOPLE LIKE US

OR

The Other Continent

OR

*Johnny Wordcount Stumbles into
a High-End Croissant Bar
on the Seine in Search
of The Kid
& Orders The Big Dream*

JASON MOTT

DUTTON

DUTTON

An imprint of Penguin Random House LLC
1745 Broadway, New York, NY 10019
penguinrandomhouse.com

Copyright © 2025 by Jason Mott

Penguin Random House values and supports copyright. Copyright fuels creativity, encourages diverse voices, promotes free speech, and creates a vibrant culture. Thank you for buying an authorized edition of this book and for complying with copyright laws by not reproducing, scanning, or distributing any part of it in any form without permission. You are supporting writers and allowing Penguin Random House to continue to publish books for every reader. Please note that no part of this book may be used or reproduced in any manner for the purpose of training artificial intelligence technologies or systems.

DUTTON and the D colophon are registered trademarks of Penguin Random House LLC.

BOOK DESIGN BY PATRICE SHERIDAN
Illustrations by Paul Girard

LIBRARY OF CONGRESS CATALOGING-IN-PUBLICATION DATA

Names: Mott, Jason, author.
Title: People like us : or The other continent, or Johnny Wordcount stumbles into a high-end croissant bar on the Sienne in search of The Kid & orders the big dream / Jason Mott.
Other titles: People like us, or The other continent, or Johnny Wordcount stumbles into a high-end croissant bar on the Seine in search of The Kid and orders the big dream
Description: New York : Dutton, 2025.
Identifiers: LCCN 2024052736 | ISBN 9798217047116 (hardcover) | ISBN 9798217047130 (ebook)
Subjects: LCGFT: Novels.
Classification: LCC PS3613.O8444 P46 2025 | DDC 813/.6—dc23/eng/20250224
LC record available at https://lccn.loc.gov/2024052736

ISBN: 9798217178704 (export)

Printed in the United States of America
1st Printing

The authorized representative in the EU for product safety and compliance is Penguin Random House Ireland, Morrison Chambers, 32 Nassau Street, Dublin D02 YH68, Ireland, https://eu-contact.penguin.ie.

To the Ones Like You:

You sing.

You dance.

You bleed like the sunrise sky.

RIGHT OFF THE BAT

Whole fistfuls of this actually happened, sister!

So, to keep the lawyers cooling their heels instead of kicking down the front door with those high-priced Italian loafers of theirs, some names and places have been given the three-card monte treatment and this whole damned thing has been fitted with a fiction overcoat. Some people—and even entire sauce-reducing countries—have been punched up a bit for the sake of laughs and the inevitable hard-sell gut punch, but, just for the record, the Frenchies are actually pretty aces once you get to know them. Really.

Now, if you read this and you think you're not one to be taken in by a con job—I mean, you feel like you know who's really on the chopping block here—and if that particular You-Know-Who that you've got all figured out has enough cash on hand to send the aforementioned loafer-wearing sharks after me because I said something ol' Daddy Warbucks wouldn't like said in public, well, then that part of the story was just coincidence and parody. Straight for laughs.

Lastly, if I ever get backed into a corner about some detail I don't want to go into, I'll just offer up a five-star smile and swear on a stack of *Raising Arizona* DVDs that I made it all up. Even if it really happened. So don't even bother.

And if I'm ever asked about whether or not we're all going to be okay in the end?

. . . Well . . . cynicism is the refuge of a world-weary heart.

—THE AUTHOR
(WITH LEGAL BREATHING DOWN HIS NECK)

PEOPLE LIKE US

Behold. Forty-four-year-old him. A low-budget, Black Jack London shivering in the frozen north called Minnesota.

Not a bad place to be—all points on the timeline considered.

He's at the age of early evening bedtimes and early morning ibuprofen. The muffin top that stalked him for the last couple of decades is finally here to stay but, depending on who you ask, he carries it well enough. This is officially midlife. Gray hair. Gentle whiffs of arthritis. Nothing really heals anymore. Every year on his birthday his doctor sticks her finger up his ass, digging for cancer like it's the last corner of peanut butter in the jar, without so much as a kiss on the cheek or a high five when she's done. Usually, she's out of the room before he can pull his pants up.

Middle age ain't for the faint of heart.

But, it's a decent life.

Outside the Minneapolis airport, he's escorted through the cold of the parking deck to a black SUV, caked with road salt and ice, by a thin-framed man with one of the best Afros he's ever seen who, from what Soot understands, was the driving force behind bringing him here to speak in the wake of the dead.

"We're so glad you could make it," the man says. "I mean, you really just don't know how much this means to us. Especially after . . . well, after everything."

Soot nods and smiles. Plays it solemn, because solemn is what it is.

In his defense, the dead weren't dead a year ago, back when he agreed to come. The living only became the dead last week. Unlucky weather.

It's under thirty degrees and dropping. There's a cold blow on the way. Billowing frost. Snow the size of horseflies. Wind that makes you regret life choices. Usual fare around these parts. Foreign landscape for him. "You all get this kind of cold often?" he asks, realizing, as his teeth chatter, that the jacket he brought from home isn't going to cut it.

"It's always on its way," the man says.

"I'm a Southern boy," Soot replies. "To me, dressing for the cold just means 'Add sleeves and pray on it.'"

Laughter.

███████████ College has paid him—in advance—to come here and talk about his book, because that's what he's done for over a decade now. It's simple enough, or at least it's become so: talk about America through the lens of his Black skin, his fear of police, and his loss.

"So, how are people?" he asks the man behind the wheel. The guy holds a phone in each hand as he drives, steering with forearms and knees over the slick roads, both phones chanting different directions at him. The car drifts, only for the guy to snatch it back after a few seconds. For sure, Soot's making conversation in part so that the man will put the phones down and keep the two of them alive.

"So, how are people?" he asks a second time.

This time, the man answers, finally looking away from the two phones and yanking the car back into its lane yet again. "People?" he says slowly, like he forgot what the word means. "People are . . . you know . . . we're . . . we're resilient." Soot hates that word. "People are doing the best they can, all things considered," the guy continues. He grins as he says the words, as if he's trying to smile to fix something that can't be fixed, but he's trying anyway. "I won't pretend like people are okay. They're definitely not okay. But what can you do? Things are the way they are." His voice trembles at the end. He clears his throat. "I'm really glad you decided to come," he says. "I mean, I don't think you understand just how much this means to all of us. I don't think you get just how much we need you."

"Just trying to help," Soot says. He still hasn't recovered from the cold, so he fidgets with the car's air-conditioning vents and the thermostat. Plenty of heat rolls out, but no warmth.

"You're definitely going to help," the man says. "I had some friends who were at Mississippi when those students got shot and you showed up there. They said you really helped out. They said you told them all the things they didn't know they needed to hear. Like about what happened to your dad, and your daughter. I respect how you can go back to wounds like that and open them up. I could never do it."

It's hard for the guy to talk and listen to his two cell phones and steer/slide over the ice and be resilient all at the same time. The car is all over all three lanes of highway and Soot starts to think it might be better to just shut up and let the guy get him there alive.

"Good to know," Soot says, deciding not to say any more for a while.

"It's all going to be okay, now that you're here," the man says.

For the rest of the drive the two of them ride in silence. Soot focuses on staying warm and on trying not to get overwhelmed by the thought that the SUV might suddenly wind up in a ditch.

The cold blow moves in as promised. It's not just the ice sliding the SUV around anymore. The wind has signed on, giving more than a gentle nudge and covering the windshield with snow. The road is crowded with cars, even as the night turns white and the windows begin to freeze over around the edges, and the pit of Soot's stomach starts to flutter as he stares out the window and imagines what might happen to someone alone in this type of world.

Eventually, Soot and the man arrive at the hotel. It's just off campus and, if it weren't covered in snow, he would see the school colors decorating the outside of the building and he would be impressed.

"Here we go," the guy says as Soot opens the SUV door. The cold grabs him by the leg. "I'll be by tomorrow evening to pick you up for the dinner with the faculty. They're eager to hear what you have to say about all this, you know?"

They shake hands.

"I'll try to do what I can," Soot says.

"Speak truth to power?" the man says.

"What?"

"I was thinking about that. That's what writers do, right? They speak truth to power. But that's not really your gig, though, is it? You sorta speak to grief. So what do you say? To grief, I mean. Something about hope?"

Soot sighs. He knows what the man wants. He doesn't want to wait until tomorrow evening, when he and the others are all together, grieving over the deaths of their students and trying to understand how this thing finally really happened to their school. He needs to start feeling something other than loss. Something other than grief and pain.

The cold keeps moving in. Everything tightens up. Hardens. But he knows he can't get out without giving the man something.

Soot steps out onto the icy ground, grabs his luggage from the back seat, and stands in the door of the black SUV with his hands in his pockets, shivering just a little already, and says, "It all comes out okay."

"You say it like you know for sure," the man says.

"Imagine that I can travel through time. And I know, for a fact, that you'll get through this," Soot says. "And imagine I tell you 'It all comes out okay.'"

The man offers a nervous smile. The kind of smile you give to a bully when you can't tell if they're being sincere or just walking you up to the moment when they punch your teeth in. "You're different" is all the man says.

"It helps though, doesn't it?"

Then he closes the vehicle door and hustles toward the hotel, losing body heat with each step, while the storm blows harder and the snow comes down fatter, and he can barely see his hand in front of his face, and everything behind him and ahead of him disappears. He stops, freezing as he is, and turns and looks back. The light shines in his eyes, centered somewhere ahead of him now, with snow dancing around it like a swarm of moths, and, somehow, Soot swears he hears a type of music buried in the wind, a gentle, delicate song, like wind chimes trying to speak.

You could feel it in your bones. You could taste it on the air. The change, I mean. You could smell it in the vendors standing outside the courthouses selling hot dogs to the angry, raised fists. You could hear the songs bouncing off every surface until they broke your ears and, even if you didn't know the words, you somehow found a way to sing along.

Yessir, sister! There was music riding on the wind! Like the flag herself was trying to speak! I swear on Nic Cage's sanctified hairline, it was one hell of a summer! Pure ticker tape! The American Dream finally came a'knocking and, sister, for once we were all at home and didn't miss out! But, hell, I don't have to tell you; you were there!

Every street in every city was full up to busting with the tomorrow we'd all been holding out for. Milk and honey fell straight from the sky. Buildings shook, from the penthouse ceiling fans right down to the basement wall sockets. Yes ma'am, all the promises that had been made were finally coming due and everything was up for grabs! And the bad things? Well, they were done for. Finally given a Chicago Overcoat by all of us. And just like everybody else, I was drunk on it. The whole thing was like watching the ocean turn upside down. Like watching a cow body-slam a crocodile. North was South and South was making love to Marilyn Monroe.

And then, when things were shining brighter than they had in decades and decades, then even the big boys got involved. Every John and Jane Bull in the upper crust looked out their tinted C-suite windows and rolled up the shades on their private jet windows and saw which way the wind was blowing. So they got on the phone and made the big calls down to all the little people and they said, "We're getting in the game, baby!"

The dollars flowed.

Money broke out of the banks like it had been convicted of a crime it didn't commit. A neo gold rush flowed from on high. A pure gully washer—as my Old Man might have put it—filling even the lowest crevices, and all aimed at the people in the dark skin.

"Put a sticker on your window, sister, and watch the bucks come rolling in!" the world said. "Hell! Don't even bother with the sticker. Your skin is your sticker! This time capitalism will find you. It'll come knocking at your front door and, even if you're not willing to let it in, it'll kick open the door and swell up the coffers and you'll be in the best state you've ever been in. You'll finally get all the things that you've been promised!"

Yes ma'am, we all know that the way capitalism apologizes for all the things it's done is with even more capitalism. And, in case you weren't there, that summer it was all on the line. It was all flowing from the font of the Amalgamation of Capital and, if you were there, it was something to see! The Summer of The Great Get Back! That's what somebody should have called it.

They never did because that's a terrible name, but you get the idea.

We were all flying high. Things were finally starting to come together. The streets were full of feet, fists, and voices. Pure inundation. Folks piled in like sediment. So much that the traffic of America and, by proxy, America herself, had no choice but to put on the brakes. Some folks will tell you that it was the plague outside that brought the Great Girl to a standstill. And I won't say that's untrue, but I'll say we did our part too.

Yes ma'am, The Great Nation herself came to a screeching halt and rolled down her windows and looked out to see what game was on the play. And, yeah, some folks in cars shook their fists and cursed certain people's names. But others got out and decided to dance and sing along. Most folks, if I'm being honest, just sat there in the chilly armpit of their air-conditioning and turned up the radio and settled back into their seats and waited for the road ahead to clear and for things to get back to normal. But that's beside the point.

The point here is that it was something to see. It was like watching Sisyphus—a man who never skips leg day—finally get that super-size rock of his farther up that hill than he ever did before. And, just for a second, you can believe that, hell, maybe he'll finally get it over the top. You're looking over at him and you find out, somehow, that drumbeat you're hearing is none other than your very own heart beating in *his* chest. You can feel his muscles straining. You can feel the pressure building with each step. You can't tell if it's him pushing that rock so close to the rim of escape or if it's you. And you don't care which. You're too far in. Too much a part of it.

That's the thing about change that promises to be on the upside: We can't help but buy in. We all love an underdog story.

So folks got onboard. Damned near the whole world got out of their cars, closed the Pornhub tabs, turned off their phones, and cheered. All it had taken to get us here was a few dead bodies.

But regardless of the buy-in, the payout was the same: There we were, watching it all change. Watching it burn with our lumber ready to rebuild it better than it had ever been. This was the turning point in the flesh. This time, when the dust settled, the scar left on Old Glory wouldn't wash off. No ma'am! This time we'd burn a demarcation line into the Stars and Stripes!

This was it. This was the "one day" Al Green sang about.

Near the height of it, during those long days under that summer sun, we ran wild with optimism. We all hugged and kissed, made apologies and promises. Even some of the cynics had to bow down in the light of the dawning day. Lady Liberty looked better than she had since she got strung out on cinematic-universe escapism.

Wooooo! What a time! Enough to leave a body breathless . . .

. . . But then the fall came.

That north wind rolled in on us. And, well, the fires turned to embers and the embers faded out, and all those tense muscles everyone had been using to change the world needed a rest.

Try not to blame them. Stamina for this sort of thing takes a lifetime to learn. You can't get it in just a single summer. But while the wind blew and the embers cooled, the streets began to clear and you could hear the old engines of America fire up again and drop into gear. Traffic started moving.

We made a promise that this wasn't a full stop, just a break. Just a chance for those who'd gotten caught up in it all to finally make it back home and cook dinner and throw in a load of laundry and walk the dog and eat a quick meal and fuck—as a way of celebrating, you understand!—and lie there sweaty and panting and still slick with satisfaction and maybe make a kid to commemorate all that they'd done and one day tell that kid about "That Summer We Changed Everything."

And outside their window, while they lay there, kissing and dreaming of tomorrow, the leaves turned. The oceans rolled over again back into their homes. The mountains we'd leveled picked themselves up and reclaimed their spots, looking down on us. The folks in the C-suites closed their windows. They had calls to take and deals to make.

Eventually, all that was left was a faint whiff, almost like a memory, of smoke in the air. Maybe the taste of blood in the backs of our throats. So easy for so many to wash away with a little wine.

We all went out looking for aloe on account of how The Great American Burn turned out to be nothing more than too much time in the sun. Destined to scab, peel, heal, and give us all a story to tell as the years rolled on.

Yeah, sister . . . it was a summer to remember. Then it was gone.

What's that? "Cynical"? Me?

No ma'am. I'm not one to sign on for that kind of thinking. Life's been too good to me for me to ever be a "bourbon glass half empty" kind of guy. Yeah, I've seen bad times swallow folks up—been shoved underwater by life a few times myself. I know the game. There's only one letter separating the brave from the grave, and we should all live accordingly.

As such, I've seen the back side of hurricanes. I've seen birds fight off bears and I've seen the northern lights dance a soft-shoe over Tuscaloosa. Seen a man get tossed into the air by an eighteen-wheeler and walk off laughing. I've seen an alpaca riding shotgun in a Toyota Camry in the middle of Atlanta. I've seen forty-year-old bare breasts dangled out of a Burger King drive-through window and given over to the dappled sunlight on an Easter Sunday. I knew a woman who sneezed every time she orgasmed. I've shook hands with a Black president and watched *Fury Road* in the same afternoon.

I'm someone who's seen rockets break orbit.

It's like I always say when folks come around with that old sales pitch about how things always gotta come up snake eyes in the end: Nothing in this life is duty bound to fall apart. Nothing.

Even when that summer ended, I was still a believer.

You'll take me at my word when I tell you it wasn't the end of that summer that sent me off to The Continent. It wasn't even the little bit of success that came my way not long after. No ma'am. It was something a lot more relatable than that. You ever been threatened with death in a back alley in LA?

I think maybe we all have when you really get down to it.

But here's how it happened for me:

Now, first off, if you've never been to Hollywood, the thing you gotta know is this: everything's magic. The streets smell like champagne, the stars all hang at eye level, and, if the mood hits you to hold the heavens in your hand, then all you gotta do is reach out and wrap your mitts around them.

Stardust.

All you need out in LA is stardust. Get your hands on enough of it and it can make your whole life shine. So, there I am, out West looking for my fistful of stardust. Looking for The Big Score. I spent a week meeting with the gods of Tinseltown. All the names. Ol' Stevie Spielberg, Spikey Lee, J. J. Abrams. You name them and I guarantee I sat on their waiting-room couches sipping fancy water—what folks out there in the biz call doing The Couch and Water Tour—waiting for my chance to sell them on book rights and glide out of there on easy street. Because if there's one thing I've been taught, it's that you ain't a writer without a movie or TV deal.

The week didn't go the best. I can admit that much. I wouldn't say that was exactly my fault though. I put on the best I had, really gave it the old college try! Picture me: five-foot-eleven (that's nearly half a foot taller than one Tommy Cruise, by the way), fit enough, dressed out in my finest gear. I'm talking the full getup: wool suit and jacket the color of the evening sea, a four-button vest to match, tie, fedora, and some of the best mud stompers you've ever seen. I look every bit like Bogart. Every bit like Poitier. Every bit like every other star the town is used to. "You look great!" they all say to me as I walk into each and every production company and studio. "You look like you come straight out of *The Maltese Falcon*!" they all shout. "And you exude the aroma of mahogany and supple leather!"

That one, in particular, always makes me feel like I'm doing things right. Hollywood right.

So, day after day and night after night, I bring my old-movie style to The Big Dream City. But my problem, of course, was that I was trying to sell a dream to the folks that specialize in selling dreams and I guess I was missing something, because by the end of the week all I had to show for it was a fistful of nothing. The closest thing I got to understanding where it was all going wrong was a producer over at Hulu telling me "America has moved on. So should you."

It felt like breakup advice she was giving me, so that's what I took it as. I decided that I'd head back to my hotel and start in on whatever was next on my menu. The walk is going aces, pure aces! The traffic is light and, since it's late, the city is lit up in its Friday finest. From the neighborhood where my hotel is I can look off and see all the lights from multimillion-dollar homes climbing the hills of the valley, twinkling in the smog. Beneath my feet the LA concrete is counting off my steps with what sounds like little bits of applause. At some point a crowd of tourists comes walking past and they see me wearing all my fine gear and I hear somebody say, "Is he famous? I think he's famous!" and it takes all I've got not to turn around and give them a hug.

Nothing like being mistaken for somebody who matters to turn your day on the right side of things, you know? There's magic in city lights. Magic in crowds. Magic in concrete and the sound of traffic and arguments and people singing love songs to one another. And as I get closer to my hotel there's magic in whiffs of kimchi coming from the shops of Koreatown and, if you never had it, you need to put it on your list. Yeah, sister, in spite of everything that's happened, the smell of good food and the lights of the right skyline can bring a body out of almost any darkness.

So imagine my surprise when, not two minutes later, I wind up on my back in the grime of an alley just on the edge of Koreatown and a guy I've never met before has me on the ground and he's got his index finger two-and-a-half knuckles deep inside my mouth and suddenly I'm questioning every life decision I've ever made and wondering where's all that stardust when I really need it?

Let me set the scene for you, sweetheart.

It's a little after midnight and I can't help but feel pretty good about the fact that the weather's playing fair. I mean, if you're going to get probed by a stranger, it may as well happen at a crisp sixty degrees with a light wind blowing down out of the north to keep the scent of your own panic out of your nostrils, you know?

Anyhow, one thing I've learned in life is that you should always respect someone who knows what they're doing, no matter what the thing is that they're actually doing. Because when you get right down to it, everything that gets done in this world has room for a talent. A natural. And when it comes to tackling guys in alleys and sticking mitts in their mouths, well, I think I mighta just found da Vinci.

"Beautiful!" the guy says after raking a fingertip over one of my back molars. "Just beautiful. You got something here. High quality!"

He pulls back about two knuckles and rubs the tip of his index finger against the point of my left canine. "Are they real? Don't feel like implants. But you ever hear about 3D-printed teeth? Whooo! It's something, ain't it! Life, I mean."

I want to answer his questions, but when I go to talk all that comes out is a train of vowels on account of how you can't make consonants with another person's hand in your mouth.

"It's okay," he says.

He looks down at me with steely gray eyes tucked behind a square brow stuck on a square head and rounded off by a square chin. He's got dark skin, backlit by the light pollution of La La Land, with some salt and pepper sprinkled around what looks like a week-old beard. Maybe it's the bad lighting or my panic, but he looks almost seventy. Like James Earl Jones, RIP, if he had ever decided to mainline creatine and wrestle bears in the Klondike. Personally, I always figured mauling people in the streets was a young man's game. Is that ageist?

"Nervous?" he asks.

I nod.

"Why wouldn't you be? Friend, I been where you are. But don't you worry none." His lips spread open into a grin of jubilation that also shows a mouth running at what I figure is about half capacity. His maw is a sort of Morse code of pearly whites and inky blackness. But, for what it's worth to the taxman, what teeth he's got are just about as shiny as anybody could ask for. "It all comes out okay," he says.

It's a smooth line. It helps, believe it or not.

Maybe out of fear, or maybe just because it feels like the thing to do, I reach my hand up. Just a small move to try to get him to take a few steps back and hand me back control over my favorite steak-eating orifice.

You ever realize you were making a mistake so fast it feels like you've made it before?

"Shhh!" he says, and his hand goes tight enough to make me think I've stuck the bottom half of my face into the slamming door of an '87 Cadillac. His grip radiates through my chompers and a highball of fear, adrenaline, and self-preservation races down my spine so fast you'd swear it was out for the NFL draft. Whole thing feels like that dream we all have where Halle Berry finally decided to use that spare key we mailed her that one time and she's slipped into the house while we're sleeping and she's waking us up with kisses and a promise of curled toes and peppermint orgasms.

Only the dream turns sideways and the plot twist is that it's actually a Kodiak bear licking at that ticklish spot behind your knee.

It's enough to make anyone go limp.

So that's what I do: a full-body erectile dysfunction right there in the middle of that alley.

"What are you working on these days?" the stranger asks, holding my whole body up by just a fistful of jaw like I was a rare wordsmith bass he'd just pulled out of a river. "Got a new book coming? What's it about? Can I read some of it?"

Old question, new context.

You see, sister, a while back I wrote a book that did well. Real well. And, when you make up a story that does well, folks always want to know what you're onto next. I've got a whole fistful of good answers for that question. A veritable roulette wheel of publicist-approved replies:

A. "You kidding? I'm always up to something new!"
B. "Of course! True fictioneers don't wait for inspiration!"
C. "Giving it all I got every second of every day, just keep an eye out on social media for updates!"

My publisher's big on option C. Like most of the players in the ever-merging and no-holds-barred book game these days, the team back in sales and marketing is stone certain that we're always one tweet away from a runaway bestseller. Personally, telling people to meet me on the socials ain't my favorite, but it's solid enough to throw into rotation now and again. For the record, my personal favorite, hands down, is option D: "It's already written, my friend! Nothing left to do but put it down on the page!"

I squeeze one of those rounds out of the chamber. I think it's the one about inspiration. Keep in mind though, he's still knuckle-deep in my mouth, so it's only a tube sock's worth of vowels that comes limping out. But he somehow gets it. He keeps the conversation moving in lockstep.

"That's great," he says. "Hot damn!"

I burble more vowels of optimistic enthusiasm.

Then his fingers go relaxed and he finally pulls his hand out of my mouth and my body barely fires up in time to keep from melting right there on the sidewalk. I wobble a little and fall back on my butt while he watches and digs into his pocket for a travel-size bottle of sanitizer, cleans his hands, squats down on these tree-trunk-size haunches he's got, and offers me the bottle.

"No, thanks," I say. "I never accept sanitizer from strange men."

"You're a good guy," he says, grinning that peekaboo smile of his. "You know that?" He eases back off his heels and takes a seat in the middle of the alleyway with his legs spread like a toddler. In spite of how old he looks, he seems full of energy.

The pale glare of a far-off streetlight bounces off his half-bald skull and makes a halo, like he might be someone from the old days of fire and brimstone that I could have avoided if I'd just spent a little more time in Jesus's local annex. That building with all the lowercase t's hanging from the walls.

Down at the end of the alley a car rolls by, its tires making an exhausted sigh on the pavement as it passes. I glance around, half thinking about running and half hoping that somebody will come walking by and notice what's going on here. But one of the trademarks of LA is that it's damned hard to get noticed.

You can live and be killed twice in this town and never get noticed.

"I'd ask you how often you brush," my new friend says, "but I don't really have to. That mouth of yours is everything I knew it would be. But . . ." He reaches forward and pats me gently on my leg. "You got a small crack in there. Second molar, left side. Top."

"Yeah?"

"Yeah."

It feels like I let him down somehow.

"Go get it looked at," he says. "Next time I see you I want you to have it fixed. I want to see a good, quality filling in there."

"Next time?"

He lunges forward so fast I hardly see it and grabs my hand and shakes with a grip that could crack oysters.

"Name's Remus." He deals it straight. Like he's at a job interview. "John J. Remus. My friends call me Remus." The palm of his hand feels like sandpaper and bad decisions.

With him out of my mouth and square in front of me, I can finally get a good look at him:

His shirt is plaid and his stained jeans seem like they rolled off the very first blue-jean assembly line ever made. And whenever it was that those boots of his came into this world, I'd bet a week's pay it was before Betty White was born. The leather worn through so that the steel toe beneath catches the streetlights and shines like a silver dollar at the bottom of a well.

Even though I'm not the biggest fan of what just happened, as much as I hate to admit it, this Remus character's got a way about him. Everything he says sorta ripples with charm. All blue skies and chocolate ice cream, this voice of his. Like he's been through his whole life and only ever met best friends, one after another. But when he finally releases me from that iron handshake and sits again in the middle of the alley, I see the scars.

Those sledgehammer paws of his have been ripped down and put back together and ripped down again. Just scars on scars on scars, especially around the knuckles. I can already tell that John J. Remus was the type of man who, if he ever had a dollar in his life, he spent ten and never stopped to worry about where he'd find the other nine to make up the difference because all of life was just a road to a final destination, and whether he reached that destination tomorrow or thirty years from now, it didn't mean shit if he didn't have a story to tell when he got there.

"You okay?" he asks. Maybe he's curious about why I've gone all quiet.

"Sure," I say.

"Good. Because I want you to be ready for this next part."

"Next part?"

"I want to tell you something and I don't want you to get all bent out of shape about it."

"Why would I get bent out of shape?" I ask. "Is this more about my teeth? Because I can promise you, I'm getting these babies checked out just as soon as this little encounter of ours is over with. Yes sir, you've scared me straight. Nothing but grade A dental care for me from here on out. You can bet on that!"

"Nah, nah, nah," he says, waving one of those torn-up hands of his.

"Okay then," I say. My stomach's starting to knot up again. For a while there it had calmed down. For a while there I felt like this was just going to turn into one of those strange stories you tell your friends and nobody believes. But now I'm starting to worry. Now I'm realizing that I'm in an alleyway with this guy and I'm not sure I can take him if he decides he wants to do something more. Something worse.

I look for the nearest exit, but all there is is that street at the end of the alley and there's no way I'll be able to get past my new friend Remus if he doesn't want me to. That street out there is just as unreachable as Beyoncé's bedroom.

"You really gotta promise me you won't get all bunched up on me," Remus says. "I just ain't got time for it. I mean, here I am being plenty respectful so all I'm hoping for is that you do me the favor of respecting me too."

"I already made a promise."

"No, you didn't," he says. "You said, 'Why would I get bent out of shape?'"

He's right.

"Alright," I say. "I gotcha. You're one of those 'letter of the law' types. You want a conversation to be a hallway full of locked doors."

"You got it."

"So let's you and me lock those doors. Let's lock them up and throw away the key. Be really on the up and up with one another."

Remus laughs. "Whooo! You're something else. Tongue slick as elephant snot. One of those niggas who thinks words are time and if you can string enough of them together you'll live forever."

"Okay," I say. "Dollar Store English: I promise not to freak out because of whatever you say."

"Pinky swear?" he asks.

I surprise both of us by laughing.

He offers me one of those thick, scarred hands of his with its pinky raised high. And just like we're back in a grade school cafeteria, I meet his finger with mine. Give it a tug.

We make a pact holy as Communion or agreeing to pick a friend up from the airport.

"Now," I say, "what's the big secret?"

My guess is he's one of those guys who's written a manuscript and wants me to read it. I run into that a lot. People just get a little nervous when it comes time to ask.

"I'm going to kill you," Remus says.

Well . . . seems I swung a bit high and wide on that one.

"Dear lord!" the woman in the seat next to me says. She clutches her Diet Coke and salted peanuts to her chest and, finally, for the first time since Remus entered the tale, she exhales.

"Life comes at you fast," I say. "Just sorta jumps out of the shadows, challenges you to a dance battle, and all any of us can do is try to keep up!"

We're at about thirty thousand feet with the whole of the Atlantic Ocean somewhere down there under our heels. There's one of the fattest moons I've ever seen hanging like a snow globe outside the airplane window, pushing and pulling all that ocean under us. Depending on who you ask, there's all sorts of things out in the ocean that have never been come across. All sorts of magicks and miracles. Don't know why I think about that just now, but I do.

"And that really happened to you?" the woman asks. "You're not just telling me a story?" Her name's Stephanie and she's somewhere around sixty or so, with a Midwestern accent. On her way to Italy for her daughter's third destination wedding.

You gotta love a love story.

"Well, I am just telling you a story," I say. "I'll own up to that much. But I swear on all things swearable, it's a true one."

She sucks her teeth and then let's out an actual "Hell's bells!"—something I didn't know you could still find in this world. "You're so brave," she says. "To be calm with someone threatening to kill you." She shakes her head. "So brave."

I wave her away. "Brave? Hardly, Dollface. Why do you think I'm on this plane letting out for all points Old World? Sure, the optimist in me figures he was just in it for the threat, but why not take a little time outside the States, you know? Get away from it all when 'it all' just happens to be a man with a promise of murder. Plus, it just so happens that I got tour business in old Euroland."

"You're on a book tour?"

"Always, Doll. Always."

"Well," she says, bathed in awe, "you tell a good story. I understand now. I understand how you won it."

"Yes ma'am," I say. "Probably the greatest night of my life, that night. Something I'll never forget."

"But the National Book Award," she whispers, glancing around as the words leave her lips, lest she speak too loudly and start a stampede of fans. "That's just such an honor. Even though I haven't read your book, I know it's wonderful. And I'm sorry about not knowing your name. You'll have to forgive me. I feel like such a fool."

"Don't you ever apologize for not knowing who a writer is," I say. "Hell, half the time we don't even know who we are. Haha!"

"You're so humble," she says. "And so honest."

"I try."

"You'll have to tell me your name again. I promise this time that I will not forget it."

"Don't you worry at all, sweetheart. It's okay. My name can be a bit tricky. You should see me try to fill out paperwork. I give people fits!"

"I'll write it down," she says. She grabs the airplane safety manual stuffed into the seat back pocket in front of her and sifts through her purse until she finds a pen. "And then, would you sign this for me? I want to remember this moment."

"Sure thing," I say. I sign my name over the picture of the little child in a flotation device in the middle of the sea after a plane crash. The kid is calmer than I would be in those circumstances.

"Thank you," she says, reading my bad scrawl of a signature with her face knotted up like she was staring down the Riddle of the Sphinx.

I offer my hand for a shake and give her my name: "My name, dear darling, is Ta-Nehisi Coates."

She inhales sudden and sharp. Her eyes go bright as LED high beams. "Oh my lord! I *have* heard of you! I've seen you on TV!"

Fun fact: Being Ta-Nehisi Coates every now and then ain't half bad, all things considered. If I wasn't Ta-Nehisi, I would have been somebody else. A few weeks back, somewhere over Arizona, I was Walter Mosley for a few thousand miles or so. Turns out I can be anyone you want me to be if I'm just willing to say the words.

I'm Ta-Nehisi Coates until she falls asleep on my shoulder. We ride the rest of the way to the Old Country like lovers. When it's all over, this trip will be something she can pull out at dinner parties and say, "There was this one time I met Ta-Nehisi Coates!" Her sentence will be greeted with awe and wonder and maybe even a little jealousy. And what's it hurting if it's only half true? Truth and fact ain't the same. But they're cousins who look a lot alike. Besides, one name is just as good as any other so long as nobody's out to kill you.

Too bad I'm not so lucky.

Up from North Carolina, where he lives now and where she doesn't, this Toronto isn't the one he's held in his head through these years. This one is warmer. The skyline has lost all of its hoarfrost and the noonday sun is bright enough that he has to shade his eyes with his hand. Her neighborhood is closer to the river than he remembers. It's louder. Not loud, exactly, but in his mind, there was no sound here. Only cold and dark and the weight of the past hanging over everything.

This time, he hears children playing somewhere nearby.

He knocks a second time and, for a second time, takes a step back from the door. He doesn't want to crowd her. Doesn't want this to scare her into thinking that he might reach out and hug her when they finally see each other again. That time has passed.

The door opens and at least this part is the way he remembers. She's still as tall as ever. Still stands with her hips square, as if every day of her life she's been facing off against the world, again and again and again, and the world has never gotten the better of her. Seeing her now, he's glad he took that step back. If he had been any closer to her, he would have reached out and hugged her, just like he feared.

"I'm sorry," he says. "Can we start there?"

She straightens her back and folds her arms across her chest, just like she's always done in both moments like this, and this moment. "Shut up and come in," she replies.

"Thank you," he says, and it's almost a sob, but he hides it with a stilted laugh and enters.

The inside of her home hasn't changed. It's still small, gently cluttered with photographs. A whisper of cinnamon hangs in the air. In the living room, the window is open and the curtain billows, bringing in more sounds of those children playing, wherever they are in this world.

He takes off his jacket and drapes it on his arm and sits and wishes he could keep his eyes away from the photographs of their daughter hung around the room.

His wife and daughter are smiling in Paris.

His wife and daughter are dancing in Rio.

His wife and daughter are laughing in Bolton.

Moments and places and times that will never come again now turned still and perpetual, never to leave again. In her own way, Tasha is doing the same thing he is.

"You two really put some miles in," he says.

"They were good times," Tasha replies.

"I'm glad."

His chest tightens. There are too many of the photos now. He fidgets with a speck of lint on his thigh and clears his throat and shifts in his seat and says, "It's warmer than I remember. How are things at work? Any promising students these days or is the next generation really falling apart the way everybody says?"

"Soot," Tasha begins, "why are you here?"

"To say I'm sorry."

"You did that at the door. Why are you really here?"

He can't look her in the eyes, but he also can't bear the photographs. He spots a candle on the far counter. "That's beautiful," he says. "Don't think I've ever seen one like it. Did you make it?"

"Yes," she says, never looking at the candle. Only watching him.

"I remember when you were just getting into making them. I'm glad that you got back to it. Looks like it's coming along really well."

"Thanks," she says. "Is that enough small talk?"

He chuckles. It lives and dies in a heartbeat. "Okay." He raises his head, straightens his back, calms his hands, and looks her in the eyes. "What if I told you that I could travel through time?"

"Excuse me?"

"I know."

"You mean that game you used to play with Mia?"

"Something like that. But for real."

"Okay," she says. "I'll play along."

"And there's something else."

"You mean time travel isn't enough?"

Sarcasm, but maybe he deserves it.

"The thing is, I've always been able to do it. The time travel. Always been able to go to any point in time in my life. I can go and relive it or I can go and just sorta watch myself. Over and over again. For as long as I want and as often as I want."

"That's called memory, Soot."

"It's not," he says.

She leans back in her chair. "Well, that's something very special. Good for you."

"You don't believe me."

"No. But it doesn't hurt anything to play along. We're not married anymore. However this goes, it ends with both of us back in our own lives. Or, in this case, I guess it would be 'in our own lifetimes.'"

"That's fair."

"Let me guess: you knew I was going to say that."

She smiles and, this time, it's sincere.

"I've been going back through it," he begins. "Back through everything. All those moments that we had. The good and bad, funny and weird. Piece by piece. Everything that led us to . . . well, to where we are now."

"Soot?"

"Yeah?"

"Can I ask you something?"

"About time travel?"

"About therapy."

"Oh," he says. "I guess I should have seen that one coming."

He watches the Canadian sun seep in through the window and dance on the floor, fracturing the light into a thousand glimmers. "I've been to therapy," he says. "My whole life. I'm not crazy. I promise. I think you know me better than that. This is real."

"So, what's it like?"

Finally, there's something in her voice that might be sympathy. Possibly even belief. It's the voice he used to hear back before they had a dead child between them and a failed marriage behind them.

He looks down at his hands as he speaks. "I've checked it all out, Tasha. From the very beginning, we did it all. We did everything. Yes, we made mistakes. But they were all just basic ones. The things every parent does along the way. Nothing bigger than that. We didn't leave the door open for the wolves to come rushing in. We didn't hand our daughter over to them. We didn't have something better to do. We didn't do anything to deserve what happened. And neither did she."

"Okay," she says.

"You've got to hear me."

"Sure, Soot. I hear you."

"Dammit, Tasha. Stop doing that. Please. That's not what this is. I'm not crazy. You need to know that we were good parents. That we made the right decisions. You need to know that it's not our fault." He's crying now. All at once and all of a sudden. Wiping his eyes and trying his best to keep his voice steady. "If you don't do something about it, if you don't come to grips with the way it came out, you won't make it. None of us will."

Tasha leans forward, places her elbows on her knees, and looks him in the eyes. "I'm saying this because it's the truth and because I love you: she isn't ever going to come back. This is the way things are now. If you ask me—"

"—I didn't."

". . . If you ask me, you should sell it all and leave before it kills you."

"Bolton didn't kill her, Tasha."

"I wasn't talking about North Carolina."

He stands. "I was wrong to come here," he says.

Before she can say anything else, he's out the door. Outside, he feels the sun on his face and washing down his shoulders and that warm wind that was in her house is still blowing out here and there's a smell coming off the water—all that beautiful blue water hidden behind the buildings and cars and concrete and pavement—and the temptation is to stay here, in this moment, with the dancing light and wafting water and all the photographs of his daughter still in his mind and with his wife only a few feet away and, if he had the courage, he could go back inside and fall on his knees in front of her and wail and weep and she would understand—the only person on this whole planet who would understand because her daughter is dead too—and then, right there in that moment this all might be something like healing, something like moving forward.

But there are no answers in forward.

Only the old question.

So, he leaves her and the falling, dappled light and the cold, lilting scent of the water, and whatever approximation of a future they might have had together. And inside of him, all of it comes along.

First, let's back up a bit. Do a little time traveling— metaphorically speaking. If we're gonna have any kind of future together, we can't be the type to speed past things that shouldn't be sped past. The Old Lady raised me better than that. Let's talk for a second about that word that guy used a little while back. You know the one.

Some words in this world you shouldn't say out loud no matter who you are. They're just too big. They hurt too many and reward too few. Words that should never roll off a civilized tongue. The N-word is one of them. And so, while I'm not one to say it—I've learned to be a little too classy for that and Sharon tells me that dropping that word can hurt book sales—I will break my own code and I'll say it here once, just to clarify that we're on the same page, and I promise I'll never say it again. No ma'am. Just the one time to clarify terms. Gird your emotional loins, my friend. Here we go. The N-word.

National Book Award.

Makes me shudder every time.

Hope I didn't scare you off. From here on out I promise I'll use, as the Frenchies say, a *name-de-plum* for it. We'll just call it "The Big One."

Yeah. A fistful of years back—before I had a man promise to kill me in a back alley in Los Angeles—I did it. I took down The Big One. "Sure was a hell of a book!" people said. And they said it all the way to the top of the dream heap.

The N-word's a pretty small club to be in. Hardly enough for a group discount at Best Western. And I wouldn't exactly say that The Big One makes you famous on account of how this writing gig actually works. It's not really a signs, billboards, and ticker tape parades kind of racket. Takes a rare bird to actually spot a writer in a crowd.

Even though it was a few years back now, everybody still wants to know what it was like. Wants to hear the against-all-odds story that turned out to be the winning ticket. A true, dyed-in-the-wool, happy ending.

So, what's it like winning The Big One? Well, let's just say it's everything and all the more. A real first-love-and-fireworks type of deal. Like waking up and finding your bed full of Nic Cage's entire catalog of work.

It all went down in the early fall, which, I guess, is as good of a time as any to have your life changed. It was the first year after The Plague and I'd finally fired off a new book and, even though the sales weren't much to write home about, the critics gave it the nod. Some folks went out and read it and, depending on who you asked, it might have even meant something to them. And then, just when I thought the book was fading into the rearview—having done a half-decent job, but not set the world on fire—one day Sharon calls me up and says, "Hey. Guess what? You're in line for The Big One."

Naturally, I thought she was yanking my crank.

"This is it," she says. "I can feel it."

For the record, Sharon's my agent. We've been paired up for quite a while. If you need an image in your head that tells you who she is, imagine that someone took the New York City skyline, wrapped it in Dolce & Gabbana, and gave it the cheekbones and skin tone of Kerry Washington. She's one of these no-nonsense boss ladies with a heart of gold. For instance: this one time, when this kid got shot, she . . .

On second thought, never mind. That's an old story. I'll come back later and give you a little about this certain Kid who's got more than a little to do with where we're going on this ride but, for now, onward and upward.

Anyhow, I've never been one to bet the farm on gut feelings but, a couple of months later, it's mid-November and I'm standing on a stage with Oprah in the swankiest hotel ballroom I've ever seen and she shakes my hand and gives me a newborn baby's worth of sculped bronze and, just like that, there I was. Freshly minted. A bona fide Author of Some Renown.

Signs and wonders, as my dear departed mama used to say.

One thing about it, rolling out into the world as a new Author of Some Renown showed me that it's better to be lucky than good. Now, that's not to say that I didn't have a part in my own success. My therapist says we all got the bad habit of buying into the bad and passing the buck when it comes to the good. She's a pretty sharp dame and I'd second-guess anybody who second-guessed her. So I won't sit here and say it was all fate and planetary alignments. I did my part just like all the other folks in the category.

But, at a certain point in the game, everybody's the cat's pajamas and it's anybody's game. I didn't win because I was better than everyone else. I just won because I won.

Most folks don't know this, but when you win The Big One they give you an eight-pound statue to take home. Handcrafted bronze. Looks like sheets of paper all rolled up and stood on end. What they don't tell you is there's a hole at the top shaped just like a shot glass and, well, when celebration time came, the team who helped bring that book to market knew what to do.

A few days after the win I'm in the Big Apple on my publisher's rooftop with about eighty bookmakers of different stripes, all doing shots of Cross-Genre from the throat of my N-word statue. A Cross-Genre is moonshine, champagne, and a dash of strawberry syrup. Someone in Cover Design tried calling it a Faulkner's Lament, but one of the ladies in Marketing said, "A title like that will never sell out West" as she tossed her bra over the guardrail and took another shot.

Fun fact: never give publishing folks an open bar and a reason.

In their defense, we'd all just come through The Plague Years so I guess everyone was trying to come out swinging, if only to prove they hadn't been broken by all the loneliness The Plague gave us. And come out swinging they did! Mardi Gras can't hold a candle to this shindig. There're more than a few fully naked partiers. A couple of people dressed as characters from books and as authors—you haven't lived until you've seen Frankenstein's monster and Jane Austen doing the Milk and Water Embrace in a bathroom stall. All the while there are flashing lights providing a rhythm to celebrate to. Yes ma'am, the bookworms turned up the heat and baked the Big Apple that night!

And I was the star of the show.

I shook hands and gave out high fives until my carpal tunnel started kicking up while that new statue of mine made the rounds, delivering good times to the mouths of anybody so inclined. And there were plenty of inclined people, take my word on that one. And, all the while, I never let it out of my sight. Not even for a moment. Because the truth is that that's what a person does when they win The Big One. They cling to it like a long-lost lover.

So, while I'm standing there watching the good times shake the heavens, Sharon comes walking over, dressed in what I can only call "wealth couture." It's a red, formfitting gown that hangs low on the shoulders and climbs high on the thigh and moves like it's made out of water and liquid cash. There's enough gold and platinum on her wrist and neck to make Mansa Musa envious. At the sight of her, the whole inebriated publishing house crowd parts and she becomes Moses slicing through the Hedonistic Sea.

"Big winner!" she says. "I've got amazing news for you!" She's bleary-eyed and her vowels hang on her tongue a little too long. She pokes me in the chest with her phone at the end of each sentence.

"I figured my life was pretty full up on good news right now," I say, watching one of the guys from Cover Design carry my statue around in his jockstrap.

Sharon leans in and pokes me in the chest with her phone again.

"The Continent is calling."

I don't have to ask what she means. I already know the score: The Old Country. Land of Gauls. The Near East. Home of Universal Health Care and unshaved nether regions.

Europe.

"That's right!" Sharon says. "An international fucking book tour. The best of Italy and France."

"When?"

"Immediately! All expenses paid. You lucky bastard!" She sounds so much like a football coach after The Big Game that I'm waiting for her to slap me on the ass.

"No foolin'?! And a full ride?"

"A full ride," she says.

"Whose dime? Publisher?"

Sharon laughs. "Hell no! You've got a benefactor over there. He wants to meet you."

"Got a name?"

Sharon pauses for dramatic effect. She actually licks her lips.

"██████ fucking ██████."

I feel my sphincter tighten and my toes curl.

"Exactly."

"You mean to tell me, ████ fucking ██████ read my book—which is already a big fish to swallow—and he's so hung up on it that he's giving me a prepaid trip to Euroland?"

"Fuck yes," Sharon says. "Everyone in Europe reads everything. They're smarter than us. And he's one of the smartest people on the planet. Shit! And all that money!" Her words are slurred a little on account of all the Cross-Genres she's had. She leans in and whispers in my ear: "They're going to love you over there," her breath smelling like paint thinner and strawberries. "They know how to treat people like *you*." One more phone poke in my chest.

"People like me?"

"You should see it," Sharon begins. She throws an arm over my shoulder and points a manicured finger out toward the east. We both look out. Past Lady Liberty. Past Brooklyn. Past JFK, Long Island, and whatever unknown sea monsters might be spending that particular moment devouring a ship in the middle of the Atlantic. We look off into the distance together, long and hard, until the City of Lights comes into view. Fuzzy and shimmering at first, like fireflies over a midnight pond. Then it comes into focus. Clear as Christmas. Every angle of the Arc de Triomphe. Every cobblestone. Every croissant and unpronounceable pastry sitting patiently in the windows of that sleeping city where existentialism first came into the world. We can both see it. Just then. In that moment. "It's not like it is over here," Sharon says slowly, weighing down each word, like she's in a dream. "Over there, you can be who you are."

And then Paris snaps away all of a sudden on account of someone from Copy Editing vomiting on my shoes. Once she's done, she plants a soft, slightly bevomited kiss on my cheek and says: "You deserve this." Then she's off back into the party, which is still, somehow, ratcheting itself up a few decibels.

"The Continent . . ." Sharon picks up, taking my face in her hands, not bothering to wipe away the vomit on my cheek. "It's gonna be everything in this world that beautiful can be. It's going to reinvent who you are and leave you a whole new man. My first time there changed me." She turns and looks back at the crowd around us. The music is thick as cotton in my ears and there's a haze of what smells like marijuana vape mist, but I can see that Sharon's looking for someone while she talks. "Once you get out of here, it's going to be earthshaking. The water is cleaner. The air is fresher. Yeah, maybe the French can be a little rude, but not to you. Hell no! Nobody on this planet treats authors better than Europeans. They've been taught to listen to people like us."

There's that phrase again.

"You know what I mean?"

I nod, pretending I do, which, sometimes, is the best way to get people to explain things you don't understand.

"They don't dice us up into pieces over there. We get to be just human, you know?"

I'm finally picking up what she's putting down. You see, and this is a well-kept secret that I'm letting you in on here: in small, private circles, in hushed tones and with frequent peeks over their shoulders, some people talk about the existence of a legendary place where everything's gravy. A place where a certain type of folks—folks that happen to feel cut off at home and isolated—fit in. Where breathing comes easy.

It doesn't really have a name. All the legends say for sure is that it's somewhere in Europe, but nobody's been able to nail down exactly where. Or, if they do know where it is, nobody's telling. Either way, Sharon seems to say it's out there.

"I've heard the legends," I say. "I just thought it was a story though. Like lottery revenue actually going to support education."

"Nope," Sharon says. "It's out there. Europe's the land of milk and honey for people like us. God! I wish I could go with you!"

"You're not coming?"

"No," she says, staring off into the crowd, looking for something. "I'm trying to get Stephen King to blurb one of my debut authors' books, and anytime you're dealing with the Stephen King Industrial

Complex, it requires three blood oaths, a fatted calf, an altar, and everything else I've got. The Obamas don't ask for as much blood as the SKIC!"

Fun fact: the Obamas are a sore subject for me. Ol' Mr. President himself came close to giving us his seal of approval on my last book, but word is he got wind of how I sat out November 2012—because I figured he already had reelection in the bag—and when you come begging for a blurb, that type of civic inaction turns out to be a bad look. All Sharon and I got from him when we asked for the blurb was an email that said "Nah, homie."

"Anyhow," Sharon says, "where is *he*?" She looks me in the eyes finally, the glow of the Big Apple washing over her brown skin. "He's part mine, you know. After all the work I put into that book. After all the work I've put into you. He owes me. You both do!"

I chuckle. "Just be gentle with him. He's bronze but fragile."

"Ain't we all?" She finally spots what she's looking for across the room and one of her eyebrows goes up like a cat that's caught wind of supper. "By the way, anything new with that guy who's out to kill you?"

"Nah," I say, a sudden shiver running down my spine. Somehow, I'd forgotten that.

"Good," Sharon says.

"I'm sure it was just a one-off. Just one of those threats that Joe and Jane Sentencewriter get."

"Not at all," Sharon says, tucking her phone into her bra. She takes a deep breath and, before she starts off in the direction of the man taking shots from my N-word statue, she says, straight out: "He's going to find you and kill you and maybe take out a few of those shiny teeth of yours in the process. Bet on it, my friend!"

My stomach is in my shoes just then because I swear, at the end there, it's Remus's voice coming out of her high-end New Yorker mouth. Just as gravelly. Just as foreboding.

Now, the thing to know, if you don't already, is that I've got a condition. It plays tricks on me sometimes. More on that a little later. But the long and short of it is this: sometimes imagination is the only weapon and the only salvation we have in this world.

Just then there's fireworks booming and crackling overhead and a rainbow of lights comes crashing down on all of us. The whole rooftop cheers. The wind rises up and so does the music and, for a moment, it's hard to breathe but I can't really say why. Sharon darts off into the party and snatches my big award out of some proofreader's bra, kisses it on the orifice, and disappears in the direction of the elevator to do god knows what to it.

Maybe I'd do something to stop her—if only so that my award doesn't get crushed in whatever sex act she's got planned for it—but I've got other concerns. Off in the distance, to the east, I can see something shadowy, way out there past the fireworks and cheers. Something that's not quite Paris but also not quite New York. Some thing. Old and wandering and wondering, rising up out of the ocean, touching air for the first time since before humans built huts. The air crackles. Lightning claps. The moon trembles, all at this *thing*.

. . . Or maybe it's not a thing. Maybe it's some place, waking up, rolling over, and marking time until we get to shake hands. Or maybe it's just my condition kicking up again. I mean, you can't feel a place you've never actually been, can you?

The next morning I wake up in my hotel room to find my N-word statue in its box outside my hotel door looking a little worse for wear and smelling like, well, I hesitate to say on account of delicate sensibilities.

I pick it up with a towel—gentle-like, the way you would a puppy that's gotten into something they had no business being a part of—and take it to the bathroom and put it under the waterworks and turn the heat up to scald-the-shame-away hot.

"You gonna make it?" I ask. "God only knows what she did to you, old boy. But I'm sure it was a novel's worth all by itself."

I stop and stare out the window for a moment. I imagine I can see Paris again, like last night. I think about ▮▮▮ fucking ▮▮▮▮▮. I think about all that milk and all that honey ahead of me. I think about Remus. I think about people like me.

"Maybe I should get a gun."

Minnesota again . . .

He fidgets with a single thread that's worked itself loose from the stitching along the hem of the white linen tablecloth and hopes that none of them knows about the gun under his jacket. He is unaware that they are all watching and waiting. "Excuse me," someone says, and he bolts up in a real-life jump scare.

He looks at each of them with a raised eyebrow, then around the room, getting his bearings.

"I'm sorry," the woman in front of him says. She's middle-aged with blond hair, a silver pantsuit, and makeup enough that it gives her skin a waxy sheen, like one of Madame Tussaud's creations come to life and forced into academic research. "Are you okay?" she asks.

He thinks for a second. Feels a gust of chilly air around his ankles as someone across the room opens the door.

The dining hall is small and cramped, but they've done their best to dress it up. The college emblem hangs on the far wall, a beautiful field of green bordered by gold. There are six tables in the room and more than thirty people, all dressed for warmth and grieving. On the far side of the room a wall of windows looks out at the ice storm as it blows in silence, a foot and a half of snow doing the best it can to brighten up the night.

"Minnesota again," he says.

Not long after realizing when he is, he notices the room staring. They lean back in their chairs. Crane their necks. All silent. All watching. He forgets about the loose thread and sits up straight—and professional—in his chair, clears his throat, and says, "Sorry about that. I drifted off. Where were we?"

"We're all fucked up," the woman in the pantsuit—Caroline?—continues. She smiles with her mouth, but not with her eyes, as she speaks. "Sorry about my language."

"Don't be."

The rest of the room turns back in their chairs, maybe to give her sadness a little privacy. Or maybe just because food can be a good distraction sometimes. The whole room smells like garlic and chicken, thyme, and, somewhere underneath it all, the scent of dark chocolate drifts over from the dessert table in the corner.

"I'm sorry," Caroline says again.

The volume of the room quickly blossoms from silence to murmur to chatter. They think that if they talk loud enough—weather, politics, recipes, vacation stories—then they won't be able to hear Caroline when she starts talking about the dead.

"They haven't even been buried yet," she says. Then she laughs, but catches it as soon as it hits the air. "Sorry," she repeats, lowering her eyes.

"It's okay," he says. "Really. You know, I offered to reschedule." The seven other people at his table, teachers all of them, nod. "Truth is, the only thing I wanted was to get out of this. To be anywhere else but here."

"So why did you come?" a man on the far side of the table asks. He's in his mid-thirties. Black. His hair is tapered low and his beard immaculate. "You shouldn't be here."

"David . . ." the middle-aged man with thick glasses and a paisley tie sitting beside him says.

"It's okay," Soot says. "Hell, he's right. It's too soon, if you ask me. I probably shouldn't be here."

"But you are," Caroline says, preempting David. "You know something about this. You've been through this before."

"Yes and no," Soot says. "I've never been where you are. I've taught here and there along the way, but never lost any students the way you have. But I've talked to people like you. It's a strange club to be in." He smiles to soften their reality, if only just a little.

"So what do we do?" Caroline asks.

"Talk about something else," David says. He leans back in his chair and folds his arms. Glowers.

"That's not a bad idea," Soot says. "In fact, I'm going to go splash a little water on my face. But I'll be right back."

He gets up from the table before anyone can stop him and walks into the bathroom. After checking to be sure that he's alone, he stretches his back and rubs his hand over his scalp and tries not to think of how old she would be if she were still alive. Tries not to think about the school colors on display, the banners hanging in the banquet room, the Minnesota Pride sign painted four feet tall on the back of the bathroom door.

He adjusts the gun beneath his jacket. Looks himself over in the mirror. The gun hardly shows.

He exhales.

"You're okay," he says. "You're okay."

Then the door opens and in walks David. He looks bigger than he did sitting at the table. He also looks more focused on his intentions. He walks past Soot and looks under the stalls to be sure the two of them are alone. Then he turns and says, "Fuck you, nigga."

"Yeah," Soot says, running his hands under the faucet.

"They were good kids, nigga. They deserved better than this. Better than a vulture like you showing up here a week after they die." He paces a little as he speaks, the soles of his shoes clicking on the bathroom tiles with each step. He walks with his chest forward and his hands trembling at his sides. Now and again, he turns them to fists, but probably only to stop the shaking.

"My daughter used to dream of coming here," Soot says. "I couldn't even tell you why. She wanted to come to this college before she even knew what college was. She was a funny kid like that. One night her, my wife, and I were watching TV and there was this show on talking about the football team here. We weren't football fans, but there was something that she hooked into while we were watching it. She couldn't have been more than six or seven. I turned the channel and she shouted, 'Banana!' Haha! It was a little game we played. If somebody turned the TV and you wanted to watch something that was on you had five seconds to scream out the name of a fruit or vegetable." Soot pauses his speech. He turns his hands over and over beneath the faucet. Then he clears his throat and continues. "So I turned back. Maybe it was the architecture or maybe it was just the colors. Whatever it was, she started googling everything she could about this place. By the time she was a teenager she knew more about this place than you probably do. Even when she and her mother moved away—after things fell apart—the plan was always for her to come back here. All that because she screamed out 'banana' one time when she was a kid. And now banana's my favorite word in the wh—"

"Shut the fuck up," David hisses. He glances at the door now and again.

"Okay."

"I should pop you in the fucking mouth," the man says. His voice gets more unsteady with each word. He decides that his hands should remain as fists. His jaw clenches. Then he says, ". . . These were good fucking kids here."

Soot dries his hands. In another time, in another place, in another version of him, he would have disappeared from moments like this. Turned invisible. But that was a long time ago.

He turns to David.

"Fuck you! . . . And fuck *him*!" David speaks with his chest, almost at a yell, but working hard to keep the others from hearing. "Fuck you."

"Fuck that nigga," Soot says.

David blinks. His chest is still heaving, but he stops pacing.

For a moment, for only a flicker in time, there is something akin to happiness on David's face, as if he has finally been given permission. "Fuck that nigga." He melts with each syllable. It's a raindrop of a sob that brings behind it a flood of tears.

"Fuck that nigga."

"Fuck that nigga," David replies. He's shuddering now, trying to cover his face with his hand so that he can cry unseen. The sobs come in waves. The volume grows. He's been holding it in too long and, now, he can't stop it. "Fuck that nigga," he weeps.

"Fuck that nigga," Soot says.

It goes this way for a long time. The two of them, alone together, here, in the middle of Minnesota, in the middle of a blizzard, just one thin door away from a room full of White folks, one of them crying like a child and the other standing with him, letting him cry, but not letting him cry alone.

"Fuck that nigga . . ."

Call.

"Fuck that nigga."

Response.

They hang at this moment in the timeline, trading the three words back and forth, again and again, saying it all in their own language. A mantra, a plea, an apology, an identifier, an old and sacred prayer that dances on the lips of two members of a wandering, displaced tribe who, for now, at this exact spot in time, have created a place where they can say what they want in the way they need to, if only just for a moment, here on this little continent given to them by a single two-syllabled word.

They sing their song together . . .
"Fuck that nigga."
(What do I do now? How do I live with this?)
"Fuck that nigga."
(You don't get to choose. None of us do.)
. . . with tears falling to the bathroom floor.

Fun fact: in spite of being born a red-blooded American, I'd never owned a gun. Never even held one, when I stop to think about it. Sure, I wrote a few of them into those bookworm stocking stuffers of mine over the years, but that was mostly a requirement of the job. It's hard to believe a story set in America if it don't have a heater. That's like writing about preachers and not mentioning getting fleeced. But in spite of what my characters might have done, when it comes to me and the real deal? Unacquainted.

So, imagine my surprise when one day before my flight to Euroland I'm standing in Bobby's Pawn & Gun City—which has a lot more *Gun* than it does *Bobby* or *Pawn*—and I've got two pounds of Pennsylvania steel in my hands that feels like it's always supposed to have been there. Like it was born there.

It's a .45-caliber Colt 1911. As American as apple pie, student loan debt, and truck nuts. Even if you don't know it by name, you've seen it. Bogart carried one in *The Maltese Falcon*. It's the gun that came home from the Big War, married Hollywood, and has been pumping out kids on celluloid and HD ever since. Chances are you've seen this gun more times than you've hugged your kids. And holding one in your hands? It's something else.

The awkward truth is there's something magic in a gun. Not exactly "You're a wizard, Harry!" type of magic. But definitely something in the wheelhouse of "I wish a motherfucker would" type of magic. Confidence is the best way that I can describe it. But "confidence" is just another word for safety. And safety's the thing all of us are working for, every single day of our lives, even if we don't know it.

You wake up in the morning, leave that warm bed of yours, shuffle off to a job you hate, and for what? Money. Anybody's that ever been down on their dollars will tell you, faster than you can ask, that not having money is one of the most unsafe feelings you can ever have. Every day's a tightrope walk over the Grand Canyon. One good breeze and you're going down. And the same goes for exercise fanatics. A good heart means a long life—at least, that's the logic. And that's a type of safety. Church folks? Having somebody out there in the universe who can, at any moment, swoop down and save the day? Even before Superman and Stan Lee, there were all those different versions of sky parents taking prayer deposits. Paying out with rain for our crops and vengeance for our enemies.

Safety. We sell our minds, bodies, and souls for it every day. So why shouldn't a gun feel a little bit like a lesser god that we can hold in our hands, sister?

"You want a holster with that?" the guy behind the counter asks. His name's Earl and he looks about like I'd bet you think he looks, being that this is a Southern American setting we're in—a little hurricane-punched town in coastal North Carolina. Tall, chunky, and with an air of Lynyrd Skynyrd about him. He wears a gun on each hip, and when I asked him about it just said "Why not?"

Pound for pound, though, he seems like an okay Joe.

Now, buying a gun is like buying a jacket. You gotta try it on first. So I'm at the counter staring down the sights of my new pistol and squeezing my hand on the grip with the barrel aimed out the window while cars scuttle past on the street outside. Everyone goes and comes about their business. It's midday so I figure most of them are on their lunch breaks. Basking in the gold autumn sun and snacking on lap belt Chipotle while they drive, completely unaware that they're crossing my gunsights here in the middle of Bobby's Pawn & Gun City.

Can't help but wonder how many times I've driven past here and been in someone else's sights.

"Feels great," I tell Earl. "I'll take it. And a shoulder holster to go with it would do me fine."

"You government?" Earl asks. He's already stacking up a couple boxes of ammunition. According to the flyer behind the counter, there's a deal going where first-time gunners like myself get two boxes of ammo for free and government employees get five percent off. Earl calls it the "Freedom and Defense Welcome Package."

"No," I say, finally placing the gun on the counter after a minivan came to a stop at the streetlight in front of the store and I wound up test aiming my gun at the kid in the back seat who just happened to look up and see me. The good news is that he seemed into it. Aimed a pair of finger guns back at me.

"Not government," I declare to Earl. "Just a writer."

"A writer?" he says, tilting his head a little. "You mean of emails and such?"

"And such."

"Oh," Earl replies. I think I disappointed him somehow. "Well, make sure you stay away from the action end. You people got a reputation, if you know what I mean."

"We got a stockpile of reputations, my friend."

"Any of them true?"

"Just the bad ones."

He disappears into the back of the shop without a chuckle. A moment later he returns with a brown leather octopus dangling in his hand and tosses it over. "Know how to put that on?"

"I can figure it."

I fumble with it for a second, trying to remember every FBI character I've ever seen on TV. A couple of moments later I finally slide my arms into all the right places. I pick up the heater. Slide it into its leather home for the first time.

I feel ten feet tall.

"You got a concealed permit?"

"No," I say.

"Don't worry. Trick question. State says you don't need 'em anymore. Praise God. You in the NRA?"

"Not that I know of."

He hands me a stack of America-colored pamphlets. "You should be. We could use a few more people like you."

"People like me?"

"Exactly."

He walks over to the register and starts ringing up all my Second Amendment ornaments.

"Don't forget that the firecrackers are free," I say.

"The what?"

"The bullets."

"Yeah," he says. From the look on his face, I think he might like to take back his NRA offer all of a sudden. Feels like all I'm doing is disappointing Earl.

"By the way," I start, "what's the law on getting these across the pond?"

"Across the what?"

"Are they legal in Europe?"

From his laughter, I think I finally make Earl happy. "Lord no," he says when he finally stops laughing. He wipes the corner of his eye. "But there's ways to get one over there. You're not the first person to want to take his freedom with him."

"Yeah?"

"Yeah."

Twenty minutes later I've been well versed in how to get this new heater of mine into the European theater. Now, for the record, my editor says the details of that conversation can't be printed here on account of liability and whatnot. But the good news is I think I redeemed myself in the eyes of Earl with my plan to take my gun to Euroland. By the end, he's smiling like I just cooked him the best steak of his life.

"You said you're a writer, didn't you?" he asks, handing me the last of everything.

"Yep. Even took home The Big One," I say.

"Good for you," Earl says. "We really do need more like you out there." He shakes my hand with all the warmth of redneck Santa Claus.

"People like me?" I ask for the second time in our conversation. But he's got his eyes on another customer and I've got some packing to do, so I grab my gun and take it on the road. Europe awaits.

A couple of days and several hours of being Ta-Nehisi Coates at thirty thousand feet later, I'm in Italy! Land of linguine, fettuccine, and Mussolini. Highs and lows, is what I'm saying.

From the air, it looks just like it does in the movies. Green hills and gray mountains. Poplars and fig trees. Vineyards and stone sculptures. Maybe even a Ferrari or two tossed in for fun. You can smell the pasta from thirty thousand feet.

I land in Milan just before lunchtime feeling top shelf. The old gal on the plane sent me off with one of the biggest hugs I've ever had. Just like Mama used to make. Outside the airport, even though it's fall, the sun is high and the air is warm. I'd never seen an Italian on their own turf before. It's a sight. Everywhere I look there's raven-haired dames in flowing dresses and half-sheer pantsuits. There are men handsome enough to test your allegiance to whoever you left back home. Everyone's thin and fit in a way that says the gospel of Krispy Kreme has yet to reach their lips.

Anyhow, it's not a bad place, I decide, sucking in a couple of lungfuls of Italiano-made air. I close my eyes and feel the sun on my face and the scent of olives on the air and it's enough to make me forget there's someone out there in this world with plans to kill me. But no sooner than I forget I open my eyes and get a quick reminder of just how fast death can show up knocking at the front door of your life.

Right there in front of me, on the doorstep of Milan herself, is the biggest man I've ever seen. He's seven feet tall if he's an inch. Arms the size of a Honda Civic and a chest like the business end of a bulldozer. He's dressed in one of the best-fitting suits this side of that crooked building in Pisa. I imagine that a man his size has no choice but to have it custom cut and, sister, he made the right call on that one. The suit is gray and his shirt is the color of the sky. It's like King Kong decided to attend a wedding reception and pulled out all the stops.

He's the very definition of a goon. Just a wall of meat wrapped in expensive wool.

I figure he's big enough to kill me with a flick of his finger if he were in the mood, but then I notice he's got one of the friendliest smiles I've ever seen. It's the only thing that keeps me from hopping the first plane off this entire continent.

"Aye," he says, sounding Scottish in a way that I thought only Sean Connery could. "It *is* yu." Before I can say a word, he's got those big goon arms around me and he's hugging me tighter and more warmly than even the old gal on the plane.

Hugged by two strangers in one day? Euroland can't be all bad.

"I'm so glad to meet yu," he says, swinging through his vowels with the music of the Scottish Highlands. "You just have no idea. I'm sooch a fan! Christ!" He sways a little bit as he hugs me, like I'm the long-lost Whoever He's Been Searching For.

When the hug ends, I realize he's squeezed all the air out of my lungs, so I pull in a deep one.

"Sorry about that," he says. "I'm joost so excited, yu know. Joost so excited."

For a moment, as I get the air back in me, all I can do is stare at him. And I think he sees it because he cuts his eyes away, like he's ashamed of something.

"Never seen a Black Scottish man," I say. And I hate myself the instant I say it.

Oh yeah. Did I mention he's Black? Yes ma'am. Looks just like the love child of Denzel Washington and Sidney Poitier.

After a moment, he grins. "We exist."

That accent and that skin . . . It's like I'm watching TV but the wrong audio track is playing. Samuel L. Jackson dubbed over by Gerard Butler.

"Right this wey," The Goon says.

"You know who I am?" I ask.

"Of course," he says. "I wouldn't be here ta pick yu up otherwise."

He reaches out the biggest paw I've ever seen and grabs my luggage and leads me across a bustling Italian street to what I can only describe as the strangest car I've ever seen. First off, it's old. And I'm talking Roosevelt Old. Too old for seat belts and high rates of passenger survival. Whole thing's shaped like a snail if that snail could pull its top back. It's got more glass and windows than a greenhouse and the skinniest tires I've ever seen. Whole thing looks like something that dropped out of World War Two and didn't survive the fall. Not the kind of thing anybody would see themselves cruising around in. Dying in? Sure. It seems built for a quick death. But cruising around Italy? Not so much.

The Goon picks up on the hesitation my face must be putting down because out of nowhere he says, "It's a Citroën and it'll tayke good care of us. Don't worry. We won't get theyre fast, but we'll get theyre feeling good."

That accent of his, it's like a massage on my ears. Really takes the edge off.

"Fair enough," I say.

I reach into my pocket and pull out my phone. Just planning to check to see if there are any fires burning back in the land of baseball and reality TV. But when it gets powered on, all it says is "No Service."

"Phone down?" The Goon asks.

"Yeah," I say. "But I'm sure I can get the tech folks back home to get me situated."

The Goon chuckles. "If I were yu, I'd leave it as it is. You can't get away if you're still anchored to what's back there."

"Is that an axiom?"

"I don't think so."

The Goon's being coy, and I like it. More than that, I like his advice. Back in my day, a phone was nailed to a wall where it belonged. And I always find myself staring off into the sunset, dreaming about the days when I didn't carry the whole world in my pocket. So maybe this is my chance. Maybe this is my time when I can do something different.

"I like your style," I tell The Goon. And, as I walk past the nearest Italian trash can, I chuck my phone inside. You can't leave the world behind if you don't leave the world behind.

Next thing I know, I'm in The Goon's little car and heading off for my adventure.

Top speed on the Citroën is about fifty if there's no headwind, and it takes its time getting up to that. So the city of Milan just sorta limps past us as we make our way in the direction of the countryside. Luckily, it looks like Milan's decided to let her hair down as we leave. Whole place is bustling. Banners and billboards and blocked-off streets. When I ask The Goon what all the fuss is about, he just says, "Fashion Week."

Sure enough, there's plenty of fashion to go around. Now, I'm not one who knows a lot about such things, but I know when people are having a good time. And Milan is that. You can feel the energy bouncing off those narrow streets and high walls. I do my best to take it all in. And while I'm doing so, I catch sight of something.

Fun fact: everywhere I go, someone like me has already been there. In this case, it's Alice Walker.

One benefit of riding in an old French car that takes a full three minutes to get up to fifty miles per hour is that you get to do some easy reading as you pass the local bookstore. There's a sign in the window declaring that Alice Walker was there just last night. Sometimes, it's good to know someone like you has already been through this part of the forest, blazing trail and leaving breadcrumbs, you know?

"It's something else," I say, craning my neck out the window, looking up Milan's skirt.

"This is Italy," he replies with a ten-euro grin.

I think I'm gonna like it here.

Because of how slow the Citroën is it takes a while for the thousand-year-old walls of Milan to fall away and the countryside to come rising up out of the earth. Cars blow past us like bottle rockets and the little French engine gets grumpy on every incline. Sometimes I think I can get out and run alongside it and get wherever we're going faster, but I gotta admit: there's something special about not being in a rush. I can count the leaves on the trees as I lean back and stare up through that open top and imagine the shapes in the clouds, none of which remind me of Remus.

It's a certain type of something, this slow ride through Italy with The Goon.

"I have a question for yu," The Goon says.

"Fire away." I'm hip deep in sunlight and feeling fine just now.

"I know that you're from North Carolina, but 'ave yu ever been to Rhode Eye-land?"

"Rhode Island?" I say. "Not that I know of. I like to think that Johnny Cash and I have been everywhere, but I can't swear on a stack of Nic Cage movies that I've given myself over to the great state of Rhode Island before."

I wait for the follow-up, but it never comes.

Sometime not long after that, jet lag catches up to me and puts me under. By the time I wake up, we're driving up the thighs of wealth and into the lap of luxury.

Now, if you know anything about ▮▮▮ ▮▮▮▮▮, then you gotta already have questions about what kind of Italian villa he'd have. I had those same questions. I mean, what does somebody do with all that money, besides bringing a writer like me to his country? What's it look like when you mold it into the shape of a house?

Well, let me lay it out for you:

The countryside leading up to the place is all poplar trees, manicured fields, and steeply inclined earth. Not quite a mountain, but definitely something where whenever ▮▮▮ ▮▮▮▮▮ says hello to his neighbors, he has to look down to do it. At the top of the hill is a second sun, burning in the sky. It takes a while for me to realize that it's not a sun but the house itself.

Rake me over the coals and I'd swear to anybody that the whole place is made of just glass and sunshine. It shimmers and dances, like a galaxy stuck on Earth. Just a glimmering dream plopped down for all to wonder at. A large metal gate lets us onto the grounds and leads to a long, winding road lined with more poplars. Our Citroën sounds like it's about to pull a hamstring trying to make it up the hill, but it gets The Goon and I there.

We step out of the car and The Goon leads me up to the house with a bit of pep in his step, while two other, thinner goons come fast-walking out of the courtyard gates and start off-loading my luggage. Lucky for me, nobody in the picture seems wise to the fact that the shoulder holster Earl sold me is doing its job of carrying all that Pennsylvania steel right next to my heart. If The Goon caught it when he hugged me back at the airport, he hasn't let on.

"So what's it like working here?" I ask while we're on the walk. The sun is starting to hang low in the sky and the air is cooling off and all the beauty of the green countryside is getting cast in gold. It's a sight to really make you stop and wonder about all the good things of the world, you know? But The Goon hardly seems to notice. I imagine he's seen this a thousand times. Lucky guy.

When I notice he still hasn't answered my question about working here I flash him a smile that says "Still waiting."

He's quiet as a church mouse all of a sudden.

"What's the big man like?" I ask.

Strike two.

I can't tell if I'm annoying him, but I feel like I'm annoying him. And with a frame like his I don't want to go too far down the annoyance road if I can help it. But I'd pay good money to hear that Scottish brogue of his again. Still, I shut my yap and follow the large, square man with the whey-protein smell deeper into the gilded bowels of ████ ██████'s homestead.

Eventually, after walking past a marble statue of a woman pouring water into a pond, backlit by the sun, that must be a thousand years old if she's a day—the woman in the statue, not the sun, I mean—we wind up in front of a pair of the largest doors I've ever seen in my life. They look like somebody slapped hinges on a pair of redwoods. I can smell the centuries used to grow these doors.

"Go ahead," The Goon says, finally giving me more of that sweet drawl of his.

"Just walk on in?" I ask. "You don't have to announce me or anything?"

He slaps me on the shoulder so hard it nearly buckles me in half. He pulls me square and looks me in the eyes, says, in his Scottish way, "Yuv got this," and does a walk-off worthy of Hank Aaron.

I reach out and grab the shiny bronze handle of the redwood-tree door and throw myself into opening it but, because of all the money at play in a place like this, even a door this big and heavy glides open like it's made of marshmallows, which means I nearly throw myself to the ground because I pulled too hard.

In the distance, The Goon cackles. "Everyone does that."

On the other side of the door is more of the same: wealth and opulence given form. All shine and cash. Ceilings so high that whoever painted these little fat angels all across them probably needed a pilot's license and a breathing apparatus. Whole place smells like fresh cucumbers and old leather.

Is this what billionaires smell like?

While I'm craning my neck up to take in all the decadence, I feel someone tap me on the shoulder. I turn around and damn near fall over from shock. My eyes go wide and I take a few steps back that turn into a stumble and it's only one of the old, probably-cost-more-money-than-my-car chairs in the middle of the room that catches me. But I'm afraid I've hurt the chair and will never be able to abide by "You break it, you buy it," so I bolt up to my feet. All the while I never take my eyes off him.

It's been years. So much time. But there he is . . .

The Kid.

It's been years. So much time. But even after all this time, after all these times being here, he's still never heard that shot that killed her. He never got the final moment. Some things can't be undone, not even when redone.

She was alone, out beyond the grapevines, in the middle of the flat, verdant acre of grass between the new growth of the muscadines and the family graves on the tail end of the property line. When he came home that sweltering afternoon, with the hard sun in the sky and the cicadas blaring like fire alarms through the August humidity, he found her note taped to the front door that read simply "Out back. I love you. I'm sorry."

He looked off in the direction of the grape rows where she liked to hide when she was a child. Then he looked past that to the mowed field where, once upon a time, they would play horseshoes until the sun was gone and Tasha had to call them both in out of the dark and from the mosquitoes that they never seemed to mind. Since the sun was getting lower in the sky, he had to make a visor with his hand. He used the opportunity to wipe the sweat from his forehead.

He sees her quickly enough. A lump of color against the fading green of the earth. And it brings him fully into that moment in time. No longer remembering. Reliving.

A breeze comes up and he can see—again, now, just like all the times he's done this before—what looks like the hem of her dress flapping gently, waving at him almost, as if to say, "Here I am. You found me" the way she had said it to him in those days past when they played their invisibility game.

"Mia?"

She doesn't move.

That's okay, he thinks. She likes to go out back and stretch out on the grass and sleep. She's been doing it ever since she was old enough to walk, even though he's warned her—her whole life—about ticks and all the other things a parent warns their child about. But she never took heed of any of that. She'd told him, "I just love the smell and the feel of it. Everything is so cool and quiet."

That was years ago. Back when they still sat and read books together on the couch or out in the yard—him in the hammock swing and her on a blanket in the grass no more than an arm's reach away. When she thought he wasn't looking, when she thought he was too far gone in his own reading to notice, she would scoot down just a little, inch by inch, until the soles of her feet were off the blanket and planted properly on the grass where her toes could paw at the blades and earth while they read.

It was instinctual. Something that, he knew, was beyond her control, so he pretended to not notice and she pretended not to know that he had noticed.

So, now—then?—as he stands, again—for the first time?—on the porch, staring at her, there's a brief moment when he doesn't know for sure. Only feels the instinct in his gut. For a moment she is not dead, just sleeping in her favorite place the way she's always done. And in the days, weeks, and years after, he'll hate himself for this moment of calm. He was supposed to know better. Supposed to know that something has happened to her. That this is not a game. He was and is her father. He's supposed to know that she's no longer a part of this world. Know that she's moved on, without permission or explanation or warning. Gone on ahead to that other continent. He should have felt her pain when the bullet passed through her.

Whether it's been seconds, minutes, or hours since she hasn't been a part of this world, he'll never be able to say.

Still on the porch, still oblivious, he turns back to the note. "I'm sorry."

Now he understands.

He shudders. His legs buckle. He folds in half right there on the porch and, for a moment, he's died with her. He doesn't breathe or hear or see or feel.

"Mia?" he calls out. "Come back," he says. "Don't do this. Stop right there. Don't go any farther. Get up, Mia. Get up and come home. You come here right now! Mia, come here! You can't leave me! You can't leave me like this! I don't know what I'll do without you. Please. It's all going to be okay. You just have to stick it out. It'll get better. We can do whatever you want. We can go wherever you want. You were right. Your mama was right. You were both right. We'll go and make everything better. I promise you! You can come with me. Minnesota. It's beautiful. Just don't do this. Just don't go without me. Don't make me go without you! Please, Mia! Get up now! There's ticks in that grass. How many times have I told you that? There's snakes out there. You'll get bit. Something will get you! You know how long a drive it is to the hospital. Get up now, baby. Please. Mia. Please. Get up! Come on, now. Please . . ."

He goes on and on. Pleading.

And yet, when people tell the story in the time after, when the neighbors on the other side of the field are asked about it, they'll only try to describe the sound they heard that snapped them out of their day and sent a chill down their spines. A horrible, lonesome sound they didn't know could live in this world. They'll say how they found Soot there, on the porch, buckled in half, curled up like a baby with that note in his clenched, trembling fist, with that horrible sound coming out of his mouth. That sound so terrible even the cicadas were cowed into silence. That scream of a father's grief.

"Like death itself," somebody will say.

. . . Time and again, the hem of her dress flaps gently, waving at him . . .

"I'm sorry," he weeps.

"I'm sorry," the note will always read.

The Kid's just standing there, alive, waving at me, like he never left. "I'm sorry" is all I want to say. But I still can't speak.

Now, I promised you a while back that I'd tell you more about a certain kid. Well, the short version is a few years back I went through a rough patch and made friends with this kid who was really on the up and up. He was only ten years old and had skin darker than anything you've ever seen, but he also had a smile brighter and more full of joy than anything you've ever imagined. The Kid and I, we made the rounds through The Land of the Free with me trying to sell some literary wares on a book tour and The Kid tagging along for laughs. It all came and went and turned out to be a hell of a ride by the end. The fact that The Kid was someone who only I could see and hear, well, that didn't mean two cents to me. He was still one of the best kids I've ever known.

Then he left. Without so much as a word goodbye. Not even a last smile to remember him by. Maybe he moved on. Or maybe he outgrew me. Or maybe he did what I've always been afraid to do: move on to something better. From the looks of him, I think that was his play.

"Kid!" I shout, and wrap my arms around him. I clap him on the back and sway back and forth like he's just come home from the Big

War. I laugh into the side of his neck and lift him up off his toes and even though my fortysomething-year-old lower back will probably give me hell for it, I don't stop. "You son of a bitch!" I shout with laughter. "Look at you! Just look at you! You grew up on me!"

He looks to be around eighteen or nineteen now. Still got that beautiful dark skin of his. He's tall and slim, dressed in skinny jeans and a button-down shirt that's the color of salmon and it suits him right down to the floor. He looks like a million bucks!

I can hardly hold myself together it feels so good to see him again, especially since things between him and me sorta ended on a strange note. "Dammit, Kid!" I say, still hugging him and rocking back and forth. "It's great to see you!"

That's about the time I feel him fighting me off, inch by inch. He's all tight and he pushes me away so that I got no choice but to let him go and return him to the earth. He flashes me a nervous, slightly embarrassed smile. Then he takes a step back and offers me a handshake like I'm a stranger.

"Ciao," The Kid says. "It's good to meet you. My name's Dylan. I'm the assistant to Mr. ▓▓▓▓▓ and I'm here to take you to him."

His voice is deeper and there's something in the lilt of his words. It's lost that beautiful Southern twang I remember. It feels like his words have been washed so many times that everything he used to be is faded out. "How's that?" I ask. I feel my high start to fade. "What are you talking about, Kid? Don't treat me like a stranger. It's just you and me here."

"Right this way," The Kid says without so much as a pause.

He starts walking and I have to almost run to keep up.

He is and isn't what I remember. Everything about him is as smooth as single malt whiskey. He looks like something out of a music video. Beautiful and full of life, a smile as big and wide as anything in this world—but he's mostly keeping it to himself. Cutting me side-glances every now and then.

"Listen, Kid," I start, as Frenchie's marble-laden villa slides by around us. "What's the score here? Where you been? *How* you been? What are you doing here? Why won't you talk to me? Was it something I did? Why'd you leave?" I'm trying not to panic, but something about all this just doesn't feel right. If there's one thing my life has taught me, it's that when the real world starts to get too hard for me, there's nothing wrong with letting it turn into a dream. But this time the dream feels like it doesn't want to be here.

"My name's Dylan," The Kid says again. "Like I told you, I'm here to introduce you to Mr. ▆▆▆▆. And, after that, I'll be helping you on your travels. I'll be your guide and interpreter on your European tour over the next few weeks. By the way . . ." He slows down here. Drops some of the formality and there's a hint of the actual Kid behind his words. ". . . I'm a big fan. It really was a hell of a book."

"Thanks," I say reflexively. But all I'm really thinking about is The Kid's accent.

It sounds like pretty clean American, but with a hint of something else on it. There's a swing to it that I can't pin down. And there's a seriousness in his eyes that says maybe, just maybe, he might not be foolin' with me. It says he might not be The Kid pretending to be someone else. Like he might just be some stranger.

"So, your name's Dylan." I say it mostly to myself.

"Yes."

"Okay. I'll dance along. Where you from, kid?"

"A little bit of everywhere," The Kid says. "I was born in Baltimore but moved to Europe when I was fourteen. Ever since then I've lived just about everywhere over here. I'm what they call a . . ." He says something in Foreign. Sounds like he's casting a spell. And even though I got no clue what *it* is, believe me when I tell you this kid has got it down pat.

"Sorry, Kid. I only speak American," I say. "But it sounds like you really got all the goods when it comes to the Foreign. Your tongue's slick as olive oil."

"Please don't call me that," he says. He says it stern but not bossy. "Like I said: my name's Dylan."

"Sure, sure," I say. "Just an old habit. Sorry about that." It's clear that he's not here to take any type of stuff from an old man like me. "I promise to call you by the name you prefer from here on out, Dylan." I slap him on the shoulder to let him know I didn't mean any harm. "That's the right way to get through life, K— . . . um, Dylan. Don't never take anything from some crackpot like me. Never ever." This whole exchange, it's like talking to an old friend who doesn't remember you anymore. "So how old are you, anyways? Always good to get a sense of where people are on this wild road of life."

"Eighteen," Dylan says. "This way."

We turn another corner in this ever-unfolding mansion. I've lost track of how many turns we made to get where we are. All I know for sure is that I could never find my way out if I wanted to. This must be what rich feels like: the ability to have people get lost in your house. But I ignore all that and turn my attention back to The Kid. I mean "Dylan."

"Eighteen and speaking so smooth and slick? Brother, that's a miracle. How many languages you got?"

"About five," he says, still leading me through the infinite house. "I guess it depends on what you mean by *got*. I can pick up most languages I come across. My mom used to say that you could drop me off anywhere on the planet and I'd be fluent in less than a week. Anyhow, do you know much about him?"

"The Big Man?"

"Yes."

"Just that he's French and loaded to the gills and a fan, right?"

"That's enough for me." Then The Kid gestures to another pair of tree-size doors that somehow snuck up on us and he says, "He's waiting for you. It'll let you meet him on your own, but I'll be back soon for dinner." Then he turns on his heel and walks off.

I don't want him to leave. I want him to stay and tell me where he's been all these years. Tell me why he went away. Tell me why he's pretending like he doesn't know me. I want him to flash that smile of his and tell me he got the fairy-tale ending I always wished he would.

But he just keeps walking away.

"Thanks again, Kid," I call out, refusing to let it end like it did last time.

He stops and turns, looks me square in the eyes. "Please don't call me that," he says. There's just enough edge in his voice to let me know he's serious. "My name is Dylan."

"Sure, sure," I say. "Sure, sure. Sorry."

I watch him walk away until the corners of the mansion swallow him up. But there's no time to linger. A billionaire has flown me across an entire ocean just to whisper in my ear. You can't keep the modern gods waiting.

"There he is!" ▮▮▮▮ ▮▮▮▮▮▮▮ screams from across the room in an accent so thick it sounds like it should come with a trigger warning somehow. He stands there—the man himself, just skin and bones and billions of euros—waving at me from across a marble-floored room the size of a plane hangar, flapping a pair of thin, pale hands with all the excitement of a kid who's just bottled lightning for himself and is finally going to get the chance to show it off and see it dance in somebody else's eyes.

Now, just between you and me, sister, I have a sneaking suspicion that, money being what money being, and power being what power being, legal's never gonna let me say his name on the page. So from here on out I'll just refer to him not by his name, but by what he let me call him: "Frenchie."

He's something else.

First thing you gotta know: in person, Frenchie doesn't look the way he does in your news feed. Photos and even 4K don't do him justice. His skin is smoother, his teeth straighter, his hair less thin. Yeah, he could use a burger or two, but that could be said of everybody in Euroland. I've never seen a Frenchman like him before—not that I've got a collection of them at home or anything.

I won't go into much detail about that distinguishing mark of his—you know, that ▮▮▮ on his face just above his ▮▮▮▮ because, again: legal. But let's just say that you know him just as well as you know any other rich-and-famous person who's famous for no reason other than the fact that they're rich and famous.

I'll give you this much, I suppose: His face is all joy. Like the whole world itself just showed up at his door. That's a lot of reaction from someone you've never met before, someone with more money than God. You'd expect people like that to be the stoic, menacing type like in all the Bond movies. But that's not the case at all. The man I see, it takes all he has not to do a backflip.

"Merci! Merci!" he screams, his voice echoing around walls decorated with paintings that are probably worth more than most countries' GDP. "Thank you! Thank you for being you!"

That accent of his? Whoo! It's full-fat butter. Sounds like it's made from croissant dough. The kind of thing where, if you heard it come out of the mouth of another living person, you'd swear they were putting you on. I'm not even gonna try to explain it to you. I couldn't put it on the page if you gave me phonetics, AI, and a decoder ring from a box of Cracker Jacks. "Thank you for being you!" he repeats again, squishing his way through the syllables.

He practically floats across the room, straight at me, with his hug-ready arms spread like he's auditioning to be in that one Creed video. The shiver running down my spine tells me he wants one of those Euro greetings where strangers hug you and then plant one on both cheeks. I can see it in his already half-puckered lips as he glides toward me from across the room. Those smackers of his are already moving for my cheeks and I don't have the heart to call him off.

I stand there waiting to be kissed on by a billionaire, but at the last second he pulls back and, instead, sticks out a hand to shake. "I'm sorry," he says. "Don't worry. I won't attack you. I won't make you uncomfortable. So I will only shake your hand. You are a professional. I will be a professional!" And then he laughs like it's an inside joke and it takes me a second to get the reference.

"Swell," I say. "Just swell. But you know what they say: when in Rome—or when you're Rome adjacent like we are—you should do as the Frenchmen do. So go ahead and bring me those lips on over here. Let's make this proper and official."

He squeals. He grabs me in his French arms and sends me one kiss east and one kiss west. Then he hugs me again and laughs like I'm the long-lost brother he never knew he was missing. It's a type of excitement I can't really remember seeing too many times before in my life. A real and true good thing.

"This is such an honor for me," he manages, choking up for just a second. He takes a deep breath to calm down. "Such a wonderful honor. I cannot think of anything in my life bigger than this moment."

"You and me both," I say. "There's nothing quite like meeting a new friend. And I can tell right away that you and me, we're destined to be the kind of friends who shake the world."

He laughs. "You're making fun of me?"

"Not even a little bit," I say. "I wouldn't make fun of someone, let alone someone who liked something I wrote. Every Johnny Backspace like me owes their salt to the person who reads their stuff. Even if they don't like it. And you, you more than like it."

"I do," he says. "I truly do love it!"

"And it shows, Frenchie."

"Frenchie," he says, grinning. "I will let only you call me this because it's funny. And because there is a type of honor in being given a nickname by someone like you. Come. Sit. We have much to talk about. I have a surprise for you, but it has to come after dinner, when our stomachs are full. That is the best time for surprises and wonderful things, wouldn't you agree?"

"I would," I say. "But you really shouldn't let people call you things you don't like. That's a rule of life."

"Nonsense! I am Frenchie now!" He squeals one more time and leads me even farther into his house.

Now, I know I keep plucking on this particular harp string, but only because, to this day, I'm still stunned by that house of his. To even call what he lives in a house is like calling Disney World the county fair.

The backstory I get from Frenchie about the place is that it used to belong to some old-money Italian family so big their name is now a household vegetable, not the other way around. That's how big the family he bought out is. They're a household name that built a household vegetable. And Frenchie had enough euro bucks to buy them out, lock, stock, and last zucchini in the fridge.

Vegetable Mansion sprawls and turns and winds back on itself. Everything's this Mediterranean auburn type of color and each room has wide, tall windows looking out on the countryside and soaking up the fading sunlight, lumen by lumen.

During the tour we swing by what's been assigned to me as a bedroom. It's bigger than the house I grew up in. It's got marble everything and there's these fat little angel children painted all over the ceiling that, from what I'm told by Frenchie, go back a few hundred years and stop on the doorstep of somebody so famous that Frenchie says, "I could tell you who painted them, but you would not believe it. I'll just let you imagine. You have a strong imagination, after all."

"You're right about that," I say.

Then comes dinner. And, with it, Dylan.

A whole line of well-suited and button-lipped servers bring out dish after dish after dish. Foods I can hardly identify and can't pronounce since Dylan tells me what each one is in that good Foreign of his. The whole while I'm just trying to figure him out. Whatever the game, he's not letting on. But, then again, I pick up quick that I'm not the only one who can see him this time.

So maybe it's like Sharon said and the rules really are different over here on The Continent.

Dinner tastes better than sex on Sunday morning. Throughout, Frenchie talks about me and about books. He asks me about writing and touring and all points in between while Dylan just watches and nods and laughs when the time comes for laughing. All the questions Frenchie asks are ones I've answered before, but they hit a little different because there's such fan service behind it all and because of all his money. That's the thing about wealth: even when you don't show it off, it's always standing right there behind you, big as a sunrise.

"You would not know this," he says, "but I have been watching you since before you were you."

I glance over at Dylan for a little explanation, thinking maybe the language barrier is fouling things up, but he doesn't say a word. "Nobody else is you," Frenchie continues. "No one else is *you*!" Then he laughs a laugh so wild it deserves four adjectives. It's a loud, happy, French, billionaire laugh.

"Thanks," I say.

"Never thank someone for telling you the facts about yourself. Now . . ." His voice stops dancing. "I bet you are wondering why you are here." He says it just like every horror-movie baddie right before the screaming starts. The fact that I don't have a phone with me feels like a mistake all of a sudden. I take a quick look down at my feet to be sure my shoelaces are tied for when the run-for-your-life phase of this particular murder trap begins. I regret the fact that I left my gun back in my room. Not getting murdered was the whole point of buying it. "I brought you here because I want to talk to you about your future." He blinks. "I want to change your fate."

"Oh?"

"You are a dreamer. And dreamers are something we desperately need more of. But you are a dreamer with poor book sales and no movie adaptation."

"Funny you should mention that. Not long ago I was actually out in Tinseltown talking with a few rainmakers over at—"

"Talks are nothing." He laughs. "Everyone in Hollywood talks. But they will not pay you. No. There will be no movie. No movie to boost book sales." He waves his hand. "Give up this dream. This will not happen. You will never write a Tax Bracket Book. Even with that award of yours. By the way, did you bring it with you?"

"He has a name."

Frenchie laughs. "That's cute. Good for him. But, still, wealth does not like people like you, unfortunately."

"People like me?"

"Wealth, however, has been very good to me. From when I was born—from even before I was born—I have been rich. And I've only gotten richer with time. I am rich enough to do almost anything and walk away laughing, you know?" I can't tell if he's bragging or if the language between us is muddying up what he's trying to make into a pretty speech. "Meanwhile," he continues, "you have never had much money."

"Can't say that I have."

"I was not asking." He reaches forward and places his hand on top of mine, maybe trying to comfort me and my lifetime of not being rich. "It is better to have money than to not. So . . . I want to give you money."

My ears perk up. "No kidding?"

"No. I am not kidding you."

"What's the score, Frenchie? We talking cab fare?"

Then he says it. Like he's said everything else this whole time. Like it's just three words and not the earthquake it really is: "███████ million dollars."

I immediately feel all that fancy food he's been feeding me threatening to come barreling back. That much money ain't even real to someone like me. It's the amount of money that, if I were a legal team, I'd redact it with that black ink that the government and poets use to hide conspiracies and bad-line integrity.

I blink.

The Frenchman and, by proxy, his offer, are still there.

"You're going to give me ███████ million dollars?" My hands are sweaty and my throat is all dried out. I feel bad for calling him Frenchie.

"Yes and no," he says. "I'm not going to give you ███████ million dollars." My heart is still beating in my ears, waiting for the other dollar-sign-shaped shoe to drop. "I am going to make it possible for you to earn ███████ million dollars."

I can't tell if I've gotten myself into a *Misery* or *Indecent Proposal*... but for ███████ million bucks I decide to pin myself to my chair and listen just a little longer. One thing I've learned is that, for enough money, most folks will moonwalk through hell. I think I'm about to find out if I'm most folks.

Maybe I won't need my gun after all.

For the first few years as a writer, while on the road, before he got here to Minnesota, before the man in the bathroom crying in his arms, he only carried his book around with him, thinking that maybe he didn't need a gun. In the beginning, he rode with his latest book in the passenger seat, sliding on the fabric when he took a turn too fast, then tumbling onto the floor when he braked too hard in heavy traffic. So, for a while, that's where it rode: on the floor. But then that didn't quite make him safe enough, so he moved it back to the seat each time it fell and that became the job that he had to do every time he went anywhere. After a few months of living in the front seat of the car, the cover was faded and pale, peeling at the edges and dotted with mud and stained with french fry grease from fast food eaten off his lap as he went from city to city, talking about the dead and about the police and about all the other things that it was his job to talk about now. Anywhere within driving distance of his home, he and his book had been there.

But then, eventually, he moved it into the little pocket in the bottom of the driver's side door. He placed it with the spine facing up so that, should the time come, if they saw it—saw it lit by the glaring flashlight that would come in through the window while he sat with his hands on the steering wheel, waiting to be told that it was okay for him to take his hands away and give them his ID—the book would be easy enough to read and they would immediately see his name in those big, bold, square letters that the publisher had decided to put his name in. He always wanted to thank the cover design people for making his name so easy to read.

For years he rode this way, with that book of his in the car door. And, more than once, it came in handy. He got pulled over. He waited with his hands on the steering wheel. The flashlight beam came in through the car window, peering into all the dark corners, searching for, well, for the things that flashlights peering into car windows search for, and all the while he sat, with his hands on the steering wheel and his tongue adding a "sir" to every answer he gave. And then he handed them his license and they shined their flashlight on the photograph and then on his face and then back to the photograph and, sometimes, he could see them finding the book. He imagined that, in their minds, there was a moment of realizing that the name on the license matched the name in the large typeface on the book spine and that the face on the license matched the face they were seeing now. And, when that happened, they would always cock their heads to the side, just a little, only for an instant, as the synapses fired and the realization kicked in and, sometimes, they would come right out and ask, "That your book?"

"Yes sir," he said.

"You wrote it?"

"Yes sir."

"I'll be right back," they said, and then the light shining in his eyes went away and they went to their car and climbed inside—behind all the computers and guns—and he would watch in the rearview mirror as the blue light of their cell phone lit up their faces. He could very nearly make out the world "Google" reflected in their eyes. Then, every time, they looked up from their phones and at him—so he cut his eyes away so they wouldn't know that he was watching—and, every time, when they came back to the car, even if they were writing him a ticket for something—which was rare, because he was always a slow driver on account of moments just like this one—they would be just a little friendlier than they had been before. "You don't have to put your hands on the wheel like that," they said. Or "I never met a real writer before." Sometimes they would get all nervous, like fans. They stammered and, more than once, asked him, "Can you recommend anything for my wife? She loves to read."

And he would recommend a book and, usually, they went on their way.

It would take a dozen or so miles for his heart to calm down and for the white-knuckled grip he had on the steering wheel to recede. His hands and forearms would ache and his stomach would be unsettled for the rest of the night or day.

Then came the gun.

He'd owned a gun in some shape or form as far back as he could remember—a .410 shotgun for quail when he was a boy; a deer rifle a little later—but it wasn't until the last couple of years that he started carrying the pistol with him whenever he went out on tour. It was a 9mm SIG Sauer that he bought from a friend. Small. Hard to notice. Not long after, he got a concealed carry permit. All of this he did without thinking. Without asking himself why he did it. It was simply what people like him did.

So, now, here in Minnesota, with the tears of the man still wet on his shoulder, he takes out his gun and places it on the bed—still in its belt holster—and goes and takes a shower, and when he comes out he eats snacks from the hospitality basket the college sent over and rests the gun on the comforter beside him while, outside, the storm blows and the world freezes and the dead are still not buried and he has a hard time remembering why it was that, back when he started selling books, he never carried a gun with him in the first place. Just now, all of a sudden, all the reasons he used to have that kept him from carrying the gun with him, from feeling the safety it gave him, all of those reasons are gone. Far, far, far off in the back of his mind, he sees a grainy video of Philando Castile sitting in the front of his car and telling the officer that he has a gun permit and then the bullets fire and then the man is dead.

But that thought is too far from his mind, too much covered up by the thought that "Hell, but I've got a National Book Award. I'll be okay."

In the middle of Frenchie's mansion, just beyond what Dylan tells me are the Van Gogh, the Rembrandt, and the second Matisse, there's another set of terrifyingly huge double doors made from what looks like the same ancient and freakishly tall slab of redwood tree as the others. They loom. They actually *loom* in front of the three of us, big enough that I swear I can feel the marble beneath them thinking about cracking up. And I'm sure all the gold doesn't help either. There's this solid gold filigree slathered over the doors like designs in a Persian rug. The old wood smells like I imagine FDR smelled: musky, and with a hint of gunpowder somehow. It's intimidating, to say the least. But I'm an N-worder . . . I'll be okay, won't I?

"I'm so excited!" Frenchie says, fishing in his pocket for what I assume is the key to the doors.

While Frenchie fondles himself for the key, just then The Goon appears out of nowhere—likely as not out of some protein- and barbell-laden pocket dimension—and he's close enough that he could check my prostate without me ever knowing. He leans in, tilting that huge, dark mass that he calls a body, and whispers, in that musical, heavy voice of his: "Layter, I'd like to ask yu again about Rhode Eye-land."

"Sure, sure!" I say, trying not to make my fear obvious as I take a small step away from him. It's not that I don't like him, you understand, I just don't like standing that close to anything that could crush me by falling on me. The Goon should come with a caution sign.

I never take my eyes off the door as The Goon says "Thank yu" and Frenchie finally finds the key. The lock thuds inside the door and the whole thing rolls open. Inside is a room with the most books I've ever seen in one place. I'm talking floor to ceiling and, somehow, even on the ceiling, thanks to some sort of bookcases carved into the rafters. As soon as the door is opened, that trademark "old book smell" that lives only in the best libraries walks up and kisses me on the cheeks and makes me twitch, just once, below the waist, if you know what I mean.

Fun fact: "old book smell" is an aphrodisiac to some people, and I'm some people.

"Come here," Frenchie says, leading me across the room. Each footfall echoes off the stone floor and the wooden walls. In the center of the room is a globe the size of a Volkswagen, spinning ever so slowly. The whole world right there in the middle of all those books.

"It turns in sync with the planet," Dylan whispers in my ear. "He'd never tell you because it sounds like bragging, but I just wanted to let you know."

"Thanks, kid," I say. "If I had that kind of dough, I'd have a fact like that tattooed on my forehead."

Frenchie makes his way over to one bookcase that stands out among the others, which is saying a whole lot in this place. He opens it with a slow reverence usually reserved for Beyoncé tickets. Then he reaches in and pulls out a small leather writing journal and hands it to me. "Open it," he says. "But only to the first page."

I do as I'm told. On the first page is written, in a scrawling, scribbled hand: *America by James Baldwin*.

It takes a minute for what I'm seeing to sink in. And when it does, it feels like a gag.

"James Baldwin who?" I ask.

"I am not your negro!" Frenchie shouts, pumping a clenched French fist to the ceiling. I glance over at Dylan and The Goon and I think I catch a little bit of an eye roll from each of them, but they do a decent job of hiding it from Frenchie.

My legs start to go a little shaky as I realize Frenchie ain't foolin'. I realize I might be holding something handwritten by Jimmy Baldwin.

"Is this real?"

"I wouldn't have shown it to you if it was not," Frenchie says. "Of course, you know James Baldwin, yes?"

"Does cocaine know a good time?"

"I do not understand."

"Yeah, Frenchie," I say, with a hint of an apology on top of it, "I know who James Baldwin is."

"One more," he says, and reaches into the shelf again. This time he pulls out a stack of papers bound with a fat, half-rusted paper clip. On the cover it says: *The Dream's Child by Langston Hughes.*

"Jesus."

"You have read him too?"

"Sure thing," I say. "I had a phase where he was the bee's knees and I tried to take in all the honey he ever made."

Frenchie hugs me like we've both just won the lottery. Like always, he's the happiest billionaire I've ever met. Sure, he's also the only billionaire I've ever met, but let's not minimize the point.

"Another!" he says, breaking the hug. He's so excited he's trembling. "I truly promise this is the last one. And I know that I am being . . . um . . . obnoxious? But you must forgive me. I am just so excited to be showing you these things. Here! Here!" He rushes across the room to a small cabinet and whips open the door. It's filled with vinyl records. He reaches past one that reads *Waywards by Redbone* and says, "Not that one. That one is for another author." Then he finds what he's looking for and, with a whole lot of relish in his turn, says, "Do you see this record here?" The album cover is simply black. No words, no designs, no images. He taps it with his index finger. "Nina Simone," he says. "A private album. Recorded in secret, just outside of Paris. Only five people on this whole planet have ever heard it. Little more than that even know about it." He takes a deep, solemn breath. "She sang so beautifully."

"How'd you get your hands on all this, Frenchie?"

"I told you: I was wealthy even before I was born. My father procured these from the artists themselves. I took them over when my father died."

I stare at Nina Simone's secret album, spellbound. "What did she sing?"

"Her private song," he says. "About her home."

"You mean North Carolina?"

"No," Frenchie says, laughing a little. "Like you, she was from North Carolina. But that was not her home. She sang about her home."

"Where's that?"

"That is only for the songs on this album to say. But my father says that she feared giving it to him, because home was difficult to describe for her. And she was afraid that she did not do it justice here. But she did," Frenchie says. "She truly did."

I stand quietly, wanting to ask to hear the song and read the books, but I already know better than that. So I only watch while Frenchie returns everything back where he got it from and closes it all up again. Then he turns to me, with the smell of all these books around me and the thoughts of just who else's work—secret and bespoke—he's got hidden away in this library of his.

"I have studied everything about you," Frenchie says. "I know you well. And here is something else that I know: yours is the final generation that will ever remember."

"Remember what?"

"America. The way it was. Those before you are already fading away and those after you are already too late. They were born into it and always will be."

"Born into what?"

He shakes his head solemnly. "Five years old, and they are already learning to hide in corners and lock doors. It is terrible. Each generation in this world remembers times that were simpler. Safer. But not anymore for you Americans. No. The tree has already fallen, as they say."

"No one says that."

"Soon," he continues, "there will be no more simpler times that anyone can remember. It will have all been devoured by the shooting and the terrorists climbing your capitol steps and your Republicans and Democrats." He makes hissing sounds like cats fighting—and if you've never seen a billionaire pretend to be two cats fighting, just take my word for it when I say it's a sight to behold. "Your politics and all the flags you cannot agree on, all the hills you plant them in and then fight over. All of it." His voice catches in his throat. There's something akin to real sadness moving through him as he speaks doom and gloom for the Land of Kentucky Fried Chicken. "You Americans . . ." He says it so low it's almost a whisper. "You are already too late. The good times? They are gone. And they will not return."

Every day of my childhood, at the start of my school day, I pledged allegiance to the flag of those same United States ol' Frenchie is laying into. I've got a natural reflex to belt him one across the jaw—and maybe that's why The Goon is here, to keep me from getting any ideas. But, even with that ball of anger churning in my belly . . . I gotta admit: there's something in what he's saying.

"So, when these good times are gone, what does this leave behind?" he asks.

"I don't know."

"You," he continues. "You are of the age that can still remember, even if it is only vaguely, the way that things used to be. It was never perfect, no. But it was different than what it has become." He puts his arm around me and walks me over to the Volkswagen-size globe—the one that's ever-so-slowly spinning in time with Earth itself—and says, "The thing to know is that I am very good at seeing the future. And no matter how much you Americans may say you want things to stop, you do not. Nothing will stop. Again, that tree has already fallen."

"Nobody says that, Frenchie."

"The way America is *now* is also the future of America. The way things are is the way things will become, only worse. It is like time travel in the science fiction books, only it's real! It is alive! Each and every day!"

"That's a dark line of thinking you got there, Frenchie. But what's that got to do with me?"

I don't like where Frenchie's going, but there's nothing I can do about it. This is his show and he knows it. I couldn't stop asking questions now if I wanted to. Curiosity's got me by the back of the neck and is pushing me straight ahead. Or maybe it's not curiosity, maybe it's just inevitability doing what it does. Whatever it is, it's making my Spidey-sense tingle.

"I want you to live here," Frenchie declares. He says it just as we're standing over Euroland on his globe that probably cost more than my house back home. "Live in Europe as an artist. Away from the guns, the racism, the Christian fundamentalism and Jesus on the Cross Nationalism that you pretend isn't as big as it is. Live here and tell me about the way it used to be, while you remember. Write books of what was and I will buy them from you, one after another, and you will grow rich and fat with each word." He laughs then.

I try to laugh with him, but nothing comes out.

"I will keep you safe," he continues. "And you will become the record keeper of the way America used to be. The way it never will be again."

My stomach says I'm going to vomit. Maybe it's the fact that we're standing over Europe. Never been one for heights. Or maybe it's just that: "I never thought I'd be given the chance to be someone's pet."

"No!" Frenchie says immediately. "That is not what this is." His face goes hard and serious. "What does a government, a country, provide? Land, safety, and the opportunity for income. This is what I am offering you. You will live in a place of your own choosing. You will have money enough for any occurrence. And the opportunity for income is obvious: Produce words. Which I will then buy. It is a complete loop. One which you may leave at any time. However, if you produce work, if you build an economy through hard work, I will pay you for it and then you may leave with that money."

There's logic to what he's saying.

"I will make you your own country. An independent citizen of the world. A whole other continent!"

Lunch is starting to come back up again. That's when I remember the others.

"Is that the offer you made to *them*?"

I nod my head in the direction of the bookcase where Jimmy, Langston, and Nina now live.

French shakes his head. "Me? No, no. I am not that old. But my father perhaps did. But they were better than you. They were not broken like you are."

"Do you mean broke? Because my finances are square. I'll admit it ain't all diamonds and champagne, but I can get extra cheese on my pizza some days."

Frenchie doesn't laugh.

"Why you? That is your question. Here is my answer: Because you are broken. America has broken you years and years ago. You will not ever be fixed. And it is those who are broken in the way that you are broken who keep the stories. And, also, I make you this offer because I think that it will do you something good. Europe is different for people like you."

"That's what I keep hearing."

"This will be a great arrangement for you. You will, as you say, make out like a robber."

"Make out like a bandit," I correct. "So let me get this straight: You're going to pay me just to live over here and write?"

"Yes. But also, you can never go back," Frenchie says.

There's that other shoe I've been waiting for.

"How's that?"

"To America," he says, and there's something ominous to it. "Ever. I will create a trust in the amount we discussed earlier. And, as long as you do not return to America, it will be yours to do with as you will while you are being this Country of One. But if you ever return to America, then the deal is off. You lose access to the trust."

"The rich really are different," I say.

"We are," he replies. "We hate the poor and we teach the poor to hate themselves, but that is another discussion. For now, you should only be agreeing to my offer. There truly is nothing for you to lose."

My head is spinning, and it's not just because we're watching Earth spin beneath us. I chew on it all for a second. ▇▇▇▇▇▇▇ million smackers, just to live as some French billionaire's personal Americana time capsule. The literal definition of selling out, trading up, or moving on, depending on how you want to look at it.

"Finally enough," he says slowly. Each word sinks into me like lotion. "Enough to pay your own way. Enough to decide for yourself what each day is. Enough to, finally, turn off the worry machine that is always running inside the heads of people like you."

"Yeah . . ."

"Enough," he repeats. "That is the deal, my friend. It is, if this were one of the old movies you like to watch so much, the ones with Humphrey Bogart and Katharine Hepburn, what you might title . . ." He finally takes his arm from around me and raises both hands in the air in front of us and makes a sweeping motion, like revealing something that only the two of us can see, and he says, ". . . The Big Score."

For an instant, I can see those three words hanging in the air, flashing like the marquee outside the TCL Chinese Theatre in Hollywood. I can hear the fanfare. I can smell the popcorn. I can hear the cash registers at the box office drumming out *ka-ching, ka-ching* to the double-time-jazz-swing rhythm. I lick my lips.

"The Big Score . . ." I say, tasting the words.

My legs are part jelly and part marshmallow. And it's not just the money or the opportunity. No ma'am. There's something else at play here.

Somewhere out in the world, buildings shake and seas boil and dogs bay at the moon. Something just woke up. There's movement behind the clouds and it sends shivers down my spine. Something's coming. Something that's been on its way for ages, been coming for me ever since the start of time, and now, right here, standing in Frenchie's elaborate library, being offered the best deal of a lifetime all on account of how the rich really are different, now that thing, whatever it is, finally picked itself up off of its eternal couch, brushed off the Cheetos of time immemorial, shambled into the bathroom, looked at itself in the mirror, and said, "Today's the day." And it said it with a picture of me staring back at it from that bathroom mirror, like whatever it is that I've been doing all my life to keep it at bay finally failed, and now, after so long, it's been let loose.

I can feel it. I can almost see it out of the corner of my eye.

My condition is starting to act up again.

"What do you think?" Frenchie asks.

I'm not sure what I say out loud, but I think it's something along the lines of "Yes" because he smiles like I've just handed him Christmas Day in sentence form. He hugs me and rocks back and forth. All the while, when I should be thinking about the payday, the ██████ million dollars of cabbage is the last thing on my mind. Instead, there's this thought of never going home. Of being bought out of the red, white, and blue for permanent. I see the house I grew up in, outgrew, and made fit again. I see the little town and the big people there. I see my folks, dead as they might be, alive again and waiting to hear what I have to say. I see Lady Liberty standing tall. I smell the cinnamon of apple pies and hear the sound of home runs cracking the autumn air. I feel the concrete of the Hoover Dam and I hear the gunfire at Sandy Hook Elementary. I see every cop that's ever pulled me over and told me I fit somebody's description.

"The Big Score . . ."

As bitter as the idea of leaving home might be up front, I gotta say that, on the back end, there's a hint of what just might be pure gravy, sister. I think that, maybe, it's the end of summer for the way things used to be. I think Frenchie might have just helped me understand that, hell, for the right price, leaving America just might be the new American Dream.

It's the end of summer. Before the death but after the divorce. And even though she is suddenly alive again, he hates coming here. The sun is still high as he stands at the end of the grape rows, not far from the spot where she did and will die. The air is still thick as syrup with humidity and, far off in the distance, the pines rustle with a breeze that does little to deal with the heat. The whole world feels like it's baking.

This is the one with the graves, he thinks to himself.

He turns and starts walking.

He crosses out into the field where it happened, careful to keep his distance from the exact spot. He keeps his eyes on the horizon, like a high-wire act. Don't look down, he thinks.

The grass is verdant and thick, just like always. There's a pinch of irony in the back of his head. Before his father died, all those years ago, this was his family's land. His grandfather's, inherited from his great-grandfather, and so on and so forth, all the way back to the day someone in his line was granted their freedom papers and an arrangement to farm the land. By the time it came to his father, the land had been doled out over the years. A few acres here, a parcel there. All of it divvied up between great-aunts and -uncles whose names he only ever saw in legal documents when he was going about the business of buying back what he could. If someone had asked him, he couldn't have said why it was so important to him to get it back. Tasha had asked him that exact question more than a few times but, thankfully, she'd never pressed him on it when he wasn't able to give anything resembling a good answer.

"Well," she'd said, "we'll get it back."

And they did. Most of it, anyhow. Damned near ten acres. Not exactly a kingdom, but just enough of the remnants of one that it could be called a legacy.

Before long he's crossed the field without falling apart in tears and made it to the acre on the far side, just at the edge of the land, where the family graves are. The first grave he sees is Daddy Henry's—his grandfather who died alone in a rest home, hated by his son, when Soot was a child.

He walks among the headstones until he finds those of his father and mother. He doesn't remember when he got used to coming out here and sitting with them like this. Can't tell exactly when he got used to them being dead and gone and accepted this place as not where the dead live but only the place where slabs of stone stuck in the ground hold up their names.

Maybe it was the time travel that had changed his view on that.

Sometimes he thinks back to the crowds that were here after his father's death. Everyone came. Celebrities. Politicians. Singers and actors. They all flooded to this small piece of earth when his father died, all angry, all with their fists clenched and their voices loud and their promises that this type of death must never happen again. There were calls for legislation and promises of change but, after they were all gone, after their voices faded away in the news headlines, life moved on. His father was just another dead body put into the ground, and now, all these years later, nothing has proven that fact more than the way that the grass and vines are threatening to grow over the dead. Threatening to swallow them up and leave little to no trace that they were ever here.

The sun rolls in the sky. The afternoon comes on. As it always does when he travels here. Eventually, he catches sight of the plume of dust coming down the dirt road, and the familiar, rattling sound of the old suspension banging and shaking over the uneven road.

It's the shabby old car Mia's friend drives, bringing his daughter home to him, alive and well.

He lets out a sigh he didn't know he was holding. He screams with joy, lets himself cry, knowing that he's far enough away that, by the time she reaches him, he'll have cleaned up his face.

Like every time, he's so focused on Mia, he doesn't hear Tasha come up behind him.

"You okay?" she asks.

He startles. Then he turns away, wiping the tears from his eyes with his palm. "Yeah," he says. "I forgot you'd be here. Sorry." He sniffles. "You know how my allergies are. Acting up today."

"Your night to cook."

"Okay," he says. Then: "It's good to see you. Good to see her."

"What do you mean? You've seen us for over a week, Soot."

"I know," he says. "It's still good to see you." She stares at him, trying, in the way that she's always been able, to get him to talk about whatever it is that's got him standing in the middle of a field crying. "How . . . uh . . . how much longer are you guys here for?" Soot asks. "My memory's a little foggy. Another week or something, right?"

"Jesus, Soot," Tasha says, her brow knotted in concern. "Are you sure you're alright?"

"Yeah. Yeah. I'm just having a brain fart, you know. Was hoping we could go over to the fair and watch the demolition derby again. Haha! But it's Saturday night. When's your flight?"

"Friday," Tasha says. Her concern dissolves from her face, all the lines of it filled in with frustration. "We talked about this. Tasha and I can't stay any longer. You know that. I've got to get her back to Toronto. School starts soon."

"Of course," he says. "I wasn't trying to get you to stay longer. I swear. I really was just sorta out of it for a second. That's all."

They both stand as, in the distance, Mia climbs out of the small, rickety car, laughing and doing a little dance to the bass line of whatever music her friends are playing. She closes the car door and watches her friends leave, waving and yelling something that, whether she knows it or not, will be the last thing she ever says to them in person. Then she turns and spots her parents across the field. She waves a large, exaggerated wave and yells. The air catches most of it. Something about changing clothes and helping.

"I guess she thinks we're mowing this stuff," Soot says.

"I wish you had come with us," Tasha says.

"I swear it comes back faster than I can mow it," Soot says.

"They would've wanted you to leave," Tasha says.

"How the hell did I let myself wind up with damned near ten acres of yard work?" Soot says.

"I'm not trying to start a fight," Tasha says. "But she needs to be away from here. You can see that, can't you?"

". . ."

Mia comes out of the house dressed for work. She wears a pair of tan coveralls and a short-sleeved shirt. He bought her an outfit just like that when she was two and asking to help in the yard and, ever since, as she's grown, it's the same thing she wears when there's any type of work to be done outdoors. Somehow, coveralls have become sacrosanct.

"I'm trying to help you," Tasha says as they both stand watching their daughter jog toward them. "And, more than anything, I'm trying to help her. She needs this."

"Not now," Soot says. "Please. We don't have much time left."

"Dammit," Tasha curses. Then: "I'll get the lawn mower."

"I'll do it."

"Helps me think," she says.

She walks the long way back to the garage, stopping to smile and hug Mia along the way. Then she continues on to the house and Mia runs up to Soot and says, "Hey, Pops," and he bursts out laughing and is almost in tears and he grabs her and hugs her and tries not to scare her with his joy at her being alive. When the hug ends, she asks: "You okay?"

"Why does everyone keep asking me that?" Soot replies. "Of course I am."

Then the lawn mower starts up in the distance with a roar and Tasha rides over acres of land that has never belonged to her family and has never been in her blood—land that she married into and then divorced out of—and starts the blades and the mower gets even louder and she begins mowing around the graves. Mia and Soot walk up to the garage and grab a few tools and come back out and get to work.

The three of them clean graves through the thinning afternoon and into the thickening evening. When it's over, they've dug up enough of the brush to start a fire and so that's what they do. They make a pile of debris at the end of the property and they start the fire and they stand around watching the fire until long after dinnertime.

When it's dark and everything is done, they come in, all tired and smelling of smoke, and while their daughter is in the shower Tasha comes over and puts her arms around him in a way that she hasn't done in a long time and he, for the first time in years, leans into her and feels her leaning back.

"You can't save anyone by staying," she says.

"I can't leave."

It's an old conversation and they're both tired of it so, eventually, she lets go and so does he.

"Can I ask you something?"

"Yeah," she says.

"Remember when Mia was in your class that year, back when she was young? Remember the way her and the rest of the kids used to laugh while they were doing those drills?"

"What about it?"

"Do you think that was the start of it? Or was it already too late by then?"

"What the hell are you talking about, Soot?" she asks.

He's seen this version of her face a dozen times or so over the years. The narrowed eyes and raised eyebrows of confusion. The tight-lipped concern.

"Nothing," he says.

He goes out and stands on the back porch and stares off at the graves and feels the ground calling to him, feels that anchor in the pit of his belly telling him that this is where he was born and this is where he belongs and that to abandon this place is to abandon them and there will be no one to tend their graves if he leaves and they will just be swallowed up by the earth and it will be like they were never here and, because of that, all that came before will be lost and he won't be able to do anything about it. He'll just be another person out there lost in the world and lost in time, trying to make their way through but with nothing rooted beneath their feet and he refuses to let it come to that. Things have to go better than that.

"I won't leave," he says to the ghosts.

Maybe the ghosts answer him back.

It's hard to say.

The language of the dead is only ever smoke and puffs of wind and, sometimes, a plot of land off in the distance, unseeable in the darkened night, but always there, beckoning us to stay or come back to it, depending on where we are in time at that moment when the evening breeze blows just so.

Even with luck suddenly falling from the sky, even with The Big Score hanging over my head, soaking up my thoughts, keeping me awake at night, the work don't stop. Frenchie brought me here for a book tour after all.

The next morning, after a long, sleepless night of staring up at those fat, little Italian-painted kid angels on the ceiling of my bedroom in Frenchie's mansion, with that offer of his dancing in my head and my answer "I'll think about it" still burning my lips, I got work to do.

So when dawn comes and The Kid—I mean, Dylan—comes knocking gently on my door to let me know we got an itinerary to keep up with, I'm two steps ahead. I pull the door open on the first knock like some sort of trapdoor spider and I grab him by the shoulders and yank him in and I ask him, straight off, "I sometimes have trouble getting square with reality, so I gotta ask: Was all that last night just in my head, or was it for real?"

"Yes," Dylan says. "Last night, and the offer, really happened."

"Okay then," I say, nodding, just to confirm it to the dream factory behind my eyes. "Okay. In that case, K— I mean, Dylan, let's get out of here and on the road. I think better in the weeds, you know?"

No sooner than the sun cigarette burns a hole through the Etruscan horizon, The Goon, Dylan, and I are in the wind. The three of us piled back into that French snail car with The Goon behind the wheel again and me riding shotgun and Dylan swiping and typing in all directions on his laptop and that little Citroën engine is, once again, abuzz with fifty horsepower of excitement as we roll down the long, well-graded road from Frenchie's hilltop getaway and, for a moment, it feels like we're really on the move! And even though it's probably going to be the slowest Euroland road trip since Hannibal got those elephants of his on the metaphorical hoof, I'm feeling like a teenager on their first-ever payday.

The Goon turns out to be a chatterbox. He starts in on a lecture about Scottish cooking—apparently a hobby of his. Everything he says sounds like music, and the novelty of that accent of his coming out of that skin color of his shows no sign of wearing off. The Goon could read Facebook's Terms and Conditions and I'd listen with a smile.

A couple of hours later, sometime after The Goon gives a long rundown on Scottish cheesecakes, we're on a road not far from the coastline and I catch The Goon locking eyes on that watery horizon a little more than he should. Something about the ocean's got him distracted and he catches me staring.

"Why haven't yu been to Rhode Eye-land?" he asks.

"Maybe I have," I say. "I find myself in all sorts of places, and only half the time do I actually know where those places are. If there's a place I haven't been, chances are I been there." I give him the finger-gun special. "Pew!"

The whole time, Frenchie's offer of money and freedom and being without a home country rings in my ears.

"I imagine yu'd remember if yu had. I think Rhode Eye-land must be the most amazing place in the whole would." It's clear that he's got some sort of soft spot for the Ocean State. "Do you know why it's so special?" he asks.

"No clue, my friend."

He takes a deep breath and takes his hands off the steering wheel just long enough to do a little flourish and say, "H. P. Lovecraft." Then he grabs the wheel again and saws it back and forth, giving our French snail a little swing step along the highway for a moment.

"Now I got you," I say. "You're a fan of the Weird One, huh?"

"More than a fan," The Goon replies. "A believer." He looks out through the windshield, half-watching the highway traffic while his focus clearly drifts to the ocean that the road is taking us closer and closer toward. "And before yu say it, I'll say it for yu. He didn't much care for people like us."

"People like us?"

"But show me a perfect person. I dare yu! The way he dreamed?" The Goon shakes his head in disbelief. "There'll never be anybody else like him. He was in touch with something special. Something wonderful. And, sometimes, I really think I can see it."

"See what?"

It's not far off early midday at this point and the sun is bright, glittering off the ocean like diamonds thrown into the sky. In the back seat, I think Dylan's catching a few unplanned z's, which leaves me alone with The Goon and all his Lovecraft passion. He looks out at the ocean, keeping the car on the road with little more than instinct, I believe. "Do yu see it?" he asks, never taking his eyes off the sea.

My eyes follow his. All I see is a bunch of salt water where a few hundred wars have come and gone in the last several thousand years. It's full of light and better tomorrows, like most times when you see an ocean.

"Hell of a view," I say.

"No," The Goon says. "Yu do not see it, but that's okay. Do yu feel it? That's more important."

"Feel what?"

The Goon breathes slowly, never really blinking that I can tell. "Some days," he begins, "it's out there."

"What is?" I ask. "And does it feel like a man you met in an alley once with designs on killing you?"

"What?"

"Never mind. Keep talking."

He lets it pass. After a moment, he takes his eyes off the ocean. He finally blinks.

"I don't have the words for it," he starts in that brogue of his, "just the feeling. But it's there. Lovecraft knew what it was. On the right days, I think I can almost see the water starting to swell because it's coming. Like it's almost about ready to burst through."

"And then?" I'm breathless at this point.

"And then it doesn't," The Goon says. "But that don't mean it didn't almost happen." Finally, his tale told, he smiles that genuine goon smile. "What is it you say? You have a condition. I think he had one too. And so do I."

"That checks out, my friend." I say it softly, with a little bit of reverence, still staring out at the water, still watching. And, for a moment, I think I see a bulge in the horizon out over the water. A bulge or a grand, massive ripple. As though something beneath not only the waves but the sea herself, had turned, slowly, as if in a fitful sleep.

A little later, when we're out of sight of the ocean, things are feeling tops. Dylan comes back from dreamland with a yawn and an apology—for some reason—and The Goon and I absolve him of his sin over lunch. The food's just as good as advertised. But there's no time to dawdle. No sooner than we can get it all swallowed down, we're back in the car and pointed toward a town that Dylan calls Pordenone.

The ride is slow and easy. Lots of time to take things in.

As we cruise, I start to notice something about myself. There's an easy feeling running through my bones that I don't know I've ever felt before. This whole place—with its olive-scented hills and lack of "Jesus Saves" church signs—somehow feels just as familiar as it does foreign. I keep expecting to catch sight of someone I know with each mile. Like my old, dearly departed mama herself, who never once set foot outside of America, might suddenly show up standing out in one of these Italian fields, watching as me and my two new friends and Frenchie's offer all go rolling past her. I feel like she might toss me a wave if I look hard enough.

It feels sorta like home. A home I've never been to, but where I'm welcome. Maybe Frenchie and that offer of his really are onto something. I take a deep breath and my lungs swell up with air and it feels like gold. I let it out and, hell, it feels even better. I do the whole process again. I pump this EU air in and out of my lungs like I've never breathed air before in my whole life.

"You okay?" Dylan asks.

"Top of the world," I say. "Just breathing."

"Good," he says, finally closing the computer he's been so focused on all morning. "I think we should talk a little bit about what's coming up. You've never toured in Europe before, right?"

"Right as rain," I say. "But I been around enough blocks to know that people are all the same pretty much wherever you go. If you think I need some sort of how-to or something, don't sweat it. I'm no rube. I'm onto the game."

Dylan thinks on it for a second. "European readers are different from Americans," he says.

"Yeah, I know. They're skinnier. We're a chunky tribe back home."

"They ask different questions over here," he says, not giving my joke the time of day.

I can tell by the seriousness in those young eyes of his that Dylan's trying to look out for me. Trying to steer me off the hook of some trap that he thinks is lying in the Tuscan underbrush, waiting. But the truth is that, right now, I can barely hear him. I'm too busy breathing. My lungs are rising and falling like never before. Every time I suck in air, it swells me right down to my toes and I'm here for it.

Dylan is still going on. Still warning me about how Italians read books but his voice is all just noise that's getting quieter by the minute as I sit here breathing, feeling lighter and lighter, like I might just float away. Maybe it's still just Frenchie's offer that's got me heady.

Maybe The Big Score can help me take out a thirty-year mortgage on this feeling of being able to breathe. Keep that other thought out of the back of my skull. That one about the man in the alley with the penchant for good teeth and promises of murder.

Maybe.

"Do you love America?"

"How's that?" I reply, choking on my water.

"Do you love America?" the woman in the front row asks.

At the end of the drive up the Italian coast was the town called Pordenone and a book festival and a seat on a stage in front of a hundred or so Italiano readers and a small, thin Italian woman standing behind a mic asking me if I love America. Signs and wonders.

"Aren't you going to ask me what my book is about?" I reply. "Where I get my story ideas? How I found my agent?"

I lean over to Dylan and whisper, maybe a little louder than I should: "She's supposed to ask me what my book is about. That's how these things go. Is this one of those language things?"

"How can it be a language thing?" he asks. "She's speaking English."

Fair enough.

The one guaranteed rule of book tours is that the first question you're up for is "What's your book about?" Trust me, I'm an author. I know how this story plays out. But, for some reason, this lady down front is missing her lines. Seems like she didn't get the memo from on high about how you're supposed to treat people like me when we come blowing through.

Book tours are all about repeatedly delivering your elevator pitch and, sister, I've got elevator experience. It's all about getting the most information across in the shortest time possible and nobody in the equation is supposed to really get down to the bare bones of things because, hell, nobody has time. And, normally, nobody reads the book.

"Do you love America?" she asks again.

I chuckle.

In an awkward situation, a good chuckle can be like kryptonite. I let one loose and broadside the whole lot of them and, while they're all staring and watching, I catch sight of someone moving along the back of the crowd. I'm staring into the sun so I can't quite make heads or tails of it, but he's thick and tall and of the melanated persuasion. He stands in the back of the room and reminds me of Remus.

I feel a bit of sweat seeping into my palms and my left knee goes to fidgeting. I make a shade with my right hand and squint to get a better look at the figure at the back of the crowd, but all I can make out is a dark shadow that just happens to be shaped like a body.

I look around for The Goon. I mean, I know he's not my goon, but he's a goon and if that really is Remus back there, I figure the best thing I can do is send The Goon in his direction.

I catch sight of him, sure enough, off by the side of the stage where he's been standing this whole while. He's still got that usual, protein-powder-and-power-cleans-driven look of contentment about him.

I give him a wave and try to turn his attention to the back of the room, but he just waves back like we're old friends that ain't seen each other in a few years. When I glance back toward the back of the crowd, the shadow is still there, watching.

"Am I asking it wrong?" the Italian woman says, looking around like she can't tell if she's speaking the right language or not. I can see her spinning her wheels over whether she somehow tuned in to the wrong station right before she opened her mouth. "Am I asking it wrong?" she repeats to the crowd. Then she says something in Foreign that I guess is the same thing and they all give her a nod to let her know that the audio's coming through just fine.

I gotta answer. But I also gotta keep my eyes on what looks like Remus at the back of the crowd—even though I can't tell for sure that's who or what it is. I think about The Goon and his shape in the water and that feeling he says he gets sometimes. Maybe we're not as far apart as I thought we were.

To get the woman off my back, I give her one of the many prepackaged-microwave-dinner answers I keep on hand for moments like this: "Do I love America? The Great Experiment? The ol' Melting Pot? Hell yeah! Who doesn't? You ever been?" I say it all without ever letting her know that I'm looking past her, keeping my eyes on the foreboding shape at the edge of the crowd.

"No."

"Damn shame, Toots," I say. "A real damned shame. You don't know what a good time is until you roll down Times Square at midnight, crowded in by a thousand different voices all talking in a hundred different languages and each and every one of you are craning your necks upward in awe, trying to soak up a few million watts of wonder as it spills down from the bright lights! It's like no other place on the planet! Everywhere leads to something and somewhere. Turn off one street and catch a Broadway show. Step off another street and meet Jay-Z. Step off another street and, hell, who knows who you might meet. You might even find yourself up there!"

A hand goes up in the back of the crowd. "That's from the Alicia Keys song, no?"

"Just because somebody else said it first don't make it not true!"

After a second of thinking on it, I can see a few nods of agreement spring up around the room. Even a chuckle or dos. Deux?

I got 'em by the good times now! Hell, I think I even see the dark stranger at the back tremble with laughter.

But the spell doesn't work on everyone.

"No," the bella ominous, who's still standing there, still giving me her thousand-yard stare, says. "I did not ask if you love New York. I asked you if you love America."

"New York is America," I say with another chuckle on the end.

I see a few more nods go around.

The woman's mouth tightens into a line thinner than an uncooked spaghetti noodle. She's not here for the laughs.

"I'm sorry," I say, giving it every iota of sincerity I got in my back pocket. "I wasn't trying to pull your leg, Dollface. I was just trying to keep it light. But I'll give you what you want. You bought my book. I owe you that much, right? That's the deal between folks like us, ain't it?"

That spaghetti noodle loosens just a little as I start to cook.

"Do I love America?" I start. For the record: I know my lines in this particular scene pretty well. "Yeah," I say. "Sure thing! Hand on a stack of Bibles, I do. Love her from sea to shining sea. But I already know what you're thinking: Why? Or maybe how? That's fair, Doll. I'm the first to admit it's got more than its fair share of problems. But, hell, who ain't loved someone who was broken? We all got that one person in our group that's a little rough around the edges, that person we warn new people about before they show up to the party. But, hell, we still invite them to see the ball drop, don't we? So that's what America is: it's that friend that you love that you also have to give a disclaimer to others about. The Land of the Free's still on my friends list. Still on the same text thread it's always been on. She still matters to me, even if she could be better. And, even more than that, she's my home."

Nailed it. Every line, every syllable.

Cut and print. That's the take. That's cinematic gold. Gregory Peck being Atticus Finch ain't got nothing on me. Put this lady square on the back foot with that one. Works every ti—

"That's not true," the woman says, breaking up my internal victory lap.

"How's that?"

"America is not your home. The continent of Africa is your home."

"Africa?" I say. "Never been. I hear good things though. Next question."

Dylan leans in real slow. "I told you Europeans were different," he whispers.

"No foolin'."

The rest of the event goes about the same. The Italians come at me one after the other, leaving the softball questions at home. Nothing but the fastballs coming fast, hard, and inside. "How does your book fit into the neo-postmodern landscape?" one of them asks.

"Three rows back," I say, giving another patented chuckle.

"Are you a Hegelian?" another asks.

"Only with the ladies," I answer. Whoever said you have to know what a word means to be able to answer to it?

"In 1942, the United States was a heroic figure on the world stage, unrivaled in . . ." and on and on and on. The questions come and go. I feel like I'm being attacked by graduate students. But all the while I keep coming back to that dame and her love question.

I've always struggled with love.

After what feels like an eight-hour stretch of bobbing and weaving, it's over. The crowd packs it in and we all make for the exits. Somewhere along the way that shadow in the back of the room faded off into nothingness. There one minute, gone the next. The good news is that as soon as I realize it's gone, that feeling of dread makes for the highway too.

"Pretty good," Dylan says. "But now we're going to take a break. Let's go out on the town for a little while. Get a bite to eat."

"Swell," I say. I take a deep breath. This air tastes pretty good.

"You really made it sound like you love America," Dylan says, clapping me on the shoulder.

"Sure, sure," I say. "I had a girlfriend once who would tell me thirty times a day—no foolin'!—that she loved me. Over and over and over again, all day long. And I'd say it back to her until I was dry in the mouth, even though I couldn't get my thinking around why she needed to say it so much. Then I figured it out: sometimes when someone says 'I love you' what they're really doing is asking 'Do you love me?' Now I probably say 'I love you' to America thirty times a day."

Pordenone after dark is a really live burg. The type of place somebody ought to sell tickets to. Not New York or London, but it's got its own type of swing. You can feel the time in this town. Centuries in the stone streets and in the steeples. The streetlamps hang like islands of light, beating back the ocean of darkness. Turn down the right street here, follow the right lights and, hell, who knows where or when you might come out.

Dylan and I make our way to a bar sans Goon. He decided to take a powder. Plus, something about a place here in town that was about to close and their ricotta cheesecake. So, by the time we make it to the bar, it's just The Kid and me. He gets a beer and I get a water. As always, I pat myself on the back for deciding to stay off the sauce yet again.

"This place is all gravy," I say, looking around the room. It's bustling. Full of thin Euro Joes and Janes dressed in tight-fitting clothes and the best shoes I've ever seen. "Pure gravy," I repeat.

"Glad you like it," Dylan says.

When the server brings our drinks, it's got to be said: she's a looker. Taller than the legs on the Parthenon and with skin like Janelle Monáe. I can tell, right off the bat, that she's got American clay in her veins and it feels good to see another wanderer over here on the other side of the world. Feels like safety in its own way.

I give her the nod that people like me do when we see each other in foreign spaces and just want to acknowledge that we've been seen and, maybe, we're not as alone in this world as we might have thought. All of this with just a quick dip of the head.

But she doesn't nod back.

She only puts down our drinks and turns away from me like I just asked for her Social Security number. She says something in Foreign to Dylan and makes to leave.

"Excuse me," I say, careful not to touch her arm. I try not to touch any dame that don't ask me to. "This ain't a come-on or anything," I say, "but I'm just curious about where you're from."

She smiles at me like I'm speaking in riddles and, again, turns to Dylan. He says something Foreign and with too many vowel sounds. She gives him back just as good as she got.

"She's from a small town in Sicily," Dylan says.

"Oh, thanks," I say, still keeping eye contact with her as best I can. "But it's okay if you and I talk, you know?"

"I don't think she speaks English," Dylan says.

"What? Of course she does. She's got south Georgia written all over her!"

Dylan says something to her, pulls out some denomination of Monopoly-money-colored Eurobucks, and hands it to her.

She walks away.

"Don't do that," he says.

"Don't do what?"

"You know she's not American, right?"

I laugh. "What do you mean? She's as American as hip-hop and using your country's flag as underwear," I say.

"No," Dylan says. "She's not. Do you think that just because she's Black that she's from America?"

"Of course not." I feel my lungs tightening again. My hand begins to fidget. "They call it a diaspora for a reason," I continue. "But people like us, we know each other when we see each other. Just like how I can spot an African or a Haitian, I can spot an American. And that woman there, she's an American. Red-blooded and pure. If it ain't Atlanta, it's somewhere else down South. South Carolina *maybe*, but my gut says Georgia. The point here is that she's an American. Me and her, we're the same."

Dylan shakes his head. He mumbles something in some language I don't recognize.

"Don't you Foreign at me," I say.

"Listen," he replies. "I don't know what you think she is, but she's not that. So just drop it and have your drink."

I look down at my water. Suddenly it doesn't seem like what I want. I get up and walk to the bar and I order a whiskey. When the bartender acts like he's slow on the uptake, like he might not speak American, I remember the Golden Rule of American Travelers: *If they say they don't speak American, make them.*

It works, of course. The bartender drops off my whiskey with a sneer and a pair of hard eyes. But I leave enough Eurobucks on the cedar that he'll get past it pretty quick, I figure.

Then I'm alone with my troublemaker.

Years now. Not a drop. But old habits die hard.

So long as I don't touch the glass, I won't drink it. I'll be fine. I've danced this dance before. Not in a long while, mind you. I've been doing better. But I know myself.

Just don't touch.

My fidgeting hand makes a go at the glass, but I catch it by the wrist just in time. It makes itself into a finger gun and, *pew pew*, I put two shots into temptation. Or so I think. Truth is, I'm dancing on the edge of the blade right now and I know it. Truth is, that drink's gonna go down warm in just a few seconds unless I find some sort of distraction.

That's when I catch sight of her: the waitress from Atlanta who pretends she don't speak American. She's on her way to the bathroom and, in spite of myself, I give chase. Not sure what I want from her, but I promise it's nothing scary.

Promise.

I catch up to her just outside of the bathroom.

"Excuse me!" I try not to block her path because I know how this looks, but I have to ask her the question that's been on my mind: "Where are you from?" I say. "Really?"

She says something in Foreign.

"No. Let's put the games down for just a second. On the square. Really. Which part of back home are you from? That's all I'm asking. I just want to know where you fit in?"

More too-fast words with too many vowels without a hint of vinegar-based barbecue or magnolias.

"Stop doing that!" I bark.

The whole bar hears that one. They turn to watch. I see it happening, know what this looks like, and I don't care. I need to know. I need her to be straight with me.

I lay it out piece by piece: "Where. Are. You. From."

She only stands there, glaring at me with this light in her eyes that makes me wonder just how fast I can duck a right hook.

On the other side of the room, Dylan stands and starts walking. A couple of others, square-shouldered Italian mustache-bearers, do the same. I know how scenes like this play out for men playing the role they all think I'm playing.

"Listen," I say, both to her and to the rest of the bar, "I'm not the baddie here!" I see a phone pop out.

I know how this looks.

"Wait! Wait!" I say to the group of guys starting to crowd in on me. "I know how this looks. I promise I'm not up to anything. I just need her to tell me where she's really from. I just need her to tell me what state she was born in. Georgia? Tennessee?"

I look into her eyes and that anger that was there a second ago is gone. Hell, if anything, I might say I catch a glimpse of pity looking back at me. Then, finally, she finds some English. She puts it to me slowly and clearly, either because her American is rusty or maybe just to be sure that I catch every part of what she's laying down: "Not American. Italiana." Then, and she delivers this to me word by word, just like I did to her. She says: "Not. Like. You."

Then she walks off and I can't move. Can't speak. Can't do anything all of a sudden.

"What the hell are you doing?" Dylan asks.

"Nothing," I say. Before I know it, I'm wiping my eyes. "I just think I need to go to the bathroom. That's all. I'm just having a rough one, you know?"

Over on the counter, the drink is still there waiting for me. It's got a neon sign floating above it with my name on it. Flashing bright and hard, giving a bit of vibrancy to the world in a way that it hasn't in quite some time.

The thing is, even though I don't let people in on it, going off the sauce didn't do anything to curb the way I see the world, if you know what I mean. One thing I've learned is that sometimes it's just easier to say that you're like everyone. Easier to smile and blend in with the crowd rather than to go it on your own and really let people know who you are and how you really live in the world. I think the trick is to save up the parts of yourself that are really important and share them only with the people that you know will understand. The Others like you.

And I know, sister, that you're just like me.

I still have a condition. And, honestly, it feels good to finally come out and say it.

"You shouldn—" Dylan says, his hand on my shoulder, stuttering a little at what I figure is the start of a pretty good laying into. A real pep talk designed to get me back to where I need to be. One of those talks to remind me that there are other people in the world and that they're real, not just figments of my imagination.

"I know," I say, resisting the urge to call him "Kid."

But he keeps on.

"You shou—"

That stutter kicks in again. But it sounds off. Makes the hairs on the back of my neck stand up.

"You shou—" he stumbles for the third time, like his Wi-Fi connection just went down and now he's stuck buffering.

"Say, what's with you, Kid?" I say, finally forgetting about the Georgia girl who refuses to admit it and really giving him the look he deserves.

There stands Dylan, staring straight ahead. Motionless as a statue. His hand that was on my shoulder hangs in the air now, frozen, just like his face.

"Hey! Hey, Kid! You okay?"

The hairs on the back of my neck have broken out into a Cirque du Soleil routine. This kid, he ain't just frozen anymore. His eyes have gone into a thousand-yard stare and everything about him is on pause. I can't even really tell how he's standing. It's like he's been dipped in wax and dropped off in front of me when I was in the process of blinking.

"Hey!" I shout! "Hey!" The whole place is looking at the two of us now. But Dylan gives no answer. He just stands there, frozen, staring off, like he sees something I can't quite get eyes on. And, whatever it is, the kid looks terrified.

He's still got a day before the high note of Minnesota. Be-fore he stands in front of the crowd and talks to them about all their pain and tries to find the right thing to say. He moves restless around in his hotel room. Sometimes standing at the foot of the bed, staring out the window for long swaths of time, waiting for something to come along and tell him the right thing to do. When nothing comes to mind, he decides that maybe work is the way to go. He's taken a part-time job teaching creative writing.

He goes to his luggage and pulls out the stack of papers all bound together by a large clip. It's a mixture of graduate and undergraduate. The main thing he worries about as he reads their work is just whether or not they're progressing. Are they learning from their mistakes? So he sits at the desk in the far corner and starts grading, with the pistol on the desk beside him—always within reach—and the wind outside howling as the storm comes on proper and the temperature drops and the world goes deeper and deeper into hibernation.

It doesn't take very long before the dead kids show up in the stack of papers. The dead are always present in writing. Death and love are the oldest tropes for a reason. When he was in college, learning about how to write, it was always dead grandmas. A person couldn't get through a week's reading without a dead grandma rearing her head in a poem or short story. It was so common that, by the end of his time in undergrad, one of his mentors—a silver-haired woman who reminded him of a swan—made the infamous "Grannies Never Die" decree.

And, after that, all the grannies began to live forever. All the work turned in became the stories of broken hearts and violence against parents and of young people trying to find their way in a world of expectation.

But that's not the way it is anymore.

When he gets to the first dead kid, it's in only the second poem he's started grading. Its title is "Because the Surgeon General Says It's a Public Health Crisis." The poem is written from the point of view of a twelve-year-old's brain that's been splattered across a dry-erase board. This takes place somewhere in Alabama. In the poem, the sun is shining. Its light "stumbles in through the window" according to the author, and its light "stomps on the red explosion from Chris's head."

Soot pauses there, looking down at the dead preteen's brain on that dry-erase board, and circles the word "stumbles" and writes: "Is stumble the word you're looking for here?"

A few lines later down in the poem: "There is a smell I will never forget."

Soot writes: "Expand on this. Describe the smell. Make it unforgettable FOR US."

The rest of the poem moves well enough. It closes with: "I don't want to be here."

Soot writes: "Where, specifically, don't you want to be?"

When he finishes reading the poem, he adds it to the stack and thinks to himself how, if this particular student can just stick with it, she might have a future as a writer.

The next paper is a short story. He leans back in his chair and settles in. In the story, a family goes on vacation and is attacked by cannibals. It's refreshing. Cannibalism doesn't get written about nearly enough these days by undergrads. The story has pacing and tension. Its twists are unexpected. He wants to pat the student on the back. At the end of the story, he scribbles, "Great job! So terrifying!"

The next story is about a student who goes over to visit her best friend and he pulls a gun on her and holds her hostage for three days. The boy is angry and the girl being held hostage tries to get him to explain why, but all he says is "I hate this" over and over and over again. The title of the story is, of course, "I Hate This." Somewhere around the story's second act the girl is locked in a bathroom with no windows and the boy with the gun strings barbed wire around it, saying that he's going to "keep you safe." He apologizes as he does it. Eventually, the girl talks the boy into opening the bathroom on the promise that, if the boy wants, she'll go with him to shoot Tommy—the perceived villain of the story.

Soot writes in the margins: "What did Tommy do to this boy? I don't see mention of it anywhere in the story. So maybe you can expand on that just a little bit. One thing that readers will always want is to be able to understand why someone hates someone else, especially if they hate them enough to shoot them."

In the latter part of the third act, just a page or two before the conclusion, the boy and the girl he's taken hostage go to school. He has the gun tucked in his jacket pocket. They walk through the halls, looking for Tommy, with the boy rabid at the thought of getting his revenge and with the girl just trying to find a moment when she can call for help or warn everyone else about the terrible thing that's about to happen.

Then, just as the boy is about to take out the gun and shoot Tommy, Tommy pulls out a gun of his own and begins picking off students one by one. "The bodies fall like leaves," the author writes.

Soot writes in the margins: "Hmmm. A little cliché. Maybe try again here."

After Tommy has shot four students in quick succession, the boy with the gun pulls out his own pistol and shoots Tommy dead. "He became the hero," the student wrote in the story's last line, "and, for what felt like forever, she just watched him revel in it and she never told anyone otherwise."

His head is hurting now so he puts the story away. The student will get an A.

For what feels like forever, Dylan is stuck there, hanging in whatever or wherever he's gone off to. That hand that was on my shoulder still outstretched, reaching for something only those distant eyes of his are able to see. The whole while, I'm standing there in front of him, shaking him by the shoulders and screaming my head off. Calling for help. Begging all these foreigners to do something. Yelling, "Doctor! Doctor! Get a doctor!" over and over again, trusting that, even in Foreign, some words just get understood.

At least that part is working.

I can tell by the cell phones suddenly shoved up against so many faces that somebody here's already called Italian 911. And since I'm a bit older and since we've both got the same-colored skin, they're all looking at me like I'm his father and asking, in the best American they can muster: "Your son?" and "Is there medicine?" and "Where is the mother?" and all I can say is "I'm not his father" and "I don't know" and "I only just met him" and, with each one, I tack on "It'll be okay."

That's the one I try to really stick the landing on. "It'll be okay."

I've found that, if you really push that optimism button hard enough, I mean really hammer it with your elbow until it damned near breaks, sometimes you can almost come to believe it. And if you do come to believe it, hell, that's just one step closer to it actually being true. When the Italianos watch me grab Dylan and lay him gently on the floor and kneel beside him and hold his hand and repeat, maybe too many times, "It'll be okay," I'm sure that, from the outside, I look like the concerned father I've never been.

"Hey, Kid," I say. "Hey. You still there? If so, send up a signal flare. I can't understand any of the Foreign these folks are throwing at me, so I need you to get back and help me out."

I don't know if any of that makes any sense to him. Don't even know if he can hear me. But it feels like a half-decent thing to say.

His hand twitches.

The whole room breathes in unison and that fresh, EU-certified air I've been sucking down since I got here starts to taste good again, bit by bit. An instant after the hand twitches, those eyes of his finally blink.

The whole room bursts into what I'd best describe as "elated Foreign." Tongues dance on vowels and two-step with consonants in unrecognizable patterns. I'm guessing it's all prayers and thank-you notes addressed to The Big Pasta Maker upstairs.

I give Dylan a little pat on the chest. "Welcome back."

There's a flash of confusion, chased down by a type of embarrassed recognition. "Shit," he says. Then, immediately: "I'm okay."

"You don't look like it, my friend."

He goes to sit up and I try to hold him down, so he can get himself together, but he's having none of it. "I'm fine," he says, shoving me off as gently as he can.

Me and one of the Italianos—some guy with thick hair and a pair of damned fine wingtips—help the kid up into his chair.

"Fuck," Dylan says. He grabs his glass of water from the table and downs it. Then: "You can cancel the ambulance." He says something in Foreign, which, I'm guessing, is the same message. He says it just as smooth as any of the locals. Sounds like he was born with those words on his tongue. "Everyone always calls the ambulance." He says it low, with a splash of shame at the end.

"What was that?" I ask.

"I've got a condition."

I chuckle. "Hey. That's my line."

He gives me a little smile.

"What's it sound like in Foreign?"

"What?"

"Those words. If I wanted to say them in some flavor of Foreign. What would they sound like?"

"Depends on where you are."

"Humor me," I say. "Imagine I'm dropped off somewhere and nobody speaks American. So I gotta tell them about my condition. What's it sound like?"

He thinks for a moment, then mumbles a whole different kind of Foreign than he did a moment ago. It's like rolling hills on the ears. It's fresh water in syllable form. Like I'm standing somewhere safe and beautiful and nobody knows I'm there. All of that from a few words in a language I can't even identify.

To keep the feeling from fading, I take a swing at repeating it. But I don't have the mouth for it. It comes out all twisted. Fingers are where my good words live, you know? A boxer don't fight underwater. They keep it in the ring. So I give up on it. "You got all the gifts," I say. "What's the story?"

"I'm fine," he says. "Just let me sit here for a second."

He looks like he's getting himself back together and I'm plenty glad. Fact of the matter is that, all of a sudden, I can't help but feel like my battery's running on low. Nothing like seeing somebody go all incommunicado for a minute or two to make you feel like it might be time to check in on your bladder and your sanity.

"I'm stepping off to the can for a second. You gonna be okay?"

"Yes," he says. He digs into his jacket pocket and I hear a little rattle of pills.

"Good," I say. "I'd be lost without you, Kid."

"Stop calling me that!"

"There he is."

Thankfully, this particular Pordenone bathroom is empty. Gives me a chance to put all my pieces back together. I walk over to the sink and lean on the counter and I sigh so heavy that I feel like I might melt straight down into the floor. Didn't know how scared I was until right then. Right now.

"Dammit, Kid," I say.

I don't know when the door opened. Don't know when he came in. All I know is that, the second I hear his voice, I already know all the bad things I thought were over with, well, they're back for another dance.

"Hidy!" Remus says, as bright as a newborn's first sunrise. He's standing not six feet away, dressed in a suit, of all things—I promise I'll get into that a little more soon. He's leaning against the wall, with his arms crossed in front of his chest, flashing that half-full smile of his. "How you been? Right as rain, I hope!"

For just a moment, while the kid was under, I'd finally managed to forget about that whole death threat, whoever it was in the back of the room earlier when the Italian bird was asking me all the hard questions . . . I'd forgotten all of it. Dumped that bucket out and filled it with my fears for Dylan. Well, I guess this is what happens when you forget the world. Eventually, it catches up.

"Well don't just stand there holding your tongue," Remus says.

I stammer. "You're uh . . . What's your name again?"

He laughs that beautiful, booming laugh of his. The walls of this bathroom take that laugh and they play Ping-Pong with it, letting it get a little louder each time it hits until it sounds like a symphony just before it's gone.

"One thing I've never been in my whole entire life, not even for the time it takes to blow a kiss, is forgettable." There's confidence and warmth enough in his words to cook a T-bone.

"Your name's Remus, isn't it?"

"Sure as shit," he says.

All the while, I'm slowly backing away from those large, scarred hands of his. Even with his arms folded in front of him, those hands of his look like clubs. But my problem is, there isn't very far to go on account of how these Euroland bathrooms are built for a skinnier population than back in the Home of the Whopper, so it doesn't take long before I find myself with my literal back against the literal wall. But just before the panic sets in I remember the heater strapped to my rib cage.

God bless America.

My right hand twitches and I think about all the gangster-movie quick draws I've seen: The hand disappears inside the folds of the jacket, then it's back again carrying a few pounds of steel. The gun shines under the stage lights. The bad guys, with all their menacing shapes and shadows, go just as stiff and motionless as Dylan did. Their violence gets put on hold.

. . . But then what?

Suppose for a second that Remus don't play his part. Suppose I pull the heater and it turns out he ain't read the same draft of the script as me. Then what? Mow him down? Shoot a man to death right here in this beautiful Italian bathroom?

I hear there's no going back after you've killed a man. And, personally, I like back. I want to be able to go there from time to time.

The moment keeps stretching out.

What if I make my play for the heater and fumble it? Then there's a gun on the ground and Remus, who might have actually just been fooling this whole time about killing me, decides to take it for real and I've just given him the push-button—or "pull-trigger"—tool he needs to do the job right. Wouldn't that be a headline? "Author Killed by Own Gun."

I'm sweating now. A flash flood from head to toe.

Meanwhile, Remus is cool as a tax collector.

He's dressed in a suit he must have inherited from his great-great-grandfather. It's one of those suits you see the high-class men in Westerns wearing. One of those formfitting deals that was skinny-fit back before skinny-fit was a thing. The problem is the suit's having trouble holding in all that is Remus. He's too broad. Too much muscle and sinew. Too many scars. Just too much to be held in by anything, and so he's busting out of everything.

When he turns to check himself in the mirror, I see the jacket is ripped halfway up the back and the seams along the sides of the pants are barely holding together. I feel like if he lets loose even so much as a light sneeze, those pants of his are gonna be splattered all over these walls.

"So, how you been?" he asks, leaning on the counter. "You're looking good. Like you got the moon on a string!" He runs those dark hands under the faucet and nothing happens. It's one of those motion jobs that sometimes struggles to know that you're real, even when you're standing right in front of it waving your hands around a pair of geese. After giving his hands a couple of passes, he gives up on it and turns to me with those eyes of his and says, "Wouldja mind?"

For reasons I can't explain, I walk over and stick my hands under the faucet. Like clockwork, it kicks on. Then his hands are under the water, and he says, "Thanks an untaxed million."

"No problem," I say, and I lean back on the wall and watch him. He's got a relaxing aura about him. And, yeah, I know what you're thinking. Hell, I know what my own mind is thinking. I know what he said before, that whole bit about killing me and all that but, right now, I just don't think he's into it.

Maybe it really was all just a gag.

He washes his hands until the faucet switches off by itself, like it still doesn't know he's there, and then he splashes what's left on his face and makes a big, satisfied noise like he just ate a whole steak for the first time in a decade. "That feels good," he says. "Yes sir, nothing like a little shot of cold water on the face to make you feel like yourself again. Why do you think that is? Just in case we fell out of a tree one day and landed in a river? 'Wake up!' them old apes is saying. 'Don't drown and waste all the fucking we worked so hard doing!'" He laughs again, particularly pleased by the image.

"I could ask how you been," I say, "but I can tell right off the bat that you've been swell."

"I already said as much, friend," he says. Then he walks straight at me and I already know what he's coming for even before he says the words. "So let me see how those teeth of yours are holding up." And without so much as a moment to prepare myself he's got those scarred-up hands of his in my mouth again.

I tighten all over and my back finds itself against the wall and I think for a second about putting my hands up to resist something but, just like before, Remus's hands go all tense and I can feel that he's a man of power and just now the best thing I can do is go with the flow.

And I figure that if it starts to go too far south, there's still the gun I keep not being able to go for.

Luckily, the inspection doesn't last quite as long this time around.

"Not bad," Remus says. "Not bad at all. And why not? It's only been two shakes of a lamb's tail since the last time we seen each other. How much trouble can teeth get into?"

"How did you find me?" I ask. I don't mean to, but the words just sorta pop out.

"You know," Remus begins, "I used to work as a driver to a rich White man. I mean a real Park Avenue type. Now, mostly all I did was drive him around, but if you know anything about New York you know that driving is a full-contact sport." He looks in the mirror as he talks, using his damp hands to tame his thinning, silver hair atop that dark skull of his.

"You're from New York?"

"Don't interrupt a good story. Where was I?"

"You were a driver for a White Park Avenue man."

"That's right," Remus says. "But I was more than a driver. We were a team. He was the king and I was his right hand. On any day he bought and sold more money than they got in all of Brazil. And, while I didn't exactly push the buttons or anything, I was a part of it. He'd always come to me, asking about the people. I'm good with people. I know what makes them tick, and that's good to have on Park Avenue. So I was his man. 'Remus,' he would say, 'you're my secret weapon.' Haha! And, brother, I knew things about him that his own loving mother didn't know. He paid me a fortune. More money in a year than a man should ever make in a lifetime."

"Sounds like a hell of a gig." I'm not really sure what exactly he's driving at. I mean, I'm a guy who tells stories for a living. I pride myself on being able to suss out what somebody's trying to tell me even when they themselves don't know what they're trying to tell me. But with this guy . . . with this guy I got nothing. All I know for sure is that he's not talking about killing me, so I'm down to hear whatever story he wants to tell. "What happened?" I ask.

"I quit," he says. "Walked out on it like it was any other job I ever had."

"Why?"

"Too much. Too much out there in the world. Too many things to see and do. Too much to reach out and grab. You ever hear about the first nigga in Japan?"

"What?"

"Happened back in olden days. This nigga went to Japan and the shogun—he was the big honcho over there—the shogun sees this nigga and can't believe his eyes. Literally can't believe what he's seeing. He thinks to himself, 'What the fuck is this guy doing? Who the hell would do this? Who the hell would cover their whole body like this motherfucker did?'" He finally turns away from the mirror. "You see what I'm saying?"

"The shogun thought it was just some crazy Joe that loved tattoos a little too much? That the deal?"

My friend Remus looks me dead in the eyes and says, "You're the storyteller. You tell me."

Then the knife is there.

I can't say where it came from or even when he pulled it. It's just suddenly there, as if it was always there, just waiting for me to catch up to it in the timeline.

As Remus walks toward me—slow, calm, with that hit-and-miss smile of his beaming—I tell my body to reach for the gun, but it doesn't. I tell my body that I'm an American. I tell my body I've got gunpowder in my DNA. I tell my body, "This is the whole reason we broke international laws to smuggle this Great Equalizer into a whole other country." And while I'm telling myself all this, Remus don't hesitate.

The knife goes in.

Tough luck.

There's as much terror in him as there is joy. His heart rises as soon as he feels the slight chill of the hotel room on his face. Toronto, again. But, this time, she's alive. A turn of luck.

Before the end, Toronto becomes her favorite place. She tells him once that she loves it because ". . . it feels like the end of the world. Like the unknown lives right out there somewhere. If someone wanted," she says, "they could just walk away from it all. Pick a direction. Head off and who knows what might come next. Canada is the edge of everything. Some whole other continent or something."

A knock at the door brings him out of the memory.

"Dad?" she calls out. "Dad! Let's go! We're gonna be late!"

She's alive now. And she always will be, here.

He opens the door and there she stands. Sixteen years old. Somehow taller than he remembers. With her hair pulled back and then blossoming out into a single Afro puff—a young Lauryn Hill—that seems to float in the air behind her head like the angelic ring in paintings of Christ from the Middle Ages.

"Mia!" he says, sighing. "Come here!"

He pulls her into his arms and hugs her so tight he hears her grunt a little. He eases up. "Ha! Sorry, kiddo," he says. But he doesn't let her go yet.

She's alive here. Now. Living and breathing and being who she is. The bullet hasn't found her. It's still months away. She's still having tomorrows.

"Daaaaaad!" she says, muffled by the hug. "Dad, you're being weird again."

He finally lets go. "Being weird is literally my whole thing," he replies.

"I'm glad you're finally here," she says. "But you're also late! We almost left without you."

"You wouldn't dare!" He says it dramatically, with one hand on his forehead and the other arm held out in front of him, like a silent movie scene.

It's enough to make her laugh, which is to say: it's everything.

"You sure you're okay?" she asks. "You seem weirder than usual."

"I'm fine," he says. "Just a little jet-lagged."

"Toronto is in the same time zone as Bolton, Old Man."

"Okay then: Canada lag."

"Ha! Let's go. Mom's downstairs in the lobby, waiting."

"Yeah. Let's go."

Then the three of them are out on the evening streets of Toronto. Soot, his recently exed wife, and his daughter who is no longer dead. The sun has just gone down and the temperature has done the same. He and Tasha walk so that Mia is in the middle. Both of them bound to and by the gravity of her. They're all silent for a while because this era, after the divorce, is new to all of them. So, silently, they head toward the river.

"Dad, isn't this amazing?" Mia says when they finally reach the riverbank. She points out to where the water has half frozen. It's ice and slush in both directions. On the other bank, evening Toronto dances with lights, and there is only the sound of the cold air and the wind rushing over the water and their family of footsteps crunching in the thick layer of fresh snow.

"Amazing," he says.

"Thanks for coming," Tasha says when Mia walks a little bit ahead of them for a moment.

"Thanks for letting me."

"I'm glad that we can do this peacefully."

"Me too. I'm not mad at you," he says. "I never was. I never will be. You made the right decision. I just didn't see it at the time."

"Wow," she replies.

"Just take it as it is," he says. "I'm feeling good. Really good. I'm in Canada with my daughter and the only woman I ever loved. I deserve to be happy."

"You know we're still divorced, right?"

As they make their way along the waterfront—emptied out by the cold—he barely notices the woman beneath a statue staring out at the blue-and-gray slush that has become the bay. She's in her late twenties, with dark hair, wearing a puffy green parka and jeans, sitting with her arms folded in front of her. He thinks of stopping, but then remembers.

Don't stop here, he thinks. This is where it starts.

"Are you okay?" Mia asks the woman.

It's too late for him to avoid it.

"I'm fine," the woman says, sniffling. "Just cold. That's all."

"Let's leave her be," Soot says, trying to undo it.

Mia waves him away, keeping her attention on the woman. "I don't think you're okay," Mia says. "I think you've been crying." The woman wipes her eyes. "What's your name?"

"Vivian."

"And I think you should come with us, Vivian," Mia says. "We're going to get some coffee. C'mon. It's freezing out here."

"I think she's right," Tasha says.

"No," Soot says. They're all looking at him now. "She'll be okay," he says. "We should get going. Let's . . . let's leave her be."

"Excuse me," Tasha says to the woman. Then she's grabbing Soot by the arm and tugging him halfway down the block so that she can be as loud as she feels she needs to be just now. "What the fuck is your problem?" she asks.

"I don't want that woman near Mia. We can't let the two of them be together."

"Be together? What the hell are you talking about? That woman is in trouble."

"I know," he says. "And I don't want her spreading it to Mia."

"What the fuck are you talking about?!"

"She went there to kill herself," Soot says.

Tasha looks back at the woman. "How do you know that?"

"Just trust me. I know. And you know it too. You said it yourself, 'That woman's in trouble.' You just didn't know exactly what the trouble was. That's all. I do know."

She thinks about this for a moment. "Then we have to help her. We can't let her leave."

"No," Soot replies. "She'll pass it on. She'll put the thought in Mia's mind. This"—he shakes as he speaks—"this is where it starts."

"Where what starts?"

"It's all her fault," Soot says. He isn't quiet anymore. Not whispering. Vivian and Mia can both hear him and he doesn't care just now. He walks back up the sidewalk, with Tasha on his heels, calling his name and tugging at his arm, but he doesn't stop. "You're the one who kills her," he hisses at Vivian.

Vivian is already rising to her feet. Already backing away, slowly, carefully, with her hands out in front of her and fear in her eyes. "I'm sorry," she says. She looks as though she's waiting to be hit. "I'm sorry," she repeats.

"No!" Mia shouts. It's loud enough that everyone stops talking. Everyone stops moving. "We're not letting you go," she says to Vivian. "My dad was just leaving. I promise. Isn't that right, Dad?"

He knows then, all at once, there's nothing he can do now. It's already too late. Even if he tried to explain it all to her, tried to make it make sense, she wouldn't get it. This was, is, and always will be the moment when his daughter and ex-wife saved the life of a lonely woman who had come down to a cold, hard river to kill herself. This will be a moment that lives with all of them.

After this, Tasha and Vivian will build a friendship up here in Canada. They'll go to movies together. Vivian will help her with her French. She'll show her the local restaurants and teach her to ski. And all the while, he will be back in North Carolina, alone in the house that used to hold a family, missing out on all of it. And then, further down the timeline, after his daughter has killed herself, Vivian will call, weeping and sobbing, wailing over the airwaves, asking how it happened. And she will ask him, "Was it me? Did I give her the idea? Did I infect her?"

And he will tell her, "No. Of course not. You can't let yourself think that." It'll go this way for years and he'll mean it each time he says it. But, eventually, one day when he's sliding back through it all, he will have a moment when he thinks that, just maybe, this was where it all started to go awry. He will try to blame Vivian, even though he knows it's not true. Knows one person's sadness didn't change his daughter any more than the rain changes the path of the moon.

I'll do us both a favor here and manicure that previous violence down to just the nubs by saying: in case you hadn't heard, or in case you heard and didn't believe, I had a knife run through my breadbasket in an Italian bathroom.

Nothing quite like it.

Here's the thing: You don't think it can happen until it does and, even then, you don't really believe it. You think you're watching a movie. You think you're dreaming. And as somebody with a certain condition that, on some days, makes it hard to tell what's real and what's a tall tale, I gotta say that when it actually went down I thought maybe I was just telling myself another story.

But then there's a blade parting the Red Sea of my belly and the next thing I know I wake up at Frenchie Memorial Hospital with an IV in my arm and my belly wrapped up like a cheese wheel and I know, finally, that sometimes, if only to keep yourself in this world, sometimes you should believe everything you see, even if you don't think it's real.

Live—get stabbed—and learn, I guess.

For the record: I call the hospital I wind up in Frenchie Memorial on account of how Frenchie owns the entire upper floor of the thing. I come to find out later that he keeps it and a small army of overpriced doctors on call all year long. I can't say why for certain, but maybe Frenchie already knows the world is full of bathrooms lousy with knives.

When I come to, I feel satin sheets under me and the air smells like teakwood and everything has this glow to it like everybody keeps saying heaven is supposed to look. There's a wall of windows—floor to ceiling—that the sunlight is coming through by the bucketful and, even though things are a bit soft around the edges, I can make out a dark-skinned silhouette hovering at my bedside flanked by another, blockier shadow.

"That you, Kid?"

"Don't call me 'Kid.'"

A few blinks of these old peepers of mine and the fuzziness starts to go away.

Sure enough, there's Dylan, still looking and sounding like a young Michael B. Jordan. And there's The Goon, still looking like an onyx mountain come down from the Highlands to say hello. "Welcome back," Dylan says.

"You're looking good," I reply. I swallow what feels like a mouthful of cotton balls.

"You've looked better," Dylan says. There's relief on his face and it feels good to see. He hands me a glass of water and, when I sip it, there's a faint hint of cucumber, just like at Frenchie's villa. Why can't all hospitals have cucumber water?

"I'm glad yu're naught dead," my big, Scotsman Goon friend bellows. He laughs and moves his bulk from behind Dylan's chair where he's been standing and slaps my thigh with one of those ham-size paws of his. "Yu lucky bastard!"

A dash of pain runs out from my stomach when The Goon swats my leg, but it's not as bad as you might expect. It feels far away, like a phone ringing in another room. My guess is that Frenchie's got me some sort of billionaire-grade painkillers; something that takes away the hurt and leaves only the taste of mint and a high-yield savings account behind.

"Not dead just yet," I say. "We got too many pages left."

I wink.

The Goon laughs again.

I try to sit up, but that ringing phone moves a little closer and Dylan and The Goon go all dark in the face like they're watching me walk out into traffic. So, maybe just to give them a break, I let out a little sigh and relax back down onto my satin-wrapped pillow. "How far'd I go?" I ask.

"What?"

"How bad is it?" I lift up the covers. I didn't know Versace made hospital gowns.

"Not too bad," Dylan says. "As far as stabbings go, you got pretty lucky. The doctors say that whoever this guy is, he wasn't trying to kill you."

"He was just joshing yu," The Goon adds.

"Could have fooled me." I chuckle, and boy do I pay for it. Fun fact: you shouldn't laugh with a stab wound to the stomach. Who would'a thunk it?

"He left a note," Dylan says.

"Yeah?"

He hands me a slip of paper. Scrawled across it in what's gotta be Remus's surprisingly elegant handwriting is "Keep brushing!"

Signs and wonders.

"What about you?" I ask. "What was that back at the restaurant?"

Changing the subject feels easier than thinking on Remus just now.

"Nothing," Dylan says. His smile turns nervous. Then he takes it down altogether. "I wasn't in any real danger. Sometimes I go away for a little while. I've got medicine. It helps."

"No fixing it?"

"No," he says.

"Tough luck." I stop myself from adding "Kid" at the end. "Say: When you take these trips of yours, where do you go and how's the rent?"

I finally get a smile out of him that's not ashamed. "I can't really say.

It's more akin to blacking out. But . . . different." He pauses, and I know there's more to it. I play it cool and give him time and space enough to keep going. If you want to hear what somebody has to say, sometimes you gotta shut up and give them the room. A moment later: "Every time I come out of it, I think about home. And I don't mean Italy, I mean home. Baltimore. Every time I have one of these . . . moments, I wake up and it's like I've been there. There's these sights and sounds and smells. Sometimes I swear I can taste my grandmama's sweet potato pie. Then I come to." He takes a deep breath and lets it out in a huff. "No memories or anything like that. Just a feeling. Crazy, huh?"

"World's full of crazy," I say. "Don't mean you should be ashamed to carry your slice of it. When's the last time you been Stateside?"

"It's been a long time," he says.

"Folks bring you over?"

"I brought me over." His voice hardens a little.

"What about your folks?" I ask.

"I'm going to get the boss." He stands up like he's been stung. "He'll want to know that you're awake." He pats my leg gently. "I'm glad you're okay." Then he's out the door.

"Something I say?"

"No," The Goon says. "Don't worry about it. He's a strong lad." The both of us stare at the doorway, as if waiting for the kid to reappear. Eventually, the moment passes. "Hey," The Goon says, "can I hug you?"

Until you've had a seven-foot-tall Black Scotsman ask to hug you, you haven't lived.

"Bring it in," I say.

The Goon almost squeals. He comes over and wraps those arms around me like I am his long-lost brother come back from the war. It's like having a bear make you its best friend. Something that could kill you and be your best friend all at the same time. "I'm glad you came back," he says. "You and Dylan both. People like us, we gotta stick together."

"Sure," I say. "You know, my friend, I think I'm starting to get an ear for that Scottish twang of yours. You don't sound quite as foreign as you used to."

"People are only foreign if you believe they are," he says, then wraps me in another bear hug.

A few moments later, Frenchie himself arrives, almost running. He screams something in Foreign as he comes in. Then he's on the edge of the bed, with my hand in his, my wrist bent in half with the back of my palm on his forehead, and then he's giving it these little Italian kisses like the two of them got history together. I think I feel an Italian tear or two touch my skin.

"Howareyou?Howareyou?Howareyou?"

He's having trouble keeping his American straight on account of how he's all choked up, so it's tricky understanding exactly what he's saying.

"Feels like I been stabbed," I say. "But take it easy. I get the feeling I'm going to be okay."

"Yes," he says, breathing deep. "Yes. You're right. I must be more calm." Finally, he sits up and gives me back my hand. He wipes his face. "This is exactly what happened to you. You were stabbed." He laughs a stiff laugh. Then smiles one of the whitest and straightest smiles I've ever seen. "Aren't you thrilled! I am so, so happy for you!"

He wipes a tear from his eye and kisses the back of my hand again. Then he stands and spreads his arms wide, in the way that he does. He's wearing a white shirt and pants that are made out of the thinnest cloth I've ever seen in public. There's no secrets between us all of a sudden.

"I'm not sure I'm understanding the vibe," I say, averting my eyes.

"You were stabbed!" He almost sings it. His face is brighter than the sun, like the roulette dealer just called out my number. "In America, this would be a bullet!"

I guess he really is a glass-half-full kind of guy.

But that's when I remember the gun. You know the one. That hunk of Second Amendment I had tucked in my shoulder holster. The one I snuck through customs. The one that's so illegal here I'm not even sure Frenchie could get me out of it if the ol' Italian beat-walkers get wind of it. And yet, here I am at Honcho Memorial and not a jail cell, so that means somebody's covering for me.

I've played enough Texas Hold 'em to know that the last thing you want to do is volunteer information. I just play it soft and wait for him to tell me how he found my gun and what he wants to do about it.

"I am so happy that you are okay! But, still, this is a happy, terrible thing. The Germans have a word for this. But is there a word for that in American English?"

"We call that a Bill Cosby."

"I don't understand."

"Never mind."

"Back home . . ." He makes a finger gun at me and pulls the trigger. "And I do not believe that you would have survived. I believe you would have been pushing up flowers."

"Daisies."

"Whatever kind. You understand what I'm saying to you. You need to get away from America. You need to leave it behind. You need to take my offer. The Big Score."

I don't tell him, but I'm starting to think he might be right. I've been letting him hang—and a little busy with Euroland—ever since he made me the offer; been trying not to let the dollar signs lead me down a dark alley. But now, at this moment, flat on my back with the knife wound in my navel, I think he really could be onto something.

Maybe I should leave home. Maybe give America the permanent goodbye kiss.

But maybe that's just these fancy painkillers talking.

"I hear you, Frenchie," I say. "You mind if we dance this jig another time? I'm pretty washed out."

"Oh!" he shouts. "My apologies. You are tired. After all, you have been almost killed. I will leave you now and let you do some healing. Luckily, this will not take long. Science is capable of so many miracles so long as you are able to afford them."

Then he leaves and The Goon leaves with him. His footfalls thud with each step, and on his way out the door he gives me a thumbs-up and says, "Push the button on the side of the bed if you need anythin'. Yu're a fighter."

Then he closes the door and as soon as he does the fatigue comes rolling in. It's a great, soft cloud of darkness that gobbles me up. Feels like sliding into a hot tub in the middle of a power outage. Just darkness and warmth and the sound of the world walking off and finally giving you the peace you've been begging for. Just before it all switches completely off, just before I'm having another Halle Berry dream, I see Dylan, back in Baltimore, laid out on a linoleum floor, with a bullet hole in his chest.

"You okay, Kid?" I ask.

Then there's Remus's voice in my ear.

But it all goes dark before I can hear what he's got to say.

Next time I come back into the world it's to the sound of my room door opening. The sun that was pouring in through the floor-to-ceiling windows in my room at Frenchie Memorial has punched out for the day. Now whatever Italian city this is has switched itself on, but there's still stars in the sky. Just a handful, but enough to remind you that you're just a small piece of punctuation in the story of the universe.

"Hey," Dylan says. He comes in and shuts the door behind him. He's got my suit jacket folded over his arm. "Mind if I sit?"

"That'd be swell," I say. The cotton balls in my mouth have eased back from choking me. Feels like I'm truly on the mend.

Dylan pulls a chair up to the edge of the bed and hands the jacket to me. The jacket's heavier than it should be, which lets me know why he closed the door behind him. "I didn't tell anyone," he says.

"Thanks." I sit up, wincing a little along the way, and place the jacket on my lap.

"After I came out of, you know, my thing, some people took me to the bathroom and there you were, bleeding out on the floor. The first guy in ran out to get help and that's when I found it. So I took it for you."

"Much appreciated," I say.

"I haven't seen a real gun in years. Outside of movies, I mean."

He stares at it. Watches it like he wants me to take it out and show it to him.

"They're something," I say. I reach over—slow, so as not to hurt myself—and open the top drawer of the bedside table—some overly ornate thing probably made out of thousand-year-old redwood—and I put the jacket and gun inside. They make a soft *clunk* sound.

It does the job of breaking whatever spell Dylan was under. He exhales and looks back at me. "But you didn't use it."

It's one of those statements that's a question. One that I don't have an answer for.

"If the poliziotti catch you with it you're gonna be in more trouble than you want."

"Can't argue with that," I say. He's still watching me. Still waiting. With that face of his that reminds me so much of The Kid that it hurts to look at him. I think I'm finally starting to believe that he's not The Kid and I think it hurts. I wish he'd stop looking at me. "Something else?"

"I knew," he begins, "even before I touched your jacket. I knew back at the villa. From the first second I saw you. I knew about the gun . . . and I felt happy."

"Happy?"

"The whole time I've been living over here, something's been missing. Something's been off. And I never knew what was missing. Then I saw you and I thought maybe it was just because of who you are. We both know I'm a fan. You're an amazing writer. I mean, you won the goddamned NBA!"

"You got the writing bug too, huh?"

He blushes. "Yeah. I thought that's what I was feeling. Meeting someone I admired. Or maybe it was just meeting another American. Another Black person, you know? It felt like home."

"Makes sense," I say. "We all want to smell home in someone else's hair, you know?"

"But that wasn't it. It was the gun. Knowing you had the gun. That's what made me happy. I realized that the second I touched it . . . Is that weird?"

The Kid's shown me something private and he wants me to make him feel okay about it. The key to a book tour is always knowing what people want from you at any moment. So I give him what he wants.

"It ain't weird," I say. "But it also ain't not weird."

And we both manage a chuckle.

A couple of Italian sunrises later, faster than you'd likely believe, I'm back on my feet and starting to feel like I'm ready to dance. It turns out Frenchie wasn't just blowing smoke when he said I'd be healed before I knew it. Who says money can't buy health?

The last few days are nice and lazy. Dylan and The Goon tag in and out, keeping me company. The nurses speak to me in Foreign and laugh at my jokes that they probably don't even understand and refill my cucumber water around the clock. Never would have thought being stabbed could lead to such a smooth ride.

But all things gotta come to an end.

Frenchie's kept an eye on my healing and the tour is still waiting.

Frenchie says we'll keep the stabbing under wraps. No sense sensationalizing things. And no sense getting his good name tied to an American N-word winner getting stabbed on Italian soil.

I go along with it. No reason not to.

On my last day at Frenchie Memorial I get up early and take my time getting dressed. There's still a little soreness in my stomach, but not enough to make me worry. Even when I put on the shoulder holster and the gun, it's almost like the stabbing never even happened.

I decide to take a stroll to stretch my legs. Dylan and The Goon want to come with me, but I tell them to hang back. The Goon doesn't like it but I'm not one for a babysitter and, besides, what are the odds of being stabbed twice in less than a week? Gotta be pretty slim.

I hop in the elevator with one of the nurses and just a couple of floors down she steps off and I'm standing there waiting for the doors to close when I hear a woman's voice screaming just off camera: "Hey! Hold that elevator for me!"

I poke my head out and look around to find the source of the voice and, lo and behold, there's a naked woman running straight for me. I mean head-on. She's at a full lope. Head high, knees high, elbows pumping. She's got real turnover, sister, I'm telling you!

And not far behind her naked form is another woman. This woman rounds a corner with some sort of hammer-shaped medical device in her hand and she's carrying it like a club and screaming something in Foreign that, even though I don't speak it, I know enough about moments like this to translate it to roughly mean "That's my goddamned husband you just fucked!"

Signs.

And.

Wonders.

Now, believe it or not, I've been where this naked dame's at. I won't go into detail, but let's just say that I've got priors. And who would I be to shut the door on this woman in need? I hold the door and I wait and

I secretly hope the appropriate gods of moments like this might look down kindly on her and bless the arches of her feet that they might knock a full half a second off her hundred-yard dash.

She's got a perfect run. Simply perfect. No flaws anywhere to be seen. She's really pulling each millisecond out of every step, you know? If the Olympic sprint team was here right now, I know for a fact that she'd make the team.

But, then, the closer she gets, the stranger things get.

I know that déjà vu is a thing that you're supposed to feel when you've been somewhere before—or, rather, you think you've been somewhere before—but this is something very different.

The elevator buzzer screams in my ears as the naked woman gets closer. I make a plan to time it so that just as she gets to the elevator, if she dives, I mean really gives her body the old heave-ho, she'll sail through the narrowing doors and safely leave the lady with the club behind to bear the burden of unrequited vengeance.

The moment comes.

I step back. I release the button. The door starts to grind closed. The running woman—who I've had contact with for the last few seconds, who I've been cheering on wordlessly—takes a dive that John Woo would be proud to set in slow motion. Her body goes horizontal and aerodynamic and the gap in the door is so small at this point I'm worried she'll lose a toe in the lunge.

Then, somehow, she makes it!

Her whole body smacks into the back wall of the elevator and she slides down it with a loud, squeaking sound like a Warner Brothers cartoon.

Then the doors are closed and the elevator is taking us both down, leaving behind the roar of the angry woman and the rhythmic *thoom-thoom-thoom* of her banging that metal club of hers in rage.

"I think you made it," I say, finally turning to get a good look at my new elevator partner. As she picks herself up off the floor, that's when the whole puzzle comes together. It wasn't just the situation that had me feeling like I was traveling through time to somewhere I've been before, it was the dame. I know this woman.

"Hiya," she says, and that voice of hers is made of even more light and wonder than I remember. "Fancy meeting you here."

Holy fuck. It's Kelly.

"I really don't understand how anyone lives here," he says. He's out of the hotel room; he's off to do this thing. And he tries to say it lightly, with a little bit of a smile so that she knows he means it gently, in that small-talk way that people use when they say things about the weather in new places.

They're halfway across campus, on their way to visit a classroom where the students are scheduled to hear him talk about his book before the bigger event tonight when the whole community is supposed to come out. Of course, none of them will. There are still burials to be done. But he's here and they won't ask him to leave and so, here the two of them are, walking across a half-frozen campus while the remnants of last night's storm continue to blow. The temperature is somewhere in the single digits. His hands are starting to go numb and it hurts a little to breathe, but he's in Rome—metaphorically speaking—and trying to do as the Romans do.

"You get used to it," she says. "Thick blood and whatnot."

"Is that true? The thick blood, I mean." His teeth chatter a little on the end so he clenches his jaw and tries again. "Does your blood literally get thicker when you live in cold places?"

"I think it's just an expression," she says. Then: "Over there is where it happened." She turns and points off into the east. It's early afternoon so the sun is sitting high and just a little behind them. In the distance, on the far side of a wide, snow-covered courtyard, sits a building whose name is blocked out by snow. Along the windows are the words ELKS SURVIVE and FOREVER AN ELK and WE WILL ENDURE. Even from here, from so far away, he can make out the yellow police tape flapping in front of the doorway of the building.

He and the woman whose name he does not remember, even though she only introduced herself a few moments ago, look at the building until the wind comes up again. "Come on," she says. "We're almost there."

"Okay."

A wall of warm air spills out of the student union building as they enter. The feeling of pins and needles comes into his hands.

"This way."

They move through the empty halls. Even though the school is open, there is no one here. All classes are optional and it seems that no one is taking the option. He's been in schools before when the students were all in class, but never when the students simply weren't there. It's eerie. Like a house that has been sitting too long without a family inside its walls, so it becomes haunted, if only to not feel so alone.

When they reach the classroom where his talk is supposed to happen, it's just as empty as all the rest. She checks her watch. "We'll give them a little more time," she says. "Someone still might show up."

"Okay."

They wait in silence for twenty minutes. He wants her to ask him about writing. Ask him about touring. Ask him how he found his agent or what it's like working with an editor. He wants all the normal conversations he's used to when promoting his book. He wants to talk about cover design and passing out from exhaustion at thirty-thousand feet. He wants to talk about three-act structure and targeted revisions. He wants to talk about outlining chapters and planning characters and, of course, unplanned characters that pop up sitting by a Euroland river in the late stages of your story and suddenly come to define the entire thing. He wants to tell her about the fun times he's had out on the road. About all the people he's met. He wants to make her laugh because he's gotten pretty good at making people laugh at his book events. Hell, he might even go so far as to say that, when the time comes, he's a pretty funny person. Not a stand-up comedian or anything like that, but he knows how to put on a show and send people home remembering that they had a good time.

But none of that discussion happens. She sits quietly the whole time, never asking him a single question. Never making small talk. She only sits and stares at the far wall—the one in the direction of the building they passed walking up, the one where everything happened.

After half an hour and still no students coming to ask him to talk about his book, she says, "I'm sorry about this. We can go."

"It's fine," he says.

Then they're back out in the cold again and it's like he never left. Things go numb almost immediately. Parts of his twitch and tremble compulsively. They walk past the building where it happened for a second time.

"I'll take you to lunch," she says, somewhere near the middle of the courtyard.

"Let me guess: ice cream?" He gives an exaggerated smile.

The restaurant is burgers and steaks and whatnot. "This is fine," he says when she asks him if it's okay. People are always asking him if the food is okay, for some reason. Maybe they think that he's only used to five-star dining or something. Whatever the reason, people always worry too much. They always want to impress. And he wants her to know that she doesn't have to impress.

Sometime after the entrées have come, when they're both silently shoving food into their mouths, she swallows a mouthful of pasta, puts her fork down, and says to him: "Why did you bring a gun here?"

He chokes a little on his steak. Then he leans back in his chair and thinks about lying, but decides against it. "Protection," he says.

"From what?"

"I don't know."

"Can I see it?"

His brow furrows. One thing he's learned from years of meeting people on tour is that, in the end, everyone wants something. Most people want information. They want to know about publishers and editors. Agents. They want to know how to get their book published. Some people just want to know about the person behind the story. They want to know how much of what they were told is real and how much imagined—which is a way of saying they want to know how much of the world in the book is the world in which they live because, if they can know that, they can understand the things they see on the news each day a little better. People want the book to explain the world, and they want the world to explain the book.

But this woman—he tries to remember her name, but all that comes up is the name of a hundred other people he's met on tour—she wants something else.

"Sorry," she says.

"When did you see it?"

"Immediately. My ex-husband used to carry a gun all the time. I got to where I could spot them."

"Oh."

"So why did you bring it here?"

Her eyes are blue and hard. Her hands are tugging at the edges of her napkin in front of her. He can't tell if she's angry or afraid.

"I take it everywhere I go," he says.

"But why?"

"I already told you."

"That's not an answer. When you say something is protecting you, you've got to be able to name the thing that you're being protected from.

If it was gloves or a jacket, you'd say it was protecting you from the cold or the rain. Hell, if it was garlic you'd say it was protecting you from vampires. But it's not any of those things. It's a gun. What's it protecting you from? Why would you bring a gun here? After what happ—"

"I shouldn't have brought it."

She blinks and, finally, she stops tearing at her napkin. She reaches across the table and places her hand on his. "You don't understand. I'm not mad at you. I promise. I just . . . I just want somebody to say it."

"Say what?"

"I want somebody, anybody, to come out and say it."

Everything is uncomfortable now. He pulls his hand away from hers and leans back in his seat. The gun, tucked away in its holster in the small of his back, digs into his skin just a little, as if it knows it's the topic of conversation. An image flashes in his head of the gun falling out and clattering onto the restaurant floor. In the image, everyone stops eating and stares at the gun. Then the screaming starts.

"Maybe I should head back to the hotel."

"Okay," she says. Her hands go back to tearing at the napkin.

They pay the check and walk, wordlessly, back to his hotel. The afternoon has gotten later and the sun is low and the storm is coming back in. Outside, in front of the hotel, she says, "You've got the rest of the afternoon free. Myself or someone else from the faculty will come by and pick you up for your event around 4:45."

"Okay," he says.

She turns to leave.

For some reason, he finally says it: "I'm scared."

A tremble washes over her.

"This is the gun that killed my daughter and I carry it with me everywhere I go. And I keep it loaded." He laughs at the end. "And I'm scared." Then, all at once, she's hugging him. Then, all at once, they're in his room. Then, all at once, she's on top of him. Then, all at once, it's over.

All the while, the gun was, is, and will be on the nightstand beside the bed. At moments, he sees her looking over at it, but he doesn't understand the expression on her face. At moments, he looks over at it, and he's not sure what he's thinking.

Then she is dressed and standing at the door. Before she leaves, she takes his hand and squeezes it. She wipes her eyes and sniffles. Then she rises up onto her tiptoes and kisses him, gently, on the forehead. "We're all scared," she says.

Even after she leaves, it is the first time in years that the two of them haven't felt alone. Sometimes, that blessing is a form of love.

A wise ol' gal once told me: "If it lasts, it's love. If it doesn't, it's just a love story." But the thing is: everyone loves a love story.

A long time ago, on a book tour far, far away . . .

I came across a woman named Kelly. She was the spring sun and the summer rain all at the same time. I don't know if she ever walked on water, but for the brief hours that I got to know her, I swear I saw daylight between the grass and the bottoms of her feet. She was a breath of air when I didn't even know I was getting choked off by life's carbon monoxide. Tall, like the memories of the one that got away always are. When she smiled, the sun had to hold its hat.

And, somehow, she cared about me. Cared in the way that you can care when you know fate isn't gonna let you be in somebody's life for long, so why not give them all that you can while you can? All of this, without the two of us getting any further than a single kiss goodbye.

This fairy-tale stage play of ours was set in San Francisco. One of the set pieces was a place called Wormfud Funeral Home. Maybe not the most expected place for one of those once-upon-a-time deals, but I don't ask questions when life throws a little magic my way.

Now, the short version is: it didn't last.

Life loaded us up on different buses, both tickets marked "Parts

Unknown," and I figured her for swallowed up by time and never given back. But now, somehow, over here on this other continent, some six thousand miles and a whole damned publishing cycle away, here she is.

Maybe Dame Luck just pinched my ass a second time.

"How you been?" Kelly says, her voice like honey on the air. We're a couple of blocks from Frenchie Memorial, walking along the Pordenone streets with her wrapped in a couple of hospital gowns we swiped on the way out, covering her north and south. The locals give us the once-over when they pass, but they keep on moving. Even money says they can smell the American on us and know that people like us are prone to odd behavior sometimes.

"I'm swell," I say. "Just swell." I stammer on the tail end and it can't be helped. After all these years, nothing has changed. She still makes me feel small, small and floating, like I'm dancing a waltz at the foot of a glacier. Forgive me if I'm not doing her justice, sister. I always struggle with writing dames. Not because I don't know any, but just because I don't know how to be anyone but me. Try as I might, Kelly and those like her are always unknowable to me, and that's what makes me feel so small in front of her. Besides, she can sing her own song, if I just sit quiet long enough to hear it.

"Good! So what are you doing here?" she asks.

"Back out on the road, sweetheart! Selling literary wares hot off the presses! Yes ma'am, the business of wordsmithing just don't stop. You churn out the words and, sometimes, you find the folks willing to believe them. It's a sweet kind of deal though. Every kid's dream, I'd say. And now it's brought me all the way over here and has me taking in The Continent real proper. It's a pure milk and honey administration these days, sister!"

"Good for you," she says, smiling—and that smile, breaks me in half every time. "But I was more asking about what you're doing in the hospital," she goes on. "You seem a little stiff too. You okay?"

"Right as rain," I say. No need to go into unsettling details with her. "Just on the mend. You?"

She gives me a quick side-eye, like maybe I said something off-kilter. No idea what though.

"I live here now," she says. "And, as for the hospital, there's a doctor there who likes to fool around at work and, apparently, who also likes to not tell me he's married. Live and learn though, I guess."

"Sister, I been there," I say, and then I laugh to stall for time on account of how I'm quietly trying to figure out exactly what it is I'm feeling now that I see her again. Like, how are you supposed to feel when you're suddenly in hand-holding distance with the one who burned themselves into you with nothing more than a kiss goodbye? It's been more than four years now since I didn't reply to her text message asking "Are you okay?"

For the record: I wasn't at the time.

I could say I skipped out on us because the world was just too crazy for me just then, but that's all just smoke and satin-swaddled lies. Fact of the matter is, our falling apart? I let it happen. I guess I must have wanted it to happen. And if I wanted it to happen, then what's that say abo—

"Do you have any idea that you're talking out loud?" Kelly asks.

I nearly walk into a wall. "What's that?"

"You know that voice we all have inside our heads? Well, right now, yours isn't. And do you really narrate your life like that? That's wild! Haha!"

The pit of my stomach goes cold. Must be some kind of gag she's pulling on me. "Strange sense of humor you've grown into," I say, grinning to let her know I'm in on the joke.

"Okay," she says.

And there's that blinding smile again.

She looks just the way she did four years ago. Like time hasn't touched her. Like she's been doing nothing but catching a few winks in suspended animation. Sleeping Beauty–style. Waiting, just for me, so that she could reappear and the two of us could take up that stage play of ours ag—

"Hey!" she says, snapping her fingers. "Do you really think I've just been in some kind of suspended animation for the last four years, waiting for you? Are you *really* that level of delusional?"

Shit.

"Um . . . Sorry." My head is starting to hurt and my stomach doesn't even want to speak to me now. What if she was right about me saying all my thoughts out loud?

"I get the feeling you're a long way from square," she says.

She walks faster, and I do my best to keep up. No sense in letting her go again just yet. "So how have you been?" I ask.

"It's not 'letting her go' if I leave," she says. "It's me leaving. There's a difference."

Dollars for doughnuts! She really can hear what I'm thinking! Or I really am talking out loud. Whatever way you want to flip that coin, the end result is the same: my therapist had better clear her calendar and stock up on prayer beads! Did it finally happen? Have I finally come across a new way to be broken?

"You're only broken if you decide you are," she says, grinning.

She starts to say something else but she's broken in on by a pair of what I'm guessing are teenage Italians. They say something in Foreign which I guess is the Italian equivalent of "Excuse me." Then they hold up a book in their hands with a pair of young, dark-skinned boys on the front. From the excitement in their eyes and the way they're holding a pen out to me, I already know what they want.

"Uh . . . sign?" one of them says.

"Sure thing," I say.

I scribble my name and the words "I hope she's not hearing all of this too" just above where I sign my name and shake their hands. "Grazie," they both say together. "Grazie, Mr. Whitehead."

"You don't know when you're signing someone else's book?" Kelly asks.

"I get that a lot. One thing I've learned is that it's okay to be somebody else sometimes. Hell, it's downright exciting every now and again! Besides, word around town is that Colson Whitehead is the tops, so if I'm gonna be him, then I'm gonna be the best Colson Whitehead I can, you know?"

I do my best to keep up with her as she walks, but the stab wound in my gut is singing a high note that's pretty hard to ignore.

"Stab wound?" She stops walking. She turns and places her hands on my stomach. "Let me see."

I pull away, even though her touch feels like all the medicine I could ever need.

"Who stabbed you?" she asks.

"A down-on-his-luck mime. Turns out Italy's lousy with them."

"Still the king of avoidance, I see."

"Not intentionally," I reply. And I think it's an honest statement. "Really, I'm just trying to figure a few things out on that front. Like, how much of what happened do I actually want to buy into? But the good news is it's not as bad as you might think. Turns out you can get a blade through the gut but, with a little luck and a rich benefactor with a fistful of Eurobucks, you can come through it okay."

She can hear your thoughts, I think. No worries. Nothing strange about that at all. Just don't open up the door in your head about the gun . . . Wait.

"Gun?"

We hang there for a second, with the word stuck in the air between us. If she can hear me, if she can hear this, I think to myself, Please, just let me have this. Don't ask. Let me pretend that there is only you and I and the sun and the way the light dances on your shoulders. Please.

She pulls her hand away from my stomach. I can't tell if she's upset or just confused.

"Okay," she says. Then we're walking again. More slowly this time. She has this lilt in her hips as she moves, as if there's a song playing somewhere and she's the only one who can hear it.

"Are you going to keep narrating things?"

"Sorry," I say. I really am trying not to.

"Don't apologize. People are full of secrets, you know? You meet someone and all you get is their ambassador. They give you this polished version of who they are that you have to invest years in before they finally show you their inner world, before you finally ever really meet them. But it looks like I won't have that problem with you, not even if you wanted me to."

"No way to hide my hole cards?"

"Exactly," she says.

My stomach tightens—and not just because of the dissolvable stitches. My heart picks up the pace and I'm pretty sure she's hearing all of that too, and I don't know what to do with that. All I really want is to get the hell out of here. Go back to hiding inside myself.

"You don't have to leave."

We're doing slow laps around Frenchie Memorial. Letting the light wash down on us. She's barefoot, and her feet seem to be just a hair above the ground, as usual.

Fun fact: I kinda like feet. Not like those people you see in the dark corners of the internet. But, well, they're not bad.

"Hahaha!" She laughs so hard it buckles her in two.

"Fuck."

Definitely time to pack it all in.

"So are you gonna ask me how I've been?" she says quickly.

"Sorry," I say. Apparently, that time, she didn't hear me. "How's the world spinning for you? Still elbow deep in stiffs?"

"I've been good," she says. "Still an undertaker when I'm not running naked through hospital hallways. Always will be, most likely. Just decided to change the venue a while back."

"How come?"

"Death is better in Europe."

"How's that work?"

We stand on the corner of a bustling street, watching the Europeans pass us by, not noticing either of us. "They kept getting younger," Kelly says. "Back home, I mean. Don't let people tell you that only the old die. It's called an average for a reason. When they came in, I treated the young ones the best I could. Not for me. Not for their parents. But for them. For all the sunrises they wouldn't get."

"That's pretty tops," I say.

"But then they just kept showing up. You remember that kid that was there the night you came, don't you?"

"How could I forget."

I'm not sure how much she knows about me and that kid. The Kid. The kid who followed me for months. The one who suddenly disappeared. The one I, some nights, had found myself hoping to run into again.

"It kept happening more and more," she says, maybe again not hearing my thoughts. "And it wasn't car accidents or illness. Bullet holes. Just bullet holes. One day I decided to try and outrun the bullets. So here I am."

"Sorry," I say.

"You didn't do anything."

"I can still be sorry though."

She turns and looks at me. No smile. "So how are you handling this situation of yours?"

"What situation is that?"

"The one with the guy that stabbed you."

"It'll be okay," I say. "Takes all kinds to make a world, you know."

"Is he going to finish the job?"

"I doubt it," I say. "Personally, I like to think that people aren't quite as bad as we make them out to be. Yeah, he got a little rowdy the last time we ran into each other. But I'm sure that's the end of it."

I don't know exactly how much of that is true. But maybe if I just keep on pushing through, then it really will be okay.

"What happens now?" I ask.

"What do you mean?"

I don't want her to leave and I don't know how to say it, so I just stand there, watching the sunlight fall down over her face and watching carloads of foreigners flow past her like the rivers of time I'm afraid will snatch her up and take her away and, this time, regardless of whose fault it is, I'll never get the chance to sit across from her like two normal people and talk about the world and maybe find out if she's still as amazing as she was the last time we hung out. I'm not sure how much of this is out loud or staying in anymore, and I don't care. I think I'm learning to like the fact that I can't keep anything in around her. That to her, I'm an open book. That she knows me and I'm not sure where to put the quotation marks.

"Where are you going next?"

"Paris," I say. "More tour stuff. Even supposed to kick it big at the French embassy."

"Is that supposed to impress me?"

"Does it?"

"Not really," she says. "But I've got some time off. And I could do with a little while in Paris."

"Yeah? Well Dylan, The Goon, and I have got a small French snail car that we're cruising around in. And there's room for one more."

"Maybe that wouldn't be so bad," she says.

"What about your doctor friend?"

I'm fishing on behalf of my heart, and I know she knows it.

"According to his wife, that's over with. And I'm not particularly upset about it. I think he was just a placeholder anyhow."

"A placeholder for what?"

"Don't you mean for whom?"

Then she turns and starts back toward the hospital, those high-arched feet of hers still hovering just ever so slightly above the ground with each step. A few steps away she turns back to me.

"Do I really make you feel small?" she asks. "Like dancing a waltz at the foot of a glacier?" She smiles like maybe she's embarrassed.

"Sure," I say softly.

You're like dancing.

Afternoon, y'all. I'm Mark. Safety Resource Officer at Southeast Carolina High School.

What? You didn't recognize me without my uniform? Haha! That's okay. I just thought I'd dress a little more casual today. But don't be fooled. This is an important conversation. Maybe even the most important conversation we can have. Stick with me and, as always, GO GATORS!

[TITLE CARD: ACTIVE SHOOTER/ATTACKER TRAINING]

First off, always remember: together, we stay alive.

To begin: there is a small window of time at the beginning of a shooting situation when responders have not yet arrived and the community—which includes yourself, your fellow students, your teachers, school staff, and perhaps even SRO personnel like myself—must depend on themselves for their immediate safety. With that in mind, we want y'all to understand actions you can take for your safety.

Did y'all know: An FBI study identified educational environments to be among the top locations of active-shooter/attacker situations in the US? Did y'all also know that there were forty-six school shootings last year alone, impacting nearly fifty thousand students in grades K–12? And these numbers don't even include active-shooter scenarios at colleges and universities.

But don't worry. Both you and your parents will be proud to know that we Gators initiated active-shooter training sessions in 2006. That was even before the shootings at Virginia Tech in 2007 that caused everybody else to jump on the wagon. Yep. We saw the way the wind was blowing, and we planned ahead.

Another thing to remember is that even when law enforcement is present, or able to respond to an attack within minutes, civilians often have to make life-or-death decisions on their own. It's important to BE AWARE. NO MATTER WHERE. Eyes up, Gators!

Common locations for active-shooter situations include, but are not limited to: Universities, colleges, and schools. Malls and shopping centers. Places of worship. Sports events. Concerts and entertainment venues. Workplaces. And more.

Now, with all that in mind, I want y'all to ask yourselves a question: What would happen if an active shooter targeted our school? And before you say "Gator Pride!" think long and hard about it.

. . .

Now that you've thought about it, here's what you should do: the first thing anyone in the affected area should do is RUN, HIDE, or FIGHT.

[TITLE CARD: RUN, HIDE, OR FIGHT]

When an emergency situation is confirmed, myself and other school police will activate the Campus Warning Sirens to sound the specific Active Shooter Campus Alarm. Now that's different from the Inclement Weather Alarm—the ol' Hurricane Howl—we're all used to here in Southeastern North Carolina. We test these sirens three times each year. You should familiarize yourself with how they sound. Now, it's easy to hear a siren and think that it's a false alarm or a drill. Around here, we sleep through thunderstorms and throw hurricane parties! Haha! However, it is absolutely critical that you learn to differentiate better and that you take campus alarms seriously, especially when you hear the Active Shooter Alarm.

[SOUND CUE: ACTIVE SHOOTER ALARM]

That's the sound.

Don't ever presume an alert is a drill. Faculty and staff will always give advance notice about test alarms. When you hear the sound of the alarm, respond in a safe and responsible manner. Show us all that Gator hustle that took us to two state championships!

School officials will notify students in various other ways as well. Monitor your text messages and school email inboxes for information from Gator Alerts. In the event of an Active Shooter, you might also receive a phone call. Students' phone numbers are automatically enrolled in our Active Shooter Alerts system when they enroll at Southeast Carolina. Parents are also encouraged to visit our website to register.

We cannot warn you if we do not know you!

[TITLE CARD: IF YOU SEE SOMETHING, SAY SOMETHING]

"Turn that off," Soot says.

"Shhh!" Tasha snaps.

—tness to what you believe is an attack on our campus, don't assume that others have contacted law enforcement. Call 911 as soon as it is safe to do so. In an active-shooter situation, don't assume someone else has already contacted police. Those around you may not be able to call 911 for a lot of reasons. Every person may have critical information that we need to better respond to an incident. Phone lines will be packed, but keep trying. Use your cell phone, a school call box, or the school safety

app to get in contact with us as soon as you are able and have taken action to secure your immediate safety.

We can't help if we don't know.

[TITLE CARD: WHAT HAPPENS NEXT?]

What should you do if you hear the siren and receive a message that an active scenario is taking place? Listed in order, the actions are as follows:

"Jesus."

—un. If there is no immediate threat to your location, seek escape via a safe route. Run. Evacuate. That's your first priority. Get the hell out!

Here's a secret safety tip, Gators: even before an active-shooter situation occurs, you should have a healthy awareness of entrances and exits everywhere you go, not just at school. Active shooters can be anywhere! Not just at school! If an emergency happens, use that knowledge of exits to get out. Your safety during a shooter scenario is also your responsibility.

Help you help you!

"Turn that off, Tasha. Please."
"We literally have to watch it before she can enroll, Soot."

—emember: run. Don't worry about your belongings. Stop for a second and you could die! Be aware of your surroundings as you move. If you're outside, don't cross campus to go to your car. Get out of the area by the most direct means possible. Those woods out behind campus? Well, the deer hide there pretty well in hunting season, don't they?

But if you don't think you can get out safely, if you don't think you can escape:

Hide. If getting out isn't doable, go to a secure area. Get others in the room to lock or barricade doors. Block windows and close blinds. Stay low and remain quiet and out of sight.

If an attacker is able to enter where you are hiding, you will have no other choice but to decide to fight! If facing an imminent threat, look for things that can be used as weapons to throw at or strike the suspect. Remember: there's strength in numbers. Work with your fellow Gators to respond to the attacker. Respond to imminent threats by yelling, throwing items and striking or hitting the attacker. Use anything you can get your hands on! When I was a student, I always carried a pocketknife with me for shop class. Now, I'm not saying you should, but I'm also not saying you shouldn't! Do anything you can to force the attacker to the floor. If possible, take the weapon from the attacker.

One more thing, Gators: Southeastern North Carolina is a hunting community. We've got a long tradition of bringing down the biggest bucks. Most of y'all here have been hunting from since before you could walk. Heck, we all know about the skip days that happen at the start of deer season every October. I never see these halls as empty as during the first week of hunting season.

So, if you are able to get the weapon away from an active shooter... Well, boys, if you feel threated, you have the right to defend yourself. Never forget that. Your safety, and the safety of those around you, is your responsibility too.

"You're a teacher, Tasha. You already know all of this. You've seen these videos year after year. You should know this by heart now. What's the big deal?"

"I think I thought it would stop," she says.

[TITLE CARD: WHAT TO EXPECT FROM LAW ENFORCEMENT WHEN THEY ARRIVE]

According to Southeast Carolina High School police policy, once help gets to the scene, they'll make every effort to stop the attacker. So your job is to try to remain calm and follow the instructions of any officers. Just know that the arrival of law enforcement doesn't mean the immediate end to the situation. Even when you hear the sirens and see the boys and girls in blue uniforms, it could be hours before anyone comes for you. Settle in.

We know that you're scared, Gators, but hang in there!

[TITLE CARD: CLOSING THOUGHTS]

Hey. Do I look a bit more familiar now? I'm back in my uniform here at the end because I know this all sounds scary. But just know that it's even more difficult to make these decisions if you've never thought about them in the past. Planning ahead saves lives. The fact of the matter is active-shooter scenarios have been, and continue to be, on the rise. This is not a problem that is going away.

If nothing else, wherever you go, do the occasional thought exercise: How can I get out of this place? Where are the exits?

Sometimes, escape can be the strongest weapon available.

Again, this has been Mark, for your Southeast Carolina High School police. Stay safe out there. You're two-time state champs. Should the day come, let's show it! Go Gators!

Tasha clicks the button confirming that she has watched the video. It's the third in a series of videos. One for parents, one for students, and one for friends and family. All three have to be watched by the parents, and they have watched all three.

It's late and the house is quiet. Tasha closes the laptop and stares off.

"We're not leaving," Soot says.

"What?"

"You're thinking it. You don't know it, but you are. Trust me."

"So maybe I am," she says.

Soot pushes the computer from her lap and places his head there. He rests his arm on her legs and holds her as best he can.

"What if I do think we should move?"

"I won't leave," Soot says. "And you'll take her away from me."

"I wouldn't ever take her away, Soot. And, besides"—she strokes his head gently as she speaks; this is one of the last times before they begin to split apart. Perhaps this is the moment it happened—"we'd all go as a family, wouldn't we?"

He doesn't respond. He lies there in her lap, holding on to her, until he falls asleep and waits for things to move on.

Sometimes escape is the best weapon.

The key to traveling around Europe with the memory of be-ing stabbed behind you and the promise of being murdered in front of you and the woman you might have once loved suddenly coming out of the recesses of the world and riding shotgun is this: Lean into it. The chaos, I mean. Save the solving for another day. Sometimes escape is the best weapon.

So that's what I do.

The next day after meeting Kelly again after all these years, the four of us are on the road. We pile into that little French snail car with The Goon behind the wheel and we light out for old Paris herself. Nothing bad ever happens in Paris, right?

Yeah, sister. At this point in the ride, I'm starting to feel like myself again!

Now, I'll admit, having the shadow of death hanging over your head puts a new sheen on Euroland. Ever since waking up with that love mark where Remus's knife went and shook hands with my innards, nothing quite feels the same. These small European roads all have an edge to them that they didn't have not so long ago. But being around the right people makes it all okay.

The kilometers come and go as slow as ever. For long stretches we all just sorta stare out the window, not talking, just letting the little fifty-horsepower engine carry us as best it can.

The Goon does all the driving—something about how this car is worth more money than any of us could ever put together and so he's responsible for it—but that's okay by us. Kelly's up front, nodding like a cat, with one foot hanging out the window and the sun on her face, while Dylan and I are in the back seat doing just fine.

Somewhere around the Alps I can't help but pay attention to the way he's on his iPad the whole time. Whatever it is, it's got all his focus. He's got his earbuds in and he's pushing and pulling, swiping and gesturing on the screen like he's running an orchestra. Since there's nothing else to do but ride, I lean over and try to get a bead on what's happening:

"What's the game over there?" I ask.

"I'm working on something," he says. From his tone, he's hardly got time for me. Whatever it is he's into, it's all-consuming.

"No kidding," I say. "Don't keep all the fun to yourself. What's the deal?"

"I'm editing a movie," Dylan says.

"Didn't know you were the Stanny Kubrick type," I say. I lean over and try to get a peek at the screen. He turns it away.

"I'm not. I didn't make it. I'm just editing it."

He still hasn't taken his eyes off the screen—which says a lot, because I know the kid's partial to me. He told me so himself. And if he's too busy to give me the time of day, then whatever he's into, it's gotta be pure gold! "Oh, c'mon, Kid," I say. "Let's pretend for a second that I'm not bothering you. Let's pretend that we're in the back of an over-priced French snail making our way through the Italian countryside at the slowest pace possible and that it might be good to chat it up. This is a chance to let your freak flag fly!"

I give him a playful elbow and a smile, and it works. For the first time in about three hours his hand stops tapping and sliding on the screen.

"Do you know who Roland Emmerich is?"

"Didn't he blow up the White House back in the nineties?"

"Yes," Dylan says, bright as a hundred-watt bulb. "He directed *Independence Day*."

"Yeah, that's the one!"

"And he also single-handedly resurrected the entire disaster genre."

"Disaster genre? Sounds like most of my dating life. Ha!"

"The disaster genre," Dylan continues—there's no stopping his excitement train now—"was a huge deal back in the 1970s but faded out. Then he brought it back. It used to be mainly natural disasters. Earthquake. Airport—though that one wasn't a natural-disaster movie, but the feeling of it was mostly the same. People ate it up. And then they didn't. But then Emmerich came along and instead of having an earthquake demolish a city, he blows up the whole world! It really was a special type of genius."

"I guess I never thought about it that way."

Dylan finally puts the screen down. "I've seen everything he's ever made. Every time he's blown up the world. I've watched them all hundreds of times."

"Never would have thought you to be that type," I say. "I guess I figured somebody with all your Foreign and travel would be into something a bit more highbrow."

"Emmerich is highbrow."

"Fair enough," I say, bowing out of the disagreement. "You're working on something Emmerich-related?"

"Yeah," Dylan says. He's full of excitement. "I personally think that Roland Emmerich has spent his entire career creating one entire movie about a single global apocalypse."

"How's that?"

"Trust me," Dylan says. He turns in the small seat to face me. He's vibrating with excitement. "You see, if you watch *2012* and *The Core*, you start to see that they're both the same movie."

"I didn't know Emmerich directed *The Core*. Which one is that one?"

"It's about the core of Earth stopping spinning and so they have to drill to the center of Earth and restart it."

"As one does."

"Yeah," The Kid says, unbothered by my little jab. "And Emmerich didn't direct it, but it's clearly in the Emmerich style, so I count it. Anyhow, if you watch *The Core* and you turn it off at just about the last fifteen minutes or so—you assume that they didn't manage to save the world and restart it, then you turn on *2012* and you skip ahead from the beginning of it and you've got one cohesive storyline of the world beginning to fall apart. And then there's *Poseidon*."

"*Poseidon*?"

"The remake of *The Poseidon Adventure*. It's about a huge ship that gets hit by a rogue wave and overturns and people have to escape. You see, in the world of an Emmerich apocalypse, rogue waves would be everywhere. If you cut that into it, then you've got a great subplot about people on this ship out in the middle of the ocean as the core of Earth has stopped spinning in the year 2012 and, well, I think you can see where I'm going and what I'm building here."

"I think I can," I say. "But Emmerich didn't direct *Poseidon*, did he?"

"No," The Kid says. "It's all about the Emmerich ethos."

"You're basically creating a supercut of the biggest apocalypse movi—"

"Emmerich-inspired."

"Sorry. A supercut of the biggest Emmerich-inspired apocalypse movies?"

"Exactly," The Kid says.

"How long is it?"

"Around seventeen hours so far."

"Jesus!"

Dylan laughs.

"It's cool to have it contained to a single place. There's something fun in it—taking all the broken worlds that all these movies made and putting them all together into a single place. Seventeen hours! Almost a whole day of the world falling apart."

I whistle in amazement. "You got a name for it yet, Kid?" I say the "Kid" part before I can catch myself. Second time I've done it. I wait for him to correct me, but he lets it slide.

"Not yet," he says.

"Well, when you do, you make sure to let me know, huh?"

"Sure thing," The Kid says.

"By the way, thanks."

"For what?"

"For letting me call you Kid. Even just a little bit."

"What happened to him?" Dylan asks. His excitement is gone now. He sounds serious, but nervous too. Like he knows he's pushing me into a place I don't want to go. "I saw that interview. The Denver one where you fell apart. And I heard after that you were seeing some imaginary kid wherever you went. But then you said that you stopped seeing him. Is all that true? What happened to him?"

While I'm waiting to answer, I notice that the whole car has gone quiet. Dylan ain't the only one listening anymore. The Goon's peeking at me in the mirror, and I don't think Kelly's as asleep as she was a little earlier. And with her being able to hear my thoughts, I figure the best thing I can do is to keep things moving. I clap The Kid on the leg and I say, "Some other time, Dylan. Promise."

The Goon's eyes go back to the road.

Kelly shifts in her seat, heading back to dreamland.

I've never toured with a team before. I could get used to it.

Picture these ex-Americans and demi-Americans and traveling Americans of the Negro persuasion moving our way from Italy to France at roughly fifty miles per hour. We stick out like a fistful of sore thumbs whenever we stop off for snacks or bathroom breaks and, frankly, I wouldn't have it any other way. It's like we're ambassadors for some unknown country. Some country with dark-skinned Scottish giants and dames that tend the dead and teenagers that dream of the world falling apart. When we go into a place for lunch, you should see the locals trying to get a bead on us. There's The Goon with all his brogue, and Kelly with all her West Coast accent, and there's Dylan with five different Foreigns, and there's me, sounding the way I sound. It's enough to give us all a chuckle.

The miles are smooth and easy.

And that's why it's all the more confusing when The Goon suddenly pulls us off the main road and switches the car off without so much as a heads-up.

"Come on, ya bunch of knobs," he says, unbuckling his seat belt. He opens the door and hoists himself out of our French snail and the car's suspension lets out a sigh of relief like grandma with an arthritic hip when grandpa finally rolls off to catch his breath. Then he walks around the car, opening the door for each of us along the way and, finally, out here, on this small, unmarked Italian backroad, flanked by hills and mountains so tall I imagine that nobody's seen the top of them since Hannibal dropped in for that surprise party all those years ago, he says: "Alright. Let's all go have ourselves a nice, real American shooting!"

Mama told me there'd be days like this.

Right off the bat, Dylan checks out: "I pass." Then he closes his door and eases back into his seat and watches us, with his face almost pressing up against the window like a kid at the zoo, and I guess he sees the look of worry in my eyes because he says to me: "He's not gonna let you get out of it. But don't worry. If he picked this spot, it's because he knows it'll be okay. Try to have fun!" He gives me a thumbs-up and a toothy smile. "I'm okay just watching."

A moment later The Goon, Kelly, and I are standing in front of the car not far from a large, shaggy green hill that leads to a large, shaggy green-and-gray mountain, which leads to a large, shaggy blue-and-white sky. The Goon rubs his hands together and shifts his gargantuan weight from one foot to the other ever so slightly, like a kid who's finally about to crack into his favorite Thanksgiving pie.

"Give us a go first, eh?" he says excitedly.

"How'd you know about the gun?" I ask.

He laughs. "C'mon, now. Do you really think I'd be any good at what I do if I couldn't tell someone like you was carrying a gun?"

"Someone like me?"

"Come on! Come on!" he says, excited as a kid on Christmas. "Don't keep me waiting. Let's see it. I'm owed this, you know?"

"You're owed this?"

Every now and then I glance over at Kelly to try and get a read on what she thinks about all this, but she's just there, listening to The Goon, and not really seeming all that bothered by the idea of firing a pistol on foreign soil.

"I'm basically an American," The Goon says.

"Really?" Kelly asks, finally seeming confused.

"I know yu can't tell it, but my grandparents were from Alabama. They went to Scotland after World War Two on account of how when my grandfather got back home, he'd already had a taste of not being treated like a nigger, you know?" Fun fact: I've never had "nigger" handed to me in a Scottish accent before. It's an experience. "They managed to get into Scotland," The Goon continues, "and they never looked back. Then came my father. Then came me." He rubs his hands together with excitement and steps toward me. It feels like a freight train knocking on my front door. "People like us," he says, "we gotta stick together. So come on, my little friend, hand it over!"

I'm not even sure why, but I do as I'm told.

With the whole team watching—two expats and one demi-American, all of the Negro persuasion—I reach into my jacket and pull out the block of Pennsylvania steel. When the sunlight hits it, The Goon's eyes light up and he lets out a sound that's a cross between laughter and a growl of excitement. He holds out both hands like he's taking Communion and I place the heater gently in those frying pan–size palms. The gun, which was like a paperback version of *War and Peace* in my hands, looks like nothing but a metallic baby bird in those paws of his.

He whistles in awe.

But then Kelly snatches it away and makes a beeline for the side of the nearby hill.

"Oi!" The Goon barks.

Before either of us knows what's happening there's the clickety-clack sound of the gun being opened up. The clip pops out into her hands and she stares into the opened gun. "Were either of you gonna make sure it wasn't loaded or was your plan just to make sure you kill each other?"

"Oh," The Goon says.

"Sorry about that."

She hands the gun back to The Goon and then gives him the clip. "Now you can play."

The Goon turns the gun over in his hand, stroking it and getting a feel for it between his fingers. "My granddad had a gun like this after the war," he says in that Highlander accent of his. "When he came back to Scotland, he brought it with him. I saw it once when I was a boy. Was in a small box my mom kept high up on a shelf. One day, when she wasn't home, I got it down from that shelf and opened the box. But the gun I saw was falling apart. It'd rusted itself down to the bone, you know? It wasn't beautiful like this."

"You never touched a gun from now to then?" Kelly asks.

"Of course I have!" The Goon says sharply. "But never a gun handed to me by a fellow American."

The Goon loads the clip into the gun and chambers the bullet and levels the gun at a small tree growing a hardscrabble life on the side of one of those emerald Italian hills in front of us. "My grandfather was a true American," he says. I'm not sure why.

The gun goes off.

It's a sound so loud my whole body trembles and I slap my hands over my ears. It knocks me back a step and the reverb of it bangs out almost as loud. It's a thundercrack that becomes a deafening heartbeat around us *THOOM! Thoom! Thoom.* With each reverb I tremble. By the time the sound fades, I'm almost on my knees.

It's the loudest gunshot I've ever heard. It's so loud I have to take a quick look up at the mountains to be sure they're not coming crashing down around our ears. Louder than it is in the movies. Louder than the gunshots that live in my memory from when my Old Man used to take me hunting on those cold Carolina mornings. It's like the gun's volume is trying its best to find its place in this new land and the only thing it knows how to do is to be even louder than it normally would.

"This is amazing!" The Goon says. "Just like I imagined. Just like I knew it would be!" And before I can get my bearings back enough to raise a hand in protest, he fires off three more shots. Each one just as loud and deafening as the last. By the time it's over I'm on one knee, with my fingers in my ears and my teeth clenched and sweat beaded up on my brow and every... *Thooom! Thooom*... gunshot and echo makes me tremble.

"My turn," Kelly says.

She takes the gun and fires off two shots in quick succession. Both of them close enough together that I can't tell she fired twice.

"Beautiful!" The Goon shouts. "Amazing! Flawless!" He grabs Kelly in a bear hug and laughs and lifts her up and cheers without so much as a thought to the gun in her hand. To my surprise, she laughs along with him.

When he finally puts her down, she takes the clip out of the gun and makes sure it's unloaded and says, smiling, "I grew up with guns."

"Of course you did!" The Goon says, like she's just answered a question.

It's about now that they finally notice me, on my knees in the Italian dirt, with my fingers in my ears and sweat dripping off my forehead.

"Oi!" The Goon says. "What happened? Are yu okay?"

"Swell," I say, sucking in a deep breath. Somewhere along the way I'd stopped breathing. For the record: breathing feels good. I stand up slowly and wipe my brow. "Don't worry about me," I say. "Just forgot how loud these heaters can be. Sorry about that."

"You're sure?" Kelly asks.

"Positive," I say. I don't know how much of it is true. Something about the gun going off brought up all sorts of things. Not even memories, really. Just . . . things. Pictures and sounds and smells: headlights of an old truck shining in the dark of a summer evening while crickets hit their high notes in the humid air; a wide hallway where the sound of my footfalls echoes and some dame I've never met before tells me she's glad I came; my Old Man—that tall, thin-framed, dark-skinned man that he was, whose clothes were always swallowing him up—sitting in the kitchen, slumped over his chair, sobbing in a way I've never seen. With each *Thoom!* and echo, the images come and go, one after another: my mother, short and round woman that she was, standing in the doorway, waving at me as I ran off the school bus; somber music playing and a choir singing at somebody's funeral; gunshots from every movie I've ever seen all ringing out at once until I almost go deaf. On and on until, finally, the echoes stop and it all goes away and I don't have the nerve to tell anyone about it.

"I think I'll pass on my turn at the gun."

"Okay," The Goon says after a moment. From his tone, I must have promised to bring home dinner and forgotten along the way, because he's all disappointment. "We'll get going," he says with a sigh. "I'm sure Dylan would like that too."

At The Goon's mention of Dylan, we all turn our attention back to the car and none of us catches any sight of the kid. We walk over to the car and find Dylan in the back seat, curled into a ball with his fingers in his ears and a slight tremble in his body.

"Jaysus."

"Hey, Kid," I say, softly opening the car door. I give him a gentle shake.

He opens his eyes and exhales. "I told you not to call me that."

"Are you okay?"

"Fine," Dylan says, sitting up.

"You don't look okay," Kelly replies. And she's right. He won't look any of us in the eyes and I can tell that he knows it. For the first time since I met him, he really does look like the kid he is. He's always had this way of looking older and smarter than his age implies, so much that, most of the time, I think he's too slick, too smart, and too worldly—what with all those shades of Foreign he's carrying around on his tongue—to actually just be a teenage boy. But right now, whatever it is that's been chasing him seems to have caught up with him.

"Can we just go now?" he asks.

"Sure thing," The Goon says. "Sure thing." Then: "I'm sorry about that, Dylan. It was just something I had to do, yu understand?"

Dylan says something in Foreign that sounds like forgiveness and shuts his door. We all load back in without another peep. For the next few hours, it's all just engine noise and the Italian wind ringing in our ears. Mum's the word. I take the front seat beside The Goon while Kelly and Dylan hold down the back seat and, the whole time, it feels like there's an apology hanging in the air and, the whole time, I think I can still hear the sounds of those gunshots ringing somewhere out there—and all the things that came along with them—running across The Continent, forever a part of the soil, like a stain that's going to seep in and, somehow, I'm the one who put it there.

His memory has gotten the better of him. He can't tell whether he's in Minnesota or Toronto or North Carolina anymore. So he calls his therapist. He says it's an emergency. An hour later they're looking at each other through the computer screen.

His therapist tells him that, oftentimes, trauma takes root in places in the body. Physical locations for nonphysical events. "Everything just trying to find a place to live," she says. "Everything just trying to find a place to belong."

"That makes sense," he says.

"Where do you exist?"

"What?"

"Where do you exist?" she repeats.

"Do you mean physically or . . . ?"

"Either," she says. "Answer that question however you want. We can start with the physical part, if you'd like." She reaches off-screen. When her hand comes back, she's holding a small globe. She spins it with a flourish.

"Where do you exist?"

He thinks for a second. "North Carolina."

"Are you sure?"

He looks out the window at the Minnesota snowscape. "Pretty sure. Damn sure not here."

"Okay. If that's your answer. But just remember, I didn't ask where you live. I asked where do you exist. Do you really exist in North Carolina? In your hometown? In that house you lived in as a child? In that town where your father was killed? Is that where you feel not only from, but of?"

He chuckles nervously and prepares to give her a fake answer.

"Try to be honest," she says.

"Did I ever tell you that I did one of those DNA genealogy tests once?"

"You didn't," she says.

"It said that, genetically, I was mostly from Ghana and Congo."

"Okay," she says. "Is that where you feel you exist?"

"You can't tell it by looking at me but, according to the same DNA test, a chunk of me comes from Europe too. Particularly France and Italy."

"That's pretty common, isn't it?" she asks.

"Yeah," he says. "Most niggas have some degree of European blood in their veins. Slavery and whatnot, you know? I went there on a book tour once. It was an experience."

She nods. "Is that where you think you exist? Europe?"

"I don't know."

"Okay," she says mercifully. "Let's try something else."

"Sure."

"In your body," she says. "Let's start there. Where do you exist in your body? If you had to put a finger on the spot within your body where you live, where you, Soot, truly exist, where would it be?" She uses a finger to demonstrate, naming various places within the body where he might live. "Is it in your head? Is it your chest? In your gut? That's the place a lot of people point to, as though they're hiding there, somewhere in their belly. But it really can be anywhere. There's no right or wrong answer. This is just something that works on feeling."

He feels foolish.

"I don't know," he says.

She thinks for a moment. "Okay then: I'll ask a different question. Where did your daughter live? In your body, where did she live? Where did you keep her when she was alive, and where do you keep the memories of her now that she's gone?"

Somehow, he has an immediate answer, as if his body knew something it hadn't yet let his mind in on.

"Here," he says, pointing to the soft spot in his neck, just below his Adam's apple. "This is where she lived."

"Are you sure?" she asks.

He nods, confident for the first time.

"Why do you think that is? Why do you think she lives there, in your throat?"

"Because since I don't have the memories of her anymore, I just have the sounds of her name and the words I want to say to her but can't." And it's in his every swallow.

"And what would you say to her?"

"I don't know," he says.

Paris. The City of Light. Birthplace of croissants and existentialism. Home of Joan of Arc, the Louvre, clown college, and Disneyland.

Me and my band of merry Americans and ex-Americans and demi-Americans broadside the city of Bogart and Bergman just before lunchtime, carrying the sun on our shoulders and with the smell of liberty, American exceptionalism, and Jim Crow heritage effervescing from our loins. If there were theme music on this page of our lives, it would be something by Onyx.

And ol' Paree? She's got legs! It's hard to hit this burg and not have a smile on your face.

As our French escargot car goes over the cobblestone and Frenchies pour out into the streets going about their day, I wonder if this is what it felt like back in '44 when the Allies came rolling down these same roads with the Stars and Stripes at their backs and French gratefulness laid out in front of them. The buildings are all oil-based brushstrokes. And the Seine herself? Well, the light glints off of her just like you've always heard. Throw a coin into that beautiful, long river and it'll give you back an eyeful of diamonds.

Yeah, sister, there's something really special going on here. No wonder Hughes and Baldwin and Simone and a thousand types whose names nobody knows got over here and never looked back. This city is full of seduction and promises of a fair shake for people like me—or so I've been told. It all makes me think that, hell, maybe I could build that "whole other continent" that Frenchie mentioned.

And, as if we needed a good omen, which we didn't, by the way: when we stop at a light the eyes of a French woman on the sidewalk go big as saucers and she runs over and tells me how excited she is to meet me and how she'd love an autograph and so I give her what she's hoping for by writing on the back of a napkin and handing it to her.

Thanks for all the love and support. Please keep reading!
—Colson Whitehead

"I thought you had longer hair," she says in an accent just as we're pulling off.

"We all changed during those plague years," I call back.

No sooner than we're in Paris proper there's a poster of Michael B. Jordan's face smiling down on us. Another sign that we're on the right path and favored by all the gods of this world. On account of how the sign is slathered in Foreign, I can't tell if it's some new movie being advertised or if it's just some sort of Michael B. Jordan appreciation billboard. If there's one thing I've learned, it's that you can't take for granted that anything works the way it does back home.

Either way, I give a nod to Mr. B. Jordan and cross myself.

The next thing I come to realize is that if you're gonna be stalked by a murderer, doing it in Paris ain't a bad choice because the odds are you'll die with a belly full of great pastries.

The hotel The Goon pulls up to is in a section of Paris I keep having trouble pronouncing no matter how many times Dylan coaches me through the syllables. Every brick looks like it's made of old money.

We all file out of the car as quick as we can because even though the slow ride in our French snail car was a hoot, there's business that needs handling. We've made it to town with not a whole lot of time before I'm slated to crash a fancy dinner at the US embassy. Definitely the highest a book tour has ever taken me.

The gig, as Dylan describes it, is centered on an annual book fair that the Frenchies have where they bring over American writers like me and spend a whole week clapping us on the back. And who doesn't like to be clapped on the back?

But enough about me—or maybe she's "heard" enough. No sooner than we've set our feet on the French pavement, Kelly says, "I'll catch you guys later."

"You got some place to be?" I ask.

"I want to start looking around for you-know-what," she replies. "Plus, I always wanted to check out the catacombs."

"The catacombs?" The Goon says.

"Still trying to tend the dead?" I ask.

"Something like that."

"Can I come with yu?" The Goon asks. "I could go for the catacombs and I want to hear more about yu being an undertaker."

"Funeral director."

"Aren't they the same thing?"

"Close enough," she says. "Let's go, Black Sean Connery." She gives me an unsolicited kiss on the cheek and it feels like heaven. And then they're both gone, leaving my heart hanging in the breeze. I hope they find what they're looking for. I hope they get a bead on that Shangri-La of theirs.

Less than an hour later Dylan and I are sharp as knives in our sport coats, I'm well-armed with the heater next to my chest, and we're standing in the doorway of the US Embassy. The place is Euro fancy. And what I mean by that is that it doesn't have all the bells and whistles, glass and LED lights of what fancy means in a town like Vegas or New York. No ma'am. Everything is stone and has an old smell to it. All the doorways are smaller than they should be and all the windows are bigger than they should be and, when you put it all together, the whole thing gives off this air of moving through a photograph you saw as a teenager.

Fun fact: calling it "university" instead of college rarely works, but to each their own.

At the door is a small security team patting people down and checking purses. My heart rate charges up a few flights of stairs. Dylan must be getting a good read on my terror because he says, "Don't worry."

"If you say so."

When our time comes to stand face-to-face with the security guard—a thick-necked man, almost as thick as The Goon, dressed in black military gear—Dylan says, "I'd like to introduce Mr. Coates."

The security guard's eyes go wide. "Huge fan," he says, offering a handshake.

"Right back atcha," I say, shaking his hand.

"Are you working on anything new?"

"Keep an eye out for the upcoming issue of *The Atlantic*," I say. Ol' Mr. Coates always has something big coming down the pike, and *The Atlantic* is as good a place as any for me . . . I mean "him."

"Yes sir," the guard says, and motions us through unfrisked.

Thanks, Ta-Nehisi.

Dinner at the embassy? Well, it's all the swank and gravy you can imagine.

Paintings and marble everything and caviar and stuff I couldn't pronounce on my best day. Since everything is stone, all the sound echoes and makes the place feel like it's even fuller than it is, like there's another party happening in some room you can't seem to find so you drift from marbled room to marbled room trying to find the end of the good times, and all the while you come up short.

As Dylan and I buzz from room to room, I start to get the info on this whole festival. Turns out it's a gas! Goes back for decades. Every couple of years the Frenchies order out for a gross of red-blooded American word nerds like myself in order to give Paris Frenchies a barometer check on what's happening back in the Land of the Free. It's kinda like inviting your neighbor's kids over to tell you stuff about whether or not your neighbors are having affairs and how much debt they're carrying.

The embassy is filled to the gills with freedom writers. Every single one of them chattering on about the décor and the macarons and doing more than a little glad-handing. This is the one place where I don't get to convince people I'm someone else. In this crowd, everyone knows who I'm not. And, sister, it really is a crowd.

The thing about writers is, well, hell, we are legion. There's so many of us out here in the world that there's no way you can know everybody. We all introduce ourselves to one another and stumble through hellos and when the other person tells us the name of their book we try to find a nice way to say that we haven't heard of it and we haven't read it and that's okay.

Can't read 'em all.

Now, I'm not the type to wilt in the middle of a crowd of unknowns. No ma'am. Over the years I've gotten the hang of making friends with strangers. Hell, a stranger is just a friend you haven't met yet. And a friend is a gift you give yourself. And speaking of which:

"My nigga!" a deep voice calls out from the crowd, aimed in my general direction.

His name's Mateo. He's the young, handsome next generation of hit-it-big word farmer. He looks like he just fell off the cover of *GQ* and landed up to his elbows in swag. Top shelf all the way! He's got that spark. That thing that says he'll swallow up the whole world someday.

He and I met out there on the road some while back and hit it off. We did a string of co-interviews where I asked him, "So what's your book about?" and he'd fire off an answer and then knock the question back across the table to me. We took turns setting 'em up and knocking 'em down. Word is we don't make a bad team.

I give him and Dylan the introductions and I can tell by the twinkle in The Kid's eye that he knows who Mateo is all too well. Might even call him a fan. Nothing wrong with having heroes but, like I said, never meet them unless their last name ends with "Cage."

Once the two of them have met and Mateo gives me another full-body handshake with all the procedures and flourish—the kind we never tell the White readers about—and he scans the room, he says, "Bro! It's been too damned long! Will you look at all this shit?" He holds up his index finger and spins it in a circle, implicating all the noise and pomp around us. "What you thinking about all this?"

"Can't really say," I tell him. "Not a bad setup, but I also get the feeling we're working against a stacked deck." I take a look around all the old French architecture and paintings and the way that, even in a roomful of Americans, he and I still seem to be drawing a lot of attention.

"I know," he says. "But this is some fancy-ass shit, right?"

"Gravy," I say. "Pure and total gravy."

"You said it, my nigga. And by the way, I heard that Ta-Nehisi's here somewhere. You seen him?"

Dylan cuts me a grin.

"No dice," I say.

"Too bad," Mateo says. "I met him once. Shoulder-checked the fuck out of him when I shook his hand. Just to let him know, you know?"

"I hear you."

"So here's the thing," Mateo begins, filling in the gap left behind by the security muscleman. "I'm hungry and the food here is shit. I say we go get some grub. I met a few locals here that you're not gonna believe and they know of a spot not far from here. You in?"

"Food and fun?" I say. "Let's make it happen."

"Okay," he says. "I'll text the gang to meet us there."

"Swell."

A half hour later Dylan and I are at a table with Mateo and a pair of bona fide writer gods. On account of the privacy promise, I won't go into their names. I'm always one to respect somebody's desire to have their name withheld. Let's just say, The Big Score? They already scored it. In spades. On their own terms. No Frenchie benefactor needed.

We settle into a small table in another unpronounceable part of town where there's singing in the distance and light from the Eiffel Tower herself trickles into your glass of wine.

"This is Toni," Mateo says, nodding to the tall, dark-skinned woman across the table. She's got locs and all of her clothes flow into one another like lines in a good poem. Now, I just gotta say, for legal reasons, that this ain't Toni Morrison. But she might as well be.

Not Toni Morrison shakes my hand.

"Big fa—"

"Big fan!" Dylan explodes with a slight stutter. "Big fan, I mean." Somewhere along the way, he started sweating. I mean, The Kid really looks like he might not make it. I didn't think a person could die from hero worship, but he just might be the one. I figure that if Not Toni Morrison so much as coughed in his general direction he'd drop down on his knees and wash her feet right there on that café sidewalk.

"Thanks," she says, then holds up a finger to get the server's attention.

While she's ordering wine Mateo points a finger across the table at Victor—not his real name, by the way. Victor, too, is a huge deal. Maybe even a bigger deal than Not Toni Morrison on account of how Victor is a semiretired rapper. I won't go into details, but he's got more Grammys than most folks have children. And with the Grammys came all the cash and notoriety. And maybe that's what made him want to step away from it all. Word is he's really the introverted type. Never cared for the stardom. That's the legend, at least. Either way, just take my word for it that if I named a single song Victor made, you'd put this book down and spend the rest of the day walking down your own Hip-Hop Memory Lane.

"Swell to meet you, Victor!" I say. "Big fan. That second album of yours? Whoo! The tops! Just the tops! How many times platinum did it go? I lost count! A pure firecracker of an album! I listen to the whole thing at least once a month. Yes sir, you really got the tiger by the tail when it comes to the music game. A pure rap legend!"

"Goddamn, nigga!" he says, laughing. His smile is just as wide as you've seen on TV and at concerts. He smells like incense, weed, and social activism. "You really talk like that, huh? I thought that was just some shit you did in interviews to move units. Thought it was just an act."

"Never been too good at acting," I say.

"Holy shit!" He glances at Not Toni Morrison and chuckles. "Okay, cool. No disrespect meant. No judgment, my nigga. Whatever you gotta do to get by in this world? You fucking do it."

Dylan gets in his handshake with Victor from across the table. When he opens his mouth to say hello all that comes out is a squeaking sound that we're all too embarrassed to acknowledge.

Around this time the waiter brings over the bottle of wine that Not Toni Morrison ordered and pours everyone but me a glass.

"Oh shit," Mateo says. "I forget you don't drink anymore."

"No worries," I say, and I give the waiter the signal for a little water.

"Wasn't it the alcohol that was making you see that dead kid?"

"Sure."

Easy answers, truthful or not, are just better sometimes.

The four of them dig into the wine and the good times start rolling. The night is beautiful and the clamor of the city is far away. Mateo leads the conversation, talking about all the good things that have been coming his way after his debut novel and the others at the table follow suit by clapping him on the back with good words. It's one of the few times

I've experienced when people like us are able to get together and really lean into being ourselves.

"So how's it feel?" Not Toni Morrison asks me. "Taking home The Big One?"

"You got a wall full of them, Doctor Not Toni Morrison. You tell me." I say it with a smile. Wanna make sure she knows I'm just pulling her leg. Just poking a little fun.

She drains her glass with a little bit of a scowl. "It's whatever," she says. "And don't call me 'Doctor.' I hate people who make you call them Doctor."

"Understood," I say. "Apologies."

"Fuck that shit," Victor says. You'd probably expect him to be draped in ten-thousand-dollar shoes, pants, and everything else. But the fact is, he looks like he just walked out of the Salvation Army. He looks comfortable as he leans back in his chair. "Don't let her silly ass fool you," he says, nodding at Not Toni Morrison. She grins like she's been caught pretending to be someone she isn't. "She's trying to play that modest shit. And she knows there ain't nothing in this world I hate more than a successful nigga that's modest. She got them awards of hers lining the walls of her house. You can't go take a shit in her bathroom without staring up at a fucking Pulitzer!"

Not Toni Morrison laughs an embarrassed laugh. You wouldn't think someone with all her success could laugh that way, but she does. And it's damned fun to hear.

"Success is great," Victor says. "It's fucking amazing! As good as advertised. Just like this city! And don't let anybody tell you different."

Not Toni Morrison pours herself another glass and the two of them clink drinkware. Mateo and Dylan join in.

"So y'all really feeling Paris?" Mateo asks.

"Fuck feeling Paris," Victor says. "Europe is the best place in the damn world."

Not Toni Morrison nods. "He's not wrong. I'm sure you've noticed by now, right?"

"Noticed what?" I ask.

"The volume."

"I've been here for seven years," Not Toni Morrison says. "Only time I go home to the States is when I gotta tour. And I don't do that very often anymore. The rest of the time, this is home. Every time I come back to it, I exhale."

"You can barely hear it," Victor says.

Mateo and I give each other a look. I think we're catching on, but you can never be sure in moments like this. Meanwhile Dylan looks like somebody just canceled Christmas. Like he went to the fridge at 2:00 a.m. and somebody had already beaten him to the last slice of cheesecake.

"All the bullshit," Victor says. "All the nigga shit. The guns . . . *The volume*. It's so much quieter here."

Now I'm starting to get my footing. "I'm onto you now," I say. "Somebody told me a nigga ain't a nigga in Paris. That true? Is there paperwork? Is there a ceremony or something?"

The whole table laughs.

"I know that story," Not Toni Morrison says. "But don't get it confused: a nigga is a nigga anywhere they go. Just ask Assa Traoré. You just gotta be willing to let this place be what it is. It's the best people like us are gonna ever get."

"People like us?"

"It's just quieter," Not Toni Morrison adds. "I go outside and, hell, when I hear something that sounds like a gunshot I don't duck under tables. I know it's just a car backfiring. For the longest, every time I went somewhere, I'd still memorize all the exits. I'd look for closets and doors I could lock in case shit went down and I couldn't get to an exit. But then, eventually, every loud sound was just that: a loud sound. It wasn't a gun. Nobody was dead. And nobody was going to be. Worst thing you get over here is a stabbing or two."

"Sister, I been there," I say.

"I'm also not as angry here," Not Toni Morrison says. "The longer I'm here, the farther away the anger gets. The harder it gets to access it directly, and I think that helps me think about it more clearly. It's harder to think about how to put out a house fire if you're still inside the house."

"The point is," Victor says, "people like us can do something different here."

"Does it feel like home?" Dylan asks. The first sentence he's said the whole time.

"Home?" Victor tests the word. "Don't think I know what home is. You know how I got this great African name, right?" He's speaking, of course, of his real name. Not the one I've given him here for the sake of Euroland privacy. "Well, a while back, I went back to Africa. Thought I was gonna show up and step off the plane and feel the Motherland beneath my feet and it would be like this bell ringing inside a nigga's soul, you know? That *Color Purple* shit. Thought I would just be at peace. Thought everything would click."

"Yep," Not Toni Morrison says, taking a swig of her wine. "That's what everyone thinks. Haha!"

"I even went to that big slave fort in Ghana," Victor says. "What's the one?"

"Cape Coast Castle," Dylan adds. His voice is shaky and his eyes are wide. He's transfixed, staring across the table at his two heroes. Not sure when it happened, but he's walking some kind of tightrope on the inside and I have no idea how he got so far out there on it or why.

"That's the motherfucker," Victor says. His words are starting to slur, but that's fair. "Went there because I heard all these stories about how niggas like us would show up there and see where it all began, see the place where we got broken off from the Mother Vine and niggas would get all overwhelmed and drop down to their knees because of all the power and history and because it would be like this great homecoming, you know? That Great Diaspora Catharsis we're all searching for."

"The what?"

"That's what he calls it," Not Toni Morrison says. "This nigga trying to patent the phrase. Haha!"

They both chuckle.

"No deal, huh?" I say.

"Was just another place," he replies. "Just a square of brick and mortar that somebody decided was sacrosanct. And even though everybody there looked a lot like us—shit, I ain't never seen that much dark skin in one place; just niggas as far as the eye can see—in spite of that, everything sounded weird and that bothered me. Like watching a movie where you know all the actors but the audio is in the wrong language. I didn't understand the clothes. I had to learn how to walk and talk to people. I had to learn all the shit I could and couldn't do. It was culture shock. To me, home is the place where you fit. Where you belong. It's a place you're not just from, but *of*, you know, nigga?"

"Yeah," I say.

"And then!" Victor is all excited now. He leans forward and bangs the table. "The wildest shit was I couldn't call them niggas 'nigga'! Can you believe that? The word didn't really work over there, no matter how I tried to use it. And I thought that was our word! 'Nigga' was always our private language. The only thing that was ours and nobody else's." He thinks for a moment, letting the excitement cool just a hair. "But, hell, I should have knew better. 'Nigga' ain't ours no more. That's why I stopped doing concerts. You got any idea what it's like to be rapping the hook of your song and have fifty thousand White people yelling, 'Get at me nigga' along with you?" He exhales long and slow. "And the fact is, I helped make that happen . . . Fuck my life."

"That was one of my favorite songs, by the way." I don't really know why I say it. Maybe just to make him feel a little better. "Sorry the Mother Continent didn't work out for you."

"We're from Africa," Not Toni Morrison says. A little solemn this time. "But we're not of it. Just like we're from America, but none of us are *of* it. I'm not *of* any place. But breathing's just easier over here. I've learned to take what I can get."

"What about those that can't get away?" Dylan says. Only his second contribution to the conversation, and it's a humdinger. "What about the ones we leave behind? Not just the Black people, but everybody else too. Don't we owe them something? Don't we owe them more than to just run away?" It sounds like a plea at the end.

Everyone at the table picks up on it. Mateo looks over at me, then nods toward Dylan as if to ask, "Yo? He good?"

"How about we change the subject?" I say.

"No!" Dylan says. "Please. Don't we owe it to the ones we leave behind to go back? Can't we go back and fix it?"

The silence settles into the table. Victor straightens his back and pushes his chest out. I can see him shifting into Rapper Mode. I can see the answer building in him, polished and elegant. He reaches over the table and pats Dylan's hand, which Dylan immediately pulls away.

"Fuck Georgia," Victor says. "Fuck Mississippi, Tennessee, Flint, and Selma. Fuck Cleveland. Fuck Atlanta. Fuck DC. Fuck Baltimore. Fuck Charleston and their goddammed slave markets turned tourist traps. Fuck Democrats. Fuck Republicans. Fuck conservatives. Fuck liberals. Fuck the Supreme Court. Fuck the red, the white, and the goddamned blue. Fuck it all. I need air. And fuck anybody that wants me to stay in a place that does nothing but suffocate me. I have no home, when you get down to it. No nigga does. And we don't need one."

Each time he sees her now, she's further away from her end.

She's fourteen years old and on the cusp of college, thanks to skipping two grades when she was younger—just like her mother—and she and Soot are getting along okay when she comes to visit. The divorce has been a strain on them both but, thankfully, she's never blamed him for it.

"So, you're thinking about Chapel Hill, huh?" he asks, standing in front of the stove, buried in the scent of pancakes and butter and it's one of the few mornings when he smiles without sadness.

It's been three months since he's seen her—or has it been three years? Shared custody isn't as shared as it was supposed to be. No one's fault. Just the way things worked out. He tries to keep it easy. He always lets her sleep in because she told him once, "I sleep better here than I do anywhere else." That little sentence sustains him when she is not around. He matters.

"Yeah," Mia says. "All locked in. It's gonna be terrific!"

"Good," he says. "And, as a proud father, I have to say that the fact that you didn't even apply to Duke proves that I raised you right."

She smiles and sips her coffee, looking more like Tasha than he would like just now. "So how have you been?"

"I'm fine," he says. He moves the pancakes around. Fiddles with bacon and eggs. "Give me a hand with this?"

"Sure."

He doesn't need her help and they both know it. But she comes over anyhow and stands watch and moves the eggs around in the skillet just like he did, the same way it was all those years ago when the two of them made breakfast together on Sunday mornings and Tasha sat in the sunlight in the corner of the kitchen, reading aloud the worst headlines she could find until Soot and Mia chanted, "Too much sad! Too much sad!"

"So how you making out on the dating front?" Mia asks.

"Excuse me?"

"You heard me."

"I don't think that's any of your business."

"Mom says you need somebody in your life."

He gives a stiff laugh. "I'm fine."

"Mom says that if you're left alone too long, you struggle. She says you daydream too much and get lost."

"I'm fine," he says a second time. He put a little firmness on the end of it, hoping that it'll do the job of making her back off a bit.

"Do you see things sometimes?" she asks.

He stops shuffling the pancakes around. "What?"

"Do you see things sometimes? Like, imagine things that you know you're imagining?"

"Why would you ask that? I don't remember you asking me that."

"Dad!" Mia calls. "You're burning the pancakes!"

"Shit!"

He scoops them out, apologizing along the way.

"Never mind," Mia says. "How's the new book coming along?"

"Better than the pancakes," he says.

Then they're at the table. The sunlight comes in hard through the windows. The sky is blue, cloudless. They eat slowly. They talk about the weather—make bets on rain. He tries to focus on the fact that she is alive now. But her question is still there, filling the house like the smell of breakfast: Do you see things sometimes? Outside the window, the blue sky has filled with birds. Blackbirds, dancing on air, spinning and funneling, with hints of blue and red around the edges of their wings. The flow spins itself into a circle.

"Dad!"

"What?" By her tone, he knows she's been calling him for a while.

"You still not ever gonna move?" She asks it between bites.

"Nah," he says. "I'll grow old and die here."

"No time soon though, right?"

"Can't do much about the growing old part. But the dying's not on the schedule for a few decades." Outside the window, the birds are gone. The sky is clear again. "I love it here," he says.

"I know you do. But Canada's pretty cool. It's . . . different. Easier to breathe, if that makes sense."

"That's what all the commercials say."

"The winters are a little rough around the edges . . . and in the middle . . . and on the top, bottom, and sides. Haha! But it's really pretty too. Some mornings you look outside and everything is just buried. And, when that happens, there's this quiet like you've never heard, Dad. Words just kinda fall straight to the ground as soon as they come out of your mouth. It's really amazing. There's magic in it."

"We get snow here."

"No, we don't. Not real snow."

He looks for the birds again, but they haven't come back. "Hey," he says.

"Yeah?"

"Do you see things sometimes?"

"Never. Do you?" When the question goes unanswered, she says, "It's not your fault."

"What's not?"

"This is family land," she says. "You don't want to leave. I get it."

"It's bigger than that."

"I know."

"Your grandparents owned it."

"I know."

"Your great-grandparents owned it."

"I know."

"Your—"

"Dad! I get it!" She sits back in her chair, again looking like Tasha. In fact, he realizes now, this is the conversation he and Tasha had for years before the divorce. Why shouldn't she replay it now? "They all lived and died here. Through slavery and sharecropping and all the rest. They all got their blood in the dirt and all that." She gesticulates as she speaks, like taking on the whole world. "So that means you can never, ever leave. I get it. Fuck!"

"I'm sorry," he says.

"You know I'm going to die here, don't you?"

"What?"

His heart pounds. His lungs tighten.

"I said: I'm never going to live here like you."

He pushes his plate away, heart still a drumbeat in his chest. "I'm gonna go out and check on the grapes. I'll have to go do some writing pretty soon."

She sighs again. "Let me finish first," she says. "I'll come."

She takes her time and he makes quick work of the grapevines while she does. The sky is still bright and blue. The air warm. The sound of the wind broken up by the drone of bees bumbling between the grape rows. He doesn't know how long he waits for her. Maybe minutes. Maybe a half hour. All he remembers is the peacock. The beautiful ebon peacock—so black it looks as though each feather were bathed in ink. He spots it out across the field, standing in the place where, years from now, Mia will lie dead. He watches it spread its feathers. Watches the plumage tremble. The feathers stare at him like black eyes. They shake and the sound of them runs through his bones, almost makes him drop the pruning shears from his hand.

I'm going to die here. And you should go back to Canada.

Mia is there, standing beside him, staring out, looking off in the same direction he is.

"What did you say?"

"Nothing. Why? You hearing things, Old Man?"

She grins and leans her head on his shoulder. Maybe she didn't say anything at all.

A second later she lifts her head. Her brow furrows and she squints. She holds one hand over her eyes, strains to see something in the same place where he sees the peacock—ebon and stunning. He wants to ask her if she sees it, if she sees the same thing he does. He wants to say, "What are you looking at?" He wants to say, "Do you already know that you're going to kill yourself?" He wants to say, "What can I say to change it?" He wants to say, "If I had come to Canada, would you still be alive?" He wants to say, "What can I do to change it?" He wants to say, "What was it? Were you sad? Lonely? Was it something else? Can you ever tell me?"

"**What the fuck was that?**" Dylan asks. I'm all but chasing him down the middle of the empty Parisian streets and my shoes aren't fans of all these old cobblestones, so after a couple of blocks of pumping my bunions they're singing like a Gregorian choir. "Jesus, kid! Hold up!"

He doesn't slow down.

"What's going on here? Why'd you bolt out of there like that? You damned near flipped over the table on those two, and they were pretty swell! What's wrong with you?"

"To hell with the both of them!" he shouts back over his shoulder, still marching with his fists thumping air to and fro like pendulums. "They don't know what the fuck they're talking about!"

"Oh," I say, spring-walking and hobbling at the same time, and barely keeping up for my troubles. "You know what they say about meeting your heroes. I ever tell you about the dame from Ohio who told me I was her Taylor Swift? Can you imagine that? Can you imagine being someone's Taylor Swift?! Well, I was struck dumb. Shook me right down to my argyle soc—"

"Would you shut up!" Dylan screams. He's almost out of breath, but I can tell that it's not anger that's got him heaving the way he is. I've danced with enough angry husbands to know the sound of anger when someone aims it in my direction.

"Well spell it out for me, kid," I say.

"Don't fucking call me kid!"

That gets him. Finally, he stops walking long enough for me to catch up and for him to turn and glare at me like he's debating whether or not he should take that fist of his and put it squarely between my eyes. "One more time," he says. Now he's marching at me like he's 1930s Germany and I smell like Poland. His takes his fist and thumps me in the chest. "Call me 'kid' one more time!" I watch his jaw muscles tighten like bridge cables. And for the first time since I met him, he sounds all American. He sounds like Baltimore. He sounds like Atlanta. He sounds like Watts. He sounds like Brooklyn and the Source Awards and my dead Geechee grandmother's chicken-and-rice recipe all rolled into one.

For the first time since I met him, with his fist in my chest and a charge of potential violence buzzing in the air around us, he sounds and feels like home.

But this is also when I finally get a bead on what I'm hearing in his voice. Yes ma'am. Like I said, it's not anger. No. What I'm hearing from the kid is panic. Pure as clarified butter. Even when he grits his teeth and hisses something to himself in what sounds like four different types of Foreign, it's still simply panic. Raw terror.

After I don't make a move that gets me slugged across the jaw, Dylan takes a step back and paces on the corner, in the cool Parisian air and beneath that beautiful French sky.

"What's got you so wound up? I mean, from the time we met you've been the coolest of cucumbers. Straight out the crisper drawer. Now look at you. What's it about? What's the story?"

"Fuck!" he spits. "Fuckfuckfuck!"

Somewhere around the third "fuck" his voice breaks. What's left behind for the final fuck is more of a sob than anything else.

"Easy." I put a hand on his trembling shoulder. His eyes dart east to west. Fight-or-flight or fix-a-ham-sandwich in action. "Just tell me the score. Whatever it is."

Finally, the crying starts.

He mumbles to himself between sobs. Sometimes in English, sometimes in various flavors of Foreign. Along the way I make out one sentence buried in the sadness: "It was supposed to be different. Those two were supposed to be able to fix it. That's who they are! But they can't fix it!"

"Fix what?" I ask.

"I'm tired," he begins. "I'm tired of being outnumbered. I'm tired of not fitting in even when I do everything I can to fit in. I'm tired of standing out. I'm tired of having to be small so that I don't make waves and I'm tired of having to scream at the top of my lungs just to keep the world from swallowing me up. It shouldn't be both ways at the same time. It just shouldn't!" He cranes his neck upward with a sigh, taking in all the lights of The Continent glowing around us. "We've been assimilated, but they won't let us be assimilated. And you can't pull the eggs out of a cake that's already been baked." The sob that comes almost chokes him.

"What? Listen, I know you're trying to say your piece, but you're losing me along the way."

"Why am I even talking to you?" he asks, another flare of anger dancing a two-step back into his tone. "You're just . . . you're just . . . you're just some *thing* that's watched too much TV and read too many books, so you hide. I don't know how I didn't see it. All you ever do is hide! Why should I listen to anything you have to say? Why should I tell you anything!? Talk about the blind leading the fucking blind!"

He chuckles then, and it's dark as death. It's one of those pain-filled crack-ups, like someone's twisting a knife in his belly and he's got no other choice but to laugh because he knows he's already dead. And, yeah, maybe he's hit a certain nail on its head. And Dylan, even with all his plumage spread out so that he looks as big as the Incredible Hulk . . . he's a born-gentle bird. He's got the whole world in his head and he just doesn't know what to do with it. "Easy," I say finally. Even though I'm not sure what my play is, I'm willing to bet on words. In my experience, if I can talk long enough, I've got a decent chance of stumbling onto the right thing to say. "Here's the hustle: I'm not saying you should listen to me. You're right: Who am I? I'm just a voice out here in the chaos. But that don't mean I can't be square with you. Don't mean I can't offer a lifeline . . . Whatever this is you're going through, let me tell you: You fit. I've seen it for myself. You're a child of the world. You're more at home in life than I could ever be. Just look at all those Foreigns you speak. You fit in anywhere. You're not like me. You're real, kid!"

I want to apologize as soon as I say that three-letter word, but he lets me get away with this one.

"I'm tired of *having* to fit!" he says. There's anger in the back of his throat again. "I just want to be somewhere where I don't have to fit because I'm already built in. I want to be *home*."

I nod. I think I know the score now, so I take a swing: "Which part of the States did you say you were from? Maryland? Georgia? You could always go back there. The peach trees and Jermaine Dupri are waiting for you! Admittedly, Jermaine is pretty much retired from the beat-making game these days, but he's still a lege—"

"That's not home," he says. "I can't go back. Ever. That whole place is burning and everyone I left there is burning with it and they don't even know it." He pauses after that last one, like he's deciding whether or not to push ahead. I guess he decides he's already bet the house, may as well bet the car too, because he keeps going: "And you know what?"

"What's that?" I'm hooked. I want to let him pour all of this out. That's how people get better, right? They gotta dump this stuff out and then that makes it all okay. That's how it works!

"I don't shed a single tear for them," Dylan says. "Not because I don't care about the people that I left behind there, but because if I start crying for them, I'll have to start crying for me. I'll have to start crying because I have no place to go. And I never did."

"I thought you dug it over here in Euroland?"

"It's not home and never will be. There's a hierarchy here, just like everywhere. You're either French-born White or Italian-born White or English-born White or Whatever-born Whatever . . . or you're an Other. Well, where do the Others go? What do you do when your home doesn't love you and all the other homes you've tried to make a life in don't love you either? And I mean, you know Victor is actually Jamaican, right?"

"Sure," I say. "I remember something about that on the backflap of that third big book he wrote."

"How fucked up is it that I'm jealous of any nigga that's from somewhere that they can call their own? People like us? What do we have? We don't even have the South, which is the closest thing we'll ever get to a homeland. How sad is that?" He shudders again. That weight he's carrying starts pressing down again. The waterworks get switched back on all the way. "I wonder what it feels like to be somewhere in this world and not feel like an outsider."

"I'm sorry, kid," I say.

Again, he doesn't correct me. But this time it's not out of kindness.

He's still staring up at the Parisian skyline like he's waiting for the Great Hand of That Great Bearded Voyeur in the Sky to come down and either pick him up or crush him into dust. I don't think he cares which.

"I'm sorry," I begin. "When I think about it, I don't know for sure if I've ever felt at home in this world. Maybe that's why I live in my head so much, you know?"

Dylan doesn't say anything. He just keeps staring up, waiting for God to intervene. And God keeps not getting involved.

"But, personally, I do think there's a fix for you out there somewhere. I'm not one to sign on for that pessimistic brand of thinking that everyone's trying so hard to sell us these days. Yeah, I've seen bad times swallow folks up—been shoved underwater by life a few times myself. I know the game. There's only one letter separating the brave from the grave. We should all live accordingly. But I've seen the back side of hurricanes too. I've seen lots of things. I've seen birds fight off bears and I've seen the northern lights dance a jig over Tuscaloosa. Seen a man get tossed into the air by an eighteen-wheeler and walk off laughing. One time I seen an alpaca riding shotgun in a Toyota Camry in the middle of Atlanta. I've seen forty-year-old bare breasts dangled out of a Burger King drive-through window and given over to the dappled sunlight on an Easter Sunday. I knew a woman who sneezed every time she orgasmed. I've shook hands with a Black president and watched *Fury Road* in the same afternoon. Yeah, kid, I'm someone who's seen rockets break orbit! When folks come around with that old sales pitch about how things always gotta come up snake eyes in the end, well, I just let it pass me by. Nothing in this life is duty-bound to fall apart. Nothing. Not even you, Dylan."

I feel good about it even before I'm finished saying it. I feel like I've finally put it out there. Finally found the words to fix him. I've sold this particular pony to people more times than I can remember, and it always works. It helps people. Just between you and me, that's all I'm ever doing—every second of every day—trying to find the words to fix people. And failing at it most days. But not today. I can feel it.

Dylan's quiet for so long that I figure him speechless. I figure he's hip deep in the word safety blanket I wrapped him in and, any second now, he's going to look away from the Big Man upstairs and look to those words of mine and say, "You're right" and that'll be the way things turn around.

Maybe it's my ego that makes it take so long for me to realize he's not thinking over what I said, he's gone away again. "Dylan?" I call out. "Hey! Dylan!"

No dice. It's just like back in Italy. I give his arm a tug, trying to pull him out of it, but that's a mistake, because he starts to topple over.

"Hey! Hey!"

I toss myself under him just in time to keep him from cracking his face open on the French stones. "C'mon, Kid!" I shout. I fish into his pockets, looking for his medicine. I come up short.

"Shit."

I look around for a Frenchie who might be able to help, but it's late at night and we're off the main strip and, unlike the Big Apple, it seems like this town actually does close up shop at night.

"It's okay, kid," I say. "You're gonna be swell." I'm not sure if I believe it, but I say it anyhow.

The kid only continues to stare ahead, like he sees the future and can't look away.

I sit there with him in my lap and my stab wound starting to speak to me in little whispers, and that cold French wind is starting to creep in from the north and, hell, I'd give just about anything to be someplace else. But I can see it in his eyes. He's out there, somewhere, and he'll come back. I don't know why I want him to come back as much as I do. Don't know why I need him to come back to me and be the smartass he is. Maybe it's because, hell, as jaded as he is, he's just a kid looking for a place to fit in.

The wind picks up and the temperature drops and, still, he's there staring into the Great Superunknown that only he can see. And that's when Remus comes rising up out of the Parisian darkness, singing a tune and smiling like a jackal.

He bundles up in the coat they loaned him so that, if he wanted, he could go walking around in the cold and not freeze to death. "You're not dressed for Minnesota," they told him as they gave him the overcoat. And that was true. So he wears the overcoat they gave him. He throws it on over his sweater jacket and jeans and he grabs his computer bag and slings it over his shoulder and tucks his book into the front zip pocket—another trick he's learned on account of he never knows where he might be when the need comes to tell someone who he is and how he stands apart and how, if something were to happen to him, then there'd be attention and, by proxy, some type of headache. And then he steps in front of the mirror and looks at himself to be sure that, between the layering of the jacket and the large overcoat, the silhouette of the pistol holstered in the small of his back doesn't show and, all the while, he tries not to think about the memory of his daughter and the way she told him to come back to Canada and the fact that it's all bleeding together.

Time travel. That's what he called it before. But now he's realizing what it is: madness.

He exits the hotel room into the always-too-quiet hallway and heads to the elevator where there's a small White woman waiting. They nod at each another politely and she takes a step to the side to allow him space enough to stand and wait for the elevator beside him. There's a window on the far side of the hallway and, as they await the elevator, they watch the wind bluster and they look out at the city hidden behind all the snow and, for now, it seems like this could be any frozen city anywhere in the world. It seems as though, if someone were staying in another hotel somewhere—some fellow author, maybe, down on his luck and trying to figure out how to survive the chaos of their life—they could look out their window and see only a city buried in snow and never have a sense of what city it was or where on this earth it was and he thinks about how disorienting that could be and—

"Are you coming?" the woman asks. The elevator has already arrived as he drifted off. It's a habit of his, to drift off into himself. Something that comes and goes of its own accord. He does what he can to get a handle on it, but some days it gets the better of him.

"Yes," he says, trying to sound chipper. He hustles into the elevator. "I'm sorry about that. Ground floor."

"Already pushed it," the woman says.

"Thank you."

The doors close and they begin their descent.

"Where are you from?" the woman asks.

"I look like I don't belong?" he asks.

"We know our own around here," she says, smiling. "You got that look about you, like you're dreading the cold. That's how locals like me know somebody isn't from around here."

"You're right," he says, smiling. "I don't know how y'all live in this. But I think I could learn to become a part of this place." He shudders and makes a dramatic action of conveying that he's cold and not expecting to be warm again anytime soon.

"People can learn to live with anything—"

She's cut off by the clatter of the pistol falling onto the elevator floor between them.

The silence returns.

"Shit," he says. He squats down and snatches up the gun. "I'm sorry. I've got a permit. I promise."

With each word she backs away. Her eyes are trembling and she has her hands in front of her, close to her body, and he can't tell if she's building up for a scream or not.

"It's okay. Really. I'm not a bad guy. This isn't anything dangerous. It's just for protection."

But she can't hear him. She's in her own place. Maybe, he thinks, she's one of those here to mourn the dead. Maybe she's even one of the people he's supposed to talk to tomorrow night when he addresses whoever decides to come to his event at the college. Maybe, right now, she's imagining the gun moving through the halls of that college, putting the living in company with the dead, or maybe she sees in him all the dangerous Black men she's been told lurk out here in the world.

Or maybe she's just seen enough guns in her day.

Whatever the answer, she keeps her scream in. The two of them ride the rest of the way down the elevator wordlessly, as far apart as they can be, with her staring at him, wide-eyed and teary, and with him staring straight ahead at the elevator doors, trying to will them open, trying to make it all end, feeling the gun in his hand.

Even when they reach the ground floor and the doors open, they are both still there, in that elevator. Days later, they're both still there, in that elevator. Years later, they're both still there, in that elevator.

"I could learn to become a part of this place," he had said.

"Looks like he's in a hard way," Remus says. He saunters up from the far end of the street. I could say he comes out of the shadows, but it's more like the shadows just sorta back away from him. They give him a wide berth. Yeah, even they know the score.

There's a buzzing in the air as he gets closer. Music almost. Some *Mo' Better Blues* jazz tune climbing up out of some unseen dive bar. At least, I'm hoping it is. The other option is that it's all in my head. Which ain't a bad play, just not the one I'd prefer. If it's in my head, that's a little bit of a worry. I always get a little on the back foot when potential murders have their very own soundtrack. Especially a jazz one. If I'm gonna be killed, let it be to something by Sade. Given a choice, "Smooth Operator" is the tune I'd like to have play me offstage when the time comes.

Remus is barefoot and bare-chested, with the soft light of Paris bouncing off his skin, darkening it somehow. His feet make loud slapping sounds on the stones as he walks, like he's trying to stomp a hole in Paris itself. All he's wearing is that same old pair of jeans he's worn the last two times we met. As he gets closer, he lets out a long whistle that bounces off the cobblestones and the walls of the streets where

Hemingway used to write about failing relationships and unwanted pregnancies.

He looks down at Dylan. "Used to know a nigga back in Mississippi that would have fits like that. Would just come over him all hard and fast. Except his—ha!—when his kicked in that nigga would just start swinging at anything that moved! Haha! You should have seen it. One minute he was running the pool tables and then you'd hear that pool cue hit the ground and his eyes would be wild as shit, and when that happened you better not move! Haha! One wrong move and he'd take your head clean off!" He laughs again, hard and loud. "Shit! Funniest part was, he wasn't a fighting kind of guy. Gentle as a mouse to anybody that knew him. Then he was fighting goddamned demons!" Remus sighs. "It was like he was seeing something nobody else could see, like you. He couldn't do nothing about it. Would just come over him. I always felt bad for that nigga. I'll tell you what though, if he'd ever learned to put an on-off switch on them fits of his, he could'a knocked out Sugar Ray!"

"I can't do this now," I say. My mouth is as dry as a dusty condom and there's something cold in the pit of my stomach and, even with all that, I'm only thinking about Dylan, still stiff as a board in my arms. I dig into his pockets, searching for his phone. Not sure what the Euroland number is for 911, but I figure I can make do. The Kid's phone is nowhere to be found though.

"Open up for me," Remus says.

"No."

I lean back as he steps within grabbing distance. But with Dylan in my lap, there's only so far I can go. I turn my head away and tighten my jaw like a four-year-old staring down the barrel of a spoonful of Benadryl.

"Grab the gun," my brain says. But maybe the muscles are all on strike because nobody's showing up for work. That's twice now. Who says a workforce united can't change the world?

I got no choice but to try and talk myself out of this. Hell, I work with words. Even won The Big One. If I can't talk myself out of a bad situation, I should put down my pen and take up—

His hand vise-grips my jaw so hard I think I feel something crack. It knocks those thoughts of gabbing my way out of this right out of my head. A few sluggish vowels of resistance spill from my mouth as he opens it by squeezing my jaw like a walnut. He tilts my head back, staring down into the dark hole of my mouth. He moves my head a little, probably trying to get a little more light in there. Then down come those grizzled, scarred fingers of his.

My eyes water from the pain and a couple of tears run down the side of my face as his fingers go in. My heart bangs out a merengue, wondering if that knife of his will make another guest appearance in tonight's episode. My stomach wound sounds off. I guess it's a little worried about if the casting director called the knife in again too.

I don't know how long we spend there, with his fingers in my mouth and my heart almost choking me to death and my bladder threatening to cut loose. I don't know why he's so worried about the health of my teeth. Maybe he thinks my teeth are where the words I write come from. Who can say? All I know is that sound, that strange, distant sound I might call music, doesn't get any louder . . . but it does get a little clearer. There's something familiar about it. Like the opening of a song I can almost remember, if the world would just be a little quieter and let me hear it all the way.

"Still looking good," Remus says finally. Then his fingers are out of my mouth and my jaw is taken from the vise. I spit and work my mouth around to see if anything's broken.

Not sure what the verdict is just yet though.

"Listen," I say, "I don't have time for this. Kill me if you want, but this kid needs help first. You get me?"

Remus take a few steps back, staring down at Dylan and me the whole time. He grins and turns and looks up at the sky and opens his arms like he's waiting for a shower to come along and pour down on him, and that's when I finally see it.

My stomach goes cold and I can feel the pumps trying to reverse and blow everything I've eaten in the last two days all over these Parisian streets. It's the kind of thing that you know you shouldn't look at, because the story behind it is only the worst kind of story imaginable. A story so dark you know that, if you ever hear the full version, you won't be able to leave it behind. It'll follow you, every step of every day, and the sun will never shine as bright or as warm as it did before you knew how something so bad ever happened.

Sister, you've never seen something so horrible.

His whole back is just a mass of haggard flesh. Like somebody ripped it off of him, ran it through a meat grinder, and somehow stuck it right back on his frame. He's chewed up and melted all at the same time. With all of that, with the horror that he must have gone through, you wouldn't think he'd even be strong enough to stalk people in the streets in the name of good dental hygiene. Don't seem like a body can go through whatever he must have gone through and still come out the other side breathing. But I guess there's all sorts of prodigies in this world.

I catch the sight of his back in just a flash before I have to look away. Even when I close my eyes, I can still see it. For his part, Remus seems to pay me no mind. I hear him let out a long, loud howl. I open my eyes just in time to see that the chill in the air has turned his breath to steam so that, somehow, this scarred, howling, would-be dentist is standing there in the middle of this French cobblestone street, just a black body cast into silhouette, with the light breaking through the steam of his breath making a rainbow halo above his head.

It's one of the most beautiful things I've ever seen. And I've seen black peacocks, snow-covered cityscapes, and Lauren Bacall.

"What's that about?" I ask, regretting it as soon as the words come out.

He flinches, like he forgot I was there. "What's what about?" He turns slowly. Takes a few steps closer. Then squats down on his haunches.

"Those . . . uh . . . those leftovers you're carrying on your back. Looks like something or somebody really put you through it."

"What scars?" he says. Then he laughs. "God! I love this city." His lips go wide and that half-filled smile of his lights up the night. "Whole place reminds me of Toronto. But better. Much as I hate to admit it. Every nigga on the planet should come through here. Mind if I sit?" He takes a seat beside me on the chilly concrete curb. Wipes his hands on his pants. "You scared of me, nigga?"

He looks at Dylan as he says it, so I can't tell if he's asking me or The Kid. But I answer on both our behalves. "Yeah."

"Smart," Remus says. "I'm goddamned dangerous. But not tonight. Ain't the right time."

"Swell," I say. "That's just swell." The cold knot in my stomach doesn't punch out for the day just yet. Which is fair, I suppose. But, since Remus hasn't lied to me about anything just yet, I figure I can press my luck a little. I say: "Well if you're not going to kill me, the least you can do is help me with the kid here."

"Sure thing." Somehow, he says it with what I can only describe as excitement.

He stands and bends down and scoops those big tree-trunk arms of his under The Kid. Lifts him out of my lap like he's weightless. He tosses Dylan over his shoulder and offers that big frying-pan of a hand of his to me. He pulls me to my feet with enough force that I feel air between my feet and the ground for a full second.

"Let's go," he says.

We start walking through the veins of Paris. Me, the unconscious kid, and my would-be killer. Never let anyone tell you life ain't an R-rated hayride.

"I ever tell you about the friend of mine that killed himself?" Remus begins after we've walked a few blocks. The streets are eerily empty, like all the Frenchies have been taken away by The Rapture. "Boy from down in Mississippi. Had everything in the world going for him and then one day he up and decides there's nothing better to do than to chew on the loud end of a Smith & Wesson. I cried over that nigga for years. Yessir, they broke the mold when they made him! But then he went out into the world and the world broke him. No shame in that, you know. We all get broken by it. And don't you ever believe anybody that tells you otherwise."

I reach into my jacket and pull out the gun. I all but give it to him. "Why can't I use this?" I ask.

"You ain't square in the head," he says. "But don't worry. I'll teach you."

"Oh."

A long time ago, back before things in my life went down the smooth and velvet road of writing success, I used to work a gig answering phones for a major cell phone company. Was a terrible way to make a living. People screaming at you all day. The bosses always wanting more. That job chewed most folks up. But I hung in, if only to keep the lights on. And, while I was there, I learned that folks want nothing more than to tell their problems to somebody. Folks would call in asking about some charge on their bill and, five minutes later, they're giving up the goods on the cheating husband, the opium-addicted wife, the kleptomaniac kid, and the racist grandma. And I never had to ask for any of it. They just gave it to me.

You see, I learned that strangers make the best therapists. They don't owe you anything and they don't even particularly care about you. They can just listen, give you their twenty cents, and then hightail it out of your life without ever spilling the beans to anybody that you might not want said beans spilled to.

Maybe that's why I say what I say to Remus next:

"Remus, my friend," I start, "you seem like the type to not let grass grow beneath his feet. Seem like you've been a few places and seen more than a few things. This world ain't never going to pull the wool over your eyes! And I'm just wondering: In all your travels, especially over here in Euroland, did you ever come across a place wher—"

"Nigger-La."

"What?"

"You want to know if Nigger-La is out there. Haha! Whooo! Boy, I knew you was pretty fucked up, but I didn't know you was a fool too." He laughs again, long and hard, like I'm doing some sort of stand-up show. He turns and claps one of those big hands of his on my back and says, "Your type thinks this world is got some special piece of land waiting out there to keep you safe? To take you out of what everybody else is going through? Ha! Hell, I know the stories. I done heard them! 'Where's Nigger-La?!' 'Where's the Brown Man's Paradise?' 'Where's the place where I can go and get my head straight? The place where I ain't gotta look over my shoulder? Where everybody there bleeds just like me? Where every night my goddamned neighbors can come over and we can eat spaghetti and drink champagne and I ain't gotta watch my back or worry about getting laughed at or getting shot through the back of the head when I ain't looking?' Hell, nigga! You think you're the first one to come hunting? And it ain't just niggas that hunt for it. I seen 'em all! Black, White, Brown, Yellow, Red. Gays and weirdos. Bastards that cry at everything in the world and can't figure out why nobody else is crying with them. The bastards who cry alone in the dark and don't tell nobody. And they all think that, somewhere, it gets better. Next thing you know you'll be telling me you want to go back to Africa. Haha!"

I feel two inches tall. Feel like I should have just kept it all to myself.

"Nigger-La," he says to himself, still chuckling. "Nigga, you're a riot."

He says it like he's answered my question. I should keep quiet. I should just shut up and let him do whatever he wants to do to me. I should just focus on Dylan and getting him mended. But I don't. I keep talking: "I can't keep living like this."

"Like what, nigga?"

Maybe it's the adrenaline. Maybe it's the stab wound that's starting to hurt. Maybe it's the buzzing—that strange sound that Remus brought with him—in my ears that still hasn't gone away. Or maybe it's just the fact that, hell, if you can't talk candidly with the man who's planning to kill you, who can you talk to?

"I think I hate everything," I say. I look down at Dylan. "I definitely hate this kid. No. That's wrong. I don't hate him. I hate how he looks at me: Like I know something. Like I know the way to that Nigger-La of yours. I hate how he clings to me. And, yeah, I know Frenchie's got him on the hook as part of his job to help me get around Euroland, but don't be fooled. He's hoping. He don't belong anywhere and he don't know what to do with that and it's killing him and he wants me to stop it."

Remus don't say a word. He just keeps marching along the empty French streets, with Dylan still slung over his shoulder like a sackful of memories.

"This condition of mine," I say. "It's chewing me up. Just like how Dylan's is chewing him up."

"Shit, nigga," Remus says. "I already knew all that stuff."

Just then, I look around and find that we've reached some sort of medical center. It's a small building, but there's a neon cross on the wall. I figure that's the easiest way to let Freedom Lovers like me know how to find a Florence Nightingale when they're in need.

He lowers Dylan to the ground. The Kid is still out. Still far off in the void. Still dreaming in that soft, beautiful way that he dreams. Wherever he is, I hope it's better than here.

"Thanks," I say. Then: "Is it really not real? That place where people that don't fit anywhere finally get to feel like they do?"

Remus turns to me. "Next time," he says. Then he hugs me. It's long and warm. The kind of hug my Old Man and Old Lady used to give me. He even smells like them: sweat and motor oil from the Old Man, sage and cocoa butter from the Old Lady. Before I know what's happening,

I hug him back. I feel those scars covering that back of his under my hands as I hug him. I shudder. But then, and I'm not sure why, I don't care about them anymore. I hold him tight, like holding on to him might heal them scars of his. Give him back whatever got taken away when those scars came along. Remus . . . right here, right now . . . he feels like love. Feels like somebody I've known my whole life. Feels like home.

Then he lets me go and says, again: "Next time."

"Next time what?"

"And don't forget to bring that gun." My body tightens. "Keep it on you," he continues. "Don't let it out of your sight. Eat with it. Sleep with it. Marry the fucker. Haha! Who knows? Maybe it'll actually save you. Maybe it'll make you a little less afraid. If it don't do that, what the hell's the point?" He slaps his hands together. "But in the meantime, I wish you and this boy here the best of luck. The two of you make a good team. All of you. That girl of yours, that big-bodied fellow. You all really got something. But weren't none of you built for this world. Not really . . . And then there's ol' Remus . . ."

He offers me that broken smile one more time and claps his hands over his head and shouts like James Brown. He spits on the pavement, turns, and saunters off into the cold nighttime city, whistling as gentle and beautiful as any songbird I ever did hear.

They were good at getting into the closet, but they weren't particularly good at staying quiet.

"Shhhhh!" Mia whispered—or, rather, tried to whisper. But what came out was more of a quiet roar followed by giggling.

"Scoot over," the other child said.

"I am scooted over," Mia replied.

"No you're not! You're all the way on my side."

"Who farted?" a third child asked. From the sound of his voice, he had his nose pinched.

"Sorry," the second child said.

"Eeewwwww!" came the shout in unison.

"You're not supposed to be talking!" Tasha said. Then, to Soot: "Do you see what I'm talking about?"

"They're kids," Soot replied, staring down at his phone. "They're just doing what kids do."

"And you don't find any of this to be even mildly terrifying?"

"Maybe that fart," Soot said, fanning the air in front of his face. "Whatever kid cut that particular slice of cheese needs to see a doctor. Jesus!"

He grinned, but Tasha was having none of it.

They both looked up at clock on the wall, checking to see how much longer the children needed to practice hiding. They were all sequestered in the small metal closets that were installed in the classroom a few years back for the day when the shootings would finally reach out their long arms and touch Columbus County. Legally, the metal closets were known as "Safety Spaces." It was an innocuous name meant to remind everyone involved—the children, the teachers, and the parents—of other innocuous names like "Bird Sanctuary" or "Prairie Dog Preserve."

"I still don't see why you wanted me to come," Soot said. "I need to be home finishing the new book."

"You really don't know why I wanted you to come?" Tasha hissed.

"Mom? How much longer?" Mia asked, her voice tinny as it filtered through the steel door of the Safety Space.

"Until you hear the alarm," Tasha said. Then she stared at Soot and said: "Hang in there, kids. Remember, this is an active shooter drill. You have to treat it seriously. Stay quiet. Your life might depend on it."

"Okay," he said gently. He stepped closer and lowered his voice. "Listen, I get it. This is surreal. Yes, I'll give you that. But they'll be fine. You know the math. The odds of anything happening at any specific school in this country are insanely low. These kids are more likely to have something happen in a hurricane, but we don't pick up and move away. Because we know that the odds of anything really serious happening are pretty slim. Yeah, the weather comes along every few years and a hard one blows down and floods things out. But people don't pick up and run away to another damned country."

Tasha grabbed him by the wrist and pulled him close and spat: "This is not the same as fucking weather. The fact that everybody acts like it is should be the last fact you need to know before deciding to take your family and leave, Soot."

"Your mom said a bad word," one of the kids said.

"I know," Mia said. "She's cool."

The alarm blared and the principal's voice crackled over the intercom declaring the faux emergency over. The children filed out of their steel-reinforced Safety Spaces, smiling as usual. Tasha walked over and removed the steel brace from behind the door and then lifted the shades meant to keep active shooters from seeing inside the classroom from the windows.

"Okay, class. You all did great!"

"Did we live?" one of the children asked.

"You sure did," Tasha said.

"I'm going home," Soot said to Tasha.

"Say goodbye to Mia. You know she hates it when we don't say goodbye."

He walked over and picked up his daughter and hugged her. "Bye, baby."

"Bye, Dad," Mia said. "I'm glad you were here today."

"Yeah?"

"Yeah. I always wanted to show you how I could hide from a shooter." She said it brightly, brimming with pride. "I would totally live if this was real," she said.

No one, not Tasha or Mia or the children, knew why Soot fell into tears then.

Not long after Remus fades off into the night—sauntering, with his old promise of death lingering behind—I lug The Kid into the Frenchie emergency center. When they see us, they come over and give us the side-eye. Really look down both barrels of their nostrils at us. Maybe it's the American I'm speaking or maybe it's something else. Either way, they don't seem particularly stressed about the fate of my unconscious friend.

"He's got a condition," I say. "Drifts off into someplace else. I feel like he's been gone too long this time though."

They got nothing for me. They check him over and make some motion that I take to mean that maybe he's had too much to drink. I argue back in the other direction, but I can tell we're hitting one of those language barriers you hear so much about. But there's one name I know they know that'll get things moving, really light a fire under their nether regions, and it ain't Jesus Christ.

"▮▮▮▮ ▮▮▮▮▮!" I shout.

The whole building screeches to a halt. The lights flicker and even folks in the ICU put breathing on hold for a second. "This kid here?" I continue, "He's ▮▮▮▮ ▮▮▮▮▮▮'s right-hand man! You got that? Practically the man's love child. If he don't get the full Florence Nightingale treatment, The Man himself is gonna rain down on all of you like them locusts your grandfolks warned you about. So my advice is that you stop dicking around and give him the tops, you hear me? The tops! Or else ▓▓▓ ▓▓▓▓▓▓ himself will come through here and burn this whole place to the ground! . . . Financially speaking, I mean."

Truth is, I probably don't need to throw in the economic threats. No sooner than I say Frenchie's name, I see it in their eyes: They know the score. We aren't just a pair of melanin-infused Americans, we're somebodies.

"YES SIR!!!"

The whole hospital sounds off at once. Even the folks with feeding tubes down their throats manage to make a two-syllabled gurgle so they can have their name counted among those who wanted to stay out of the French billionaire's path. The thirteen-week guys and gals down on Parris Island couldn't have done it better.

The French doctors are all hands-on now. They catapult Dylan out of my arms and onto a gurney with a type of gentleness I didn't know existed in this world. Someone runs to a room and comes back with a tall glass of cucumber water for me and says, clear as day, "Mercy."

"Mercy to you too," I say.

Then the French doctors are all talk. They're just a deluge of soft vowels and vibrating jawlines. They give me entire dissertations and, even though it's in Foreign, I read between the lines: "Jesus-Baguette-Baking-Christ! You know Frenchie?! *The* Frenchie! We're sorry! We'll take real good care of this friend of yours. Really give him the soft touch. We promise! Just you wait and see!"

After swearing allegiance to the billionaire in my back pocket, they wheel Dylan on into the bowels of the emergency center. I finish off my glass of cucumber water and step outside to get some air. The doctors paw at me, telling me not to leave. I think they're afraid that I'm going to run off and say something bad about them to Frenchie. But I pat them on the head and promise to give them a good grade on their report card when the time comes.

Outside, the night has cooled and the air feels wet. There's a chill, like the kind that blows off lakes in the spring when the sun is too hot and the shade is too cold. I fold my arms over my chest and, for the first time in a while, I can hear my heart beating. It's still dancing that merengue that started up when it saw Remus and, all of a sudden, I'm tired in a way I didn't know I could be. I take the cue from my body and I just sorta melt down onto the sidewalk, stretch out on my back, and stare up at the sky.

Then . . . there's that peacock again. That beautiful black peacock. It's circling around, with those ebony wings of its stretched out like fans. It glides in silence, blotting out the stars as it loops around and around until, finally, it lands on the roof of the emergency center and stares down at me.

We stare at each other for almost a full minute.

"You gonna say something or what?" I say.

The bird lets out this howl of sorts. Sounds like a mixture between a scream and a jazz trumpet letting out one long note.

"Sure, sure," I say. "But what do I do?"

Before the bird can answer, I hear a *whup-whup-whupping* sound that does nothing but get louder, until soon the air is shaking and the bird is gone and a black helicopter—the same shade of black as the peacock—is hovering over me. Slowly, it lands on top of the hospital.

I rush inside.

The helicopter brings The Goon and Kelly. Not sure how they got word of what happened, but I'd bet money on the doctors here putting in an emergency phone call once they found out just how connected Dylan and I were.

"How is he?" Kelly asks.

"Not sure," I say. "He switched himself off again. But, well, I'm not sure he's gonna turn back on this time."

"What do you mean?"

"I'm not sure," I say. "Just a feeling."

"He'll be fine," The Goon says, sounding jolly as usual. He grabs me around the shoulder and pulls me close. "Don't ye worry. Dylan's one of the immortals! Nothing can touch him!"

"I hope so," I say.

"I know so," The Goon says. "It's going to be okay. Plus, we're moving."

"Moving?" I ask. "What's the play?"

"It'll be better," he says. He snaps his fingers and everybody in the place—even some of the patients—jumps three feet into the air and doubles their speed. They really find their hustle. "It'll be better," The Goon says one more time.

Whether he's making promises or just trying to convince, who can say. All I know for sure is that it turns out The Goon's got a gift for understatement because a few minutes later the four of us are in a private helicopter and *whup-whup-whupping* our way through the Paris sky and, not long after that, we touch down on the lawn of what I can only describe as an honest-to-god mansion in the middle of the city.

Mansion.

Sister, whatever that word brings to mind, just don't tell it. You hear the word "mansion" and you see a big lawn and a huge, dominating square-shaped house with spired gables and velvet curtains, and the sunlight that makes its way through the floor-to-ceiling windows is bright and maybe the whole place smells like old furniture. Or maybe you hear the word "mansion" and all you see is a pile of money in the shape of a house.

Well, I'm here to tell you that they're both true and they're both wrong.

Frenchie's Paris mansion? Sister, it's unlike anything you've ever seen.

Paris ain't even supposed to have mansions. It's all built up. Every inch used for something. But, in the middle of the night, we all take this chopper into the heart of Paris and, all of a sudden, the lights sorta fade away and, even though we're still in Paris, we land on this huge field of open grass and I can't see another house or streetlight or anything. All I see is a huge complex that I can't even call a house because the word just don't work for something this big.

I don't get much of a chance to take it all in—the quarter-mile-long gravel driveway, the servants, the head butler, the security people tucked away but visible at the same time—on account of it being night and on account of me still worrying about Dylan. But when the sun finally comes up, that's when I'm able to really get a look at it.

Dylan's in a bed upstairs, watched over by a small squad of sawbones and nurses, and I'm outside looking back at this place. The grass is so green it looks like something Willy Wonka dreamed up. Like if I reached down and grabbed a few blades and chewed it down, it would taste like the sour apple Now and Laters of my childhood. Well, for the record, the grass tastes slightly sweet. Who says money can't buy a different world.

The house itself is too big to take in all at once. You stare at it straight on and all you get is a side of it. And that one side is bigger than most Walmarts you've shopped at. But then, if you're willing to take the long walk around it, to see it from the other sides, it just keeps getting bigger. Personally, I don't know how anyone could live in a place like this and not get lost, but the servants seem to know their way around pretty well.

I could spend another hundred pages talking about this place, but we ain't got the time, sister. Let's get back down to business.

Here on The Honcho's home turf, all that money of his is like a solid fist sitting square in the middle of everyone's shoulder blades. Just something you can't ignore, no matter how much you want to. I walk around trying to figure out how anyone can have so much. My whole life would fit in just one of Frenchie's bathrooms. Dylan has got a whole wing of this mansion devoted to him getting better. I call it Honcho Memorial: Part Deux. For three whole days, it's like an episode of *ER*. Helicopters land and doctors from other parts of the world get out and they come in and do tests and consult and do examinations. Equipment is brought in that I can't even pronounce. Dylan gets poked and prodded and, through it all, he's still checked out. Nobody sleeps but Dylan. He just lies there, eyes closed, but with a stiffness in his body that makes it seem like whatever sleep he's in, it ain't exactly one you'd want to sign up for. And all the while, the only news that keeps coming back is as simple as two words: no news.

When the three days come and go, and the days keep coming and Dylan is still MIA, we get into a routine. The Kid stays tucked into his dreamworld while his body sits in satin sheets in a room at the top of the stairs that's about the size of a Whole Foods. The three of us take turns sitting with him and bending his ear. None of us can really be sure if he hears us, but we give him what we can anyhow. The Goon usually takes the morning shift, giving The Kid stories about Scottish history. Kings and battles and haggis. He really gives him the world.

When it's Kelly's turn, she mostly just talks about the news. She keeps him up-to-date on all the goings-on back in the States even though The Kid ain't been there in a fistful of years. She's a considerate dame, so she does the right thing of editing the info as best she can. There're shootings and protests and people storming the Capitol building, but she keeps that to herself.

I can really get behind what she's doing. One of the problems with knowing all the bad things in the world is the fact that, when you really get down to it, there's no reason to fill up the world with bad things if you can help it. If you've got somebody who drifts off into their own world, why not let their world be the best version that you can, you know?

And then, when it's my turn to talk with the kid . . . Well, let's not worry about that. I really do try to make things better. We go on like this for a week. No time on the road. No interviews or book events or anything like that. Just the four of us there on that great big French estate, letting the days come and go, one after another.

And the word is: we can stay as long as we want to.

If you live anywhere long enough, I guess you start to get sucked in by it. Whether you want to or not. But that's what it is. A week turns into more weeks. Then a month. All the while, rhythms form.

Some days the three of us don't even bother to leave the place. As good as Paris is to all of us, there are times when we all make the decision to just stay in. To stay right where we are. We roam Frenchie's house, looking at paintings, trying on suits of armor, trying to find the kitchen, wondering if the gold trim along the walls is real or not, but knowing all the while that it is. Some days we loaf around outside on the grounds—yeah, this place is so big it has grounds, plural. On those days, we walk in shade with that sweet grass beneath our feet. Or we stretch out on the earth and let the sun wash over us like dogs that are finally getting to have their day.

But we're not all joined at the hip all the time either. Some days, the sun peeks its head up, dances a two-step over the sky, and dives down behind the horizon with the three of us never once setting eyes on each other. That's just how big this place is. On those days, I go into the three-story library on the northern side of the house, shut the door, read first editions of books older than some countries—and I don't come out again until it's my time to visit with The Kid. At most on those days, I'll hear someone drop off food outside the door of the library—a perfectly cooked steak with baked sweet potatoes and some of that cucumber water Frenchie's gotten me hooked on. But I don't see the person who put it there, and I hate to say it but I start to get used to that too. I don't have to thank anyone or make small talk, and I dig it.

But even with that feeling of space, of not seeing another soul for a whole day, we all know that we're there. We all know that, if we want, there's just a quick yell separating one from the other. We get to be alone without ever being lonely.

Maybe money, in big enough stores, really can do anything.

The thing about time is that there isn't much you can do to stop it. Not even taking photographs and painting stuff you saw really does anything to slow down that old river. Moments come and go at the same pace they've always come and gone since before light ever shined in the sky, and we're just here trying to grab hold of water in our bare fists.

All that to say that, well, time rolls on out there on that little expensive plot of Parisian land.

None of us knew how it happened or when it happened, but it—that place—was right there, and it was beautiful. The days were peaceful and the nights were long. The French fall wasn't nearly as harsh as it could have been—like it knew we were there and that we deserved some sort of a break and it was doing the best it could to give us just that.

The world kept spinning and burning and, all the while, we didn't catch a whiff of smoke. Didn't hear a scream. We had finally made some Other Continent to call our own: The Scottish Goon, The Woman Who Swaddles the Dead, The Always-Dreaming Kid, and me . . . whatever I am.

Yes ma'am, it was good days.

And the nights weren't half bad either.

Kelly and I finally found the formula we never could all those years back. There wasn't a warm-up to it. No transition paragraph from the way we were to the way we became. No lead-in from across the table to holding hands. One day it was just there, a part of our lives, as if it had always been.

The details? I'll keep those in my pocket. Some things writers get to keep for themselves.

Was it everything I hoped it would be?

Yes and maybe.

"Do you think he wants to come back?" she says to me one night. It was a couple of months in. The French fall was heave-hoing outside and the winter was knocking in the distance. Maybe she could feel how we were slipping away from the rest of the world. And maybe she didn't like it.

She took on a habit of sleeping on my chest and, most nights, it was the most beautiful thing in the world. For all these months, she's been able to hear my thoughts. So, in a sense, I've got nothing left to hide from her and nothing left to reveal. She's seen me, she's heard me, from the inside out, and she's still here, making me feel small in the best way—even with all the awards and fanfare behind me, even with people mistaking me for Ta-Nehisi and Colson and all the rest—but she knows I'm not any of them. She knows I'm just who I am. And that's a little slice of perfect, if you ask me.

Yeah, it's been good between us here. But, this night, I can feel the anxiety dancing around in her head. "Of course," I say. I know full-on what she's talking about. Even though we almost never talk about The Kid directly, he's always in the room—metaphorically speaking. "He'll bounce back. He's the type with a destiny, you know? The type promised to take this world by the horns. So don't you worry about that none at all." I should stop there, but I don't. "Why wouldn't he want to come back?"

"He did once," she says. "Why not do it again?"

I sit up in bed. "How's that?"

"His parents," Kelly says. She rolls over onto her back and looks up at the ceiling. There's a night sky painted there. It's all ink blotches and specks. Probably put up by Jackson Pollock somehow. In this place, that would fit.

I'm ashamed to say it, but I never thought much about Dylan's parents. "Something go down with his folks?" I ask.

"Didn't he tell you how he got here?"

"Can't say that he did. But also can't say that I asked. I've got a condition."

"Being an asshole?"

"Sometimes."

She sighs. Then: "He's a runaway. Grew up in a small town outside DC. Came over here with his folks when he was nine or ten. He said he begged them to stay. Told them he didn't ever want to go back home. Said all he wanted was to stay over here because he could breathe better over here."

"Asthma or something?"

She rolls her eyes.

"Sorry," I say. "Jokes ease the tension sometimes."

"His folks took him back home," she continues.

"And then what? They came back?"

"They didn't," she says. "He did."

"You mean he ran off from his folks?"

I whistle in amazement.

"That's what he told me," she says. "He didn't exactly say how, but I believe him. Somehow, he ended up working for You-Know-Who. Never went back. Never had to."

"And his folks never came and found him?"

"It's a big world. They probably think he's somewhere in DC. Or maybe they just think he's dead."

"Shit," I say. "What would make a kid do something like that? Were his folks the all-hands-and-no-hugs type? Did they do something to him?"

"I don't think so," she says. "I think life back home did."

I imagine Dylan back in DC. A fresh-faced kid with dreams of grabbing the world by the wrist and leading it into the future. I imagine his parents: A pair of parent-shaped shadows, looking down at Dylan as he sits on the living room floor, playing with toys or watching the tube. There's Christmas. There's a birthday. There's laughter and a dream of good things. Then he's gone, and those two parent-shaped shadows are searching, crying, screaming. They're on television, begging for help. They offer cash. "Anything to get our son back," they say, even though they don't know for a fact that he's been taken. They imagine him killed by drunk drivers, killed by cops, killed by a classmate. They imagine him lying in a shallow grave, eaten by worms. They imagine centipedes burrowing into the hollow of his skull. Their imagining keeps them up at night blaming one another. Then, one day, they're placing a Dylan-shaped casket into the ground. Inside the casket is just photographs and the last pieces of hope that hurt too much to hold on to.

"What would make a kid do something like that?" I ask.

"I don't know," Kelly says.

"Maybe, right now, while he's underwater, he's back home with his folks. Maybe each time he drifts away, they're there, trying to convince him to stay. Trying to convince him that he's not alone in this world. And maybe this time they finally nailed their pitch. Maybe they finally talked him into staying."

"Or maybe he's just a kid who needs help," she says.

"You ever stop to think about how long exactly this song will keep playing? How long before we have to leave and get pulled back into everything out there beyond the fence?"

"That's a tomorrow problem," she says.

"Yeah," I say. Then: "I think I'm gonna go check on The Kid."

It's The Goon's turn to sit with Dylan, so he's there when I get there. Nothing's changed. The Goon is sitting on the far side of the room, reading Lovecraft. He smiles when he sees me.

"This has been the best," The Goon says. He leans back in his chair, with all of his heavy muscle giving the antique chair beneath him fits. "We should all just stay here for years. Dylan too. I think maybe he just needed to catch his breath. So he did. And it made all of us slow down and catch our breaths. No reason we can't just stay here forever. The boss wouldn't mind. He said that you can live wherever you want, just so long as it's not in America. So why not here with all of us?"

"What about Rhode Island?" I ask. "I thought you were gonna make a go of high-fiving Lovecraft's tombstone—or something along those lines."

The Goon blushes. "I don't think I'd belong there, my friend."

"Why not?"

"Can I ask you a question?"

"My brain door's always open," I say.

"Are you afraid of America?" The Goon asks. "I mean, does us living there ever just make your blood run cold some nights?"

But before I can answer, there's a gentle *thumpthumpthumpthu—* that catches our ears. It's like the sound of mice dancing a two-step over a cotton blanket. The Goon and I both look over to find out the source of the sound and there, for all the world to see, are Dylan's fingers twitching against those high-dollar, ivory-colored bedsheets of his. The Goon and I watch in silence as the fingers on Dylan beat out a quirky rhythm.

"What's that?" The Goon asks.

All I can do is shrug—even as Dylan's hand turns over, palm up, and the fingers keep right on twitching.

"Seizure maybe?" I don't really mean it, but it's the best thing I can come up with.

"Should we call somebody?"

But it's around then that I start to understand the play. He's not having a seizure. That hand of his goes from thumping out some rhythm to twisting around into a rectangular shape perfectly fit for a phone. It's his thumb that's doing all the movement. And when I look over at his left hand, that thumb is filling in the gaps too, texting away a million words per second.

That's when Dylan, the dead man, the kid in perpetual limbo, finally says it: ". . . M . . . Mom." His voice is flat as shoe leather, like the sound you'd hear on an old recording. ". . . Mom!" The kid says it again, and it gains a little steam until, after a few more misfires, with his eyes still shut and his hands still texting the air, he finally belts one out hard and thunderous: "Mom! . . . Mom!!!"

All of a sudden, he's screaming.

The Goon and I freeze.

"Oh god, Mom! He's coming for me! I can hear shooting! He's coming for me! Mom! Dad! Dad!!"

"Jaysus," The Goon says.

Dylan's arm twitches. His fingers are moving a thousand miles a second. He keeps talking: "Mom! Mom! I'm scared! There was a fight yesterday. One of the boys who got beat up came back with a gun. He's shooting! We're locked in the classroom! God! Mom! I love you! I love you, Mom! Please! I love you!"

"Wake him up!" The Goon says. "We gotta wake him up!"

I'm already there. I'm shaking The Kid, jostling him like a bag of concrete, but it's not doing any good. He's screaming and typing in midair in the palms of his hands. Sending out what he thinks are his final words. His last chance to tell somebody he loves them: "Mom! I'm so fucking scared! Tell Dad I love him! Tell Dad I'm sorry. Tell Dad I'm just a smart-ass because I'm scared of everything all the time. I'm sorry! I'm sorry! I'm sorry!"

"Kid!" I scream.

And just like that, he's awake.

He stands on the stage and begins:

Picture her mother: Short. Medium complexion. Former high school athlete turned mid-twenties grade-school teacher. She's smart. When she was the age of most of her students, she'd skipped two grades in a single year based on her reading scores and impressive strength with numbers and a general unwillingness to be talked down to. The only weakness that ever gave her grief, over her whole life, was her bladder.

As the legend goes when she explains the story, she was born with the smallest bladder in the history of human existence. "A pecan with cracks in it" is how she described it to him on one of their first dates, back before their daughter ever came into the picture. Every night when she went to bed, she was a guaranteed yo-yo. All night long there was the sound of her footfalls thumping on the floor. Wake up. Piss. Flush. Sleep. Wake up. Piss. Flush. Sleep. As orchestrated as a Broadway musical. I could almost set my watch to it.

From the supple days of her youth, through wifehood, and beyond, there was nothing to be done about it. Sometimes she thought the smartest thing she could do was find a way to sleep in that bathroom, if only to save herself all the time she spent hiking back and forth each night. Over a lifetime, if somebody was to pull out the abacus and add up all those little leaky trots, I bet there was miles to go before she slept. Ol' Rob Frost had nothing on her mama!

It went this way for decades. Through rain, sleet, snow, hail, marriage, and motherhood. All night every night. It was like she'd left the better parts of her life on the john and she was always in there trying to find them.

And then she came along. The year was 2003. The back side of July, to be precise.

George W. was in the White House. The towers were still freshly fallen and we were all trying to pick ourselves up. Not exactly salad days, but we got through them.

And in the middle of all this: 'Twas a balmy, humidity-bathed Carolina night when she decided it was time to vacate that fetal brownstone we all share at the start of this life. The landlord—my ex-wife, Tasha—decided our daughter had had enough time to herself. Enough time getting ready for whatever was waiting for her out here. She sent the word down the line: "Vacate immediately. Head for the nearest exit. Happy birthday!"

As for my daughter? Hell, she didn't mind it. She knew she couldn't stay there forever. Knew there was a whole word of sunlight and Star Trek *waiting for her out here. She would have been out of there in no time, if it wasn't for one little thing.*

Just imagine her there: making her way down the exit chute, happy as she pleased, and then looking over and catching sight of that little, rickety bladder of her mama's. Now, for the record, it wasn't her bladder that was the problem. But her pelvic floor. Just wasn't plumb. And my daughter, being who and what she was, immediately picked up on the fact that that floor of hers needed shoring up. The last thing she wanted to do was move out of this apartment and leave a mess for the landlord, you know?

She got to work. She wrapped her little baby mitts around whatever tools she could find and just went to repairing that thing—knowing all the while that she was on the clock. Knowing that before long the bottom was going to drop out and she'd be evicted from that ten-month lease agreement—security deposit be damned! And so, you can imagine my daughter there, working hard and fast and steady, trying to get that pelvic floor braced up. Put things right before her time ran out. Trying to fix the world before she'd even set foot in it.

Now, why she waited until the last minute for this particular job, lord only knows. But let he who has never procrastinated cast the first stone, you know?

The job took hours. One of those labors of legend. Hercules himself would have been proud. My daughter worked through storms and blizzards in there. Constant earthquakes. Everything around her trying to shove her out the front door and into this world of ours. All the while, her poor ol' mama was out here screaming and crying, fighting and cussing. Yes sir, she birthed our daughter uphill! Both ways!

Trials and tribulations!

The hours came and went like this. My wife and my daughter pushing and pulling at each other and me watching from the sidelines. Contractions shoving my daughter one way and birth canal exit alarms blaring in her ears. But she held on. She planted her feet and refused to leave on anybody's time but her own.

But just fixing her mama wasn't ever going to be enough for someone like her. No sir, no ma'am. The doctor who delivered her—a round, sweaty fellow by the name of Doctor Dennis—had been struggling with more than a few back issues for years of his life coming into all of this. Had one of those bad discs. Herniated it decades back and, ever since, he'd become something of a mythological creature.

You see, the thing was, on account of his back ol' Doc Dennis spent every day of his life taking ibuprofen and grunting every time he stood up. He couldn't sit in one position for too long, nor could he stand for too long. He was a man cursed. One of those old curses like the Greek gods used to dole out when somebody looked at them the wrong way or turned down a roll in the hay. It was a petty curse that said that Doc Dennis would never be able to find comfort for more than a few moments at a time. And so he was always shifting, always moving, always seeking comfort in some other place, in some other position.

Stand for a while. Sit for a while. Lean for a while. Twist and stretch for a while.

And all that ever happened in all that moving and stretching was that there would be a brief reprieve from the discomfort, and then the soreness would start to seep in like fog and turn to stiffness and the stiffness to pain and, just like clockwork, he'd be on the move again. Seeking out comfort in some other place. It was a brutal existence. In olden days philosophers would have written entire books about Doc Dennis's plight. "The Perpetual Motion Man," they might have called him. Barnum & Bailey would have sold tickets. But nowadays this legend, this marvel of a bygone era, just went to work.

So, there my daughter was coming down the pike. And there was Doc Dennis, being all miserable and uncomfortable like he always was. Staring down the barrel of the birth canal and chewing Advil like it was cud. He needed to stand and stretch. Needed a cigarette. But he could see her shiny little head coming at him like a slow-motion meteor, a vaginal shooting star, and he needed to be there to catch it. He stayed and groaned and watched and rubbed his back and waited, suffering the whole while.

And then: My daughter stalled. Right there at the end of the runaway. Got full-on stuck. Maybe she saw something else in that pelvic floor that needed to be fixed, so she held up a tiny little finger and told the birthing process, "Hold on a minute!" and went back to hammering and banging and sanding on whatever it was that needed to be fixed.

I can't say that's exactly what it was that kept her at the end, but I know it had to be something important.

Well, that last stop probably would have been fine and dandy under other circumstances, but by this point she was putting one hell of a strain on my wife. She was already over a day into all this and wasn't quite sure how much more she could handle. If she'd been asked about the time-consuming repairs our daughter was making to that pelvic floor of hers—if she'd known that it would cause this whole birthing to be delayed by a full thirty-six hours and that she'd have to pay for it in suffering—well, she might have just canceled the whole job and went through life getting up at all times of the night to pee. Sometimes a person just learns to live with a thing. Sometimes the cost of a repair job is too high, so she might have passed on this one if she'd been given a choice in the matter. But, well, she wasn't given a choice. Our daughter was incommunicado.

There she was, stalled at the entrance, stuck like that tanker in the Suez Canal that one time, backing up the forward progress of the whole damn capitalist world! But Doc Dennis, he knew that the state of things couldn't persist. He knew that, well, something needed to be done because her mama was at the end of her rope. One thing to remember is that everybody has an ending to their ability to hang on, to persevere, to endure. Don't let the T-shirts and posters and Live, Laugh, Love branding fool you: everybody has a breaking point.

That whole thing about how something that doesn't kill you serves only to make you stronger is one of the biggest lies ever told. Sometimes a thing happens and it breaks you, makes you weaker, and there ain't no getting back to the way it was. Sometimes it's physical. Sometimes it's mental or emotional.

Even love has been known to decimate.

And Doc Dennis—still shifting back and forth on his stool, watching that birth canal and trying to figure out why my daughter wasn't here yet—he knew that my wife was running up on that delicate point. Love or no, this couldn't go on. So he made the call.

"Take a deep breath," he told my wife. "Time to bring an end to all this."

Even though he might not have looked it, Doc Dennis was a tough old guy. And that's not to say that being tough is the way to be in this world, it's just to say that, to look at him, you wouldn't have thought that he was the type to headbutt a problem in place of talking it through. But that's what he was. He was the guy who had slammed his way past every problem he'd ever had—not counting the back thing. So that's what he was going to do now. He was going to headbutt, slam, and shove my daughter out into this world.

"Okay, kiddo," Doc Dennis said. "That's enough of that. It's time to show up to the dance."

So he got his fingers on the top of her crown—gently though, he was a good doctor after all—and he looked my wife and me in the eyes and he saw the fear and worry and pain and exhaustion there and he said, "It's gonna be alright" and he nodded—but didn't smile—and my wife nodded back and clenched her teeth and he said, "Take a deep breath" and she did and he firmed up his grip and said, "Now push when I tell you. Push harder than you've ever pushed before" and my wife tightened her grip on the bed railings and nodded firmly—she knew that this all needed to come to an end and now she and Doc Dennis were going to go for this, so this girl of hers would stop dawdling around in there and get out here and say hello— and the two of them hung there in that moment for a second before Doc Dennis barked "Push!" and BLAM! *my wife pushed and my daughter shot out like a little mahogany rocket and hit Doc Dennis square in the chest— Joe Montana couldn't have done it better!—and Doc, because he was a veteran at these things, made the catch perfectly; but he got off-balance and the stool slipped out from beneath him and he fell to the floor with a crash— still holding my newborn child in his arms. And, at the same moment, he let out a scream on account of how he landed in a bad way for his back and my wife and I, we let out screams of our own because we were afraid the Doc had landed on our showroom-fresh baby and crushed her and the nurses all let out their own little sound effects of terror and the whole thing* added up to become one of the most horrifying birth scenes any of us had ever lived through.

My daughter's birth would go on to become a story that each of them would tell in the years that followed. It was a saga they told at parties and family reunions and any time when a group of people needed a tale of life and wonder and the unbelievable. People's breath caught in their lungs and their faces went white—assuming they were of a certain genealogical background that allowed for such coloration—every time a storyteller got to the part where Doc Dennis fell to the floor on top of the baby and let out that scream of pain and the storytellers would always pause here, always drag the moment out—because that's what a good storyteller does: they keep the best parts of a story just over the horizon, because any yarn-spinner worth their salt knows that it ain't the sunrise but the split second before the sunrise that we really want to hold on to. That's the moment we keep coming back for because it's a moment where we can imagine anything and everything being possible when that sun finally does come crack up the horizon into that dazzle of colors.

Yes sir, yes ma'am, my daughter's birth made everyone in that room into better storytellers.

After the long pause, whoever was telling the story would go on to say that a long, deep silence filled the room after the scream. Everyone was motionless. Waiting. Suffering to find out what had just happened. All of them hoping that it wasn't Death that had shown up unexpectedly just now. Hoping that it wasn't Injury and Maiming that had come by either. Everyone just prayed to whatever gods would listen: "Please let the baby be okay." All eyes followed the thread of the umbilical cord down beneath Doc Dennis's motionless body.

". . . Shit!"

The word broke the silence like an AR-15. Out of nowhere Doc Dennis was on his feet again. Out of nowhere the room was filled with the wailing of a newborn. Out of nowhere Doc Dennis was laughing. And out of nowhere my wife was crying tears of joy. Out of nowhere, everything looked to be okay.

Doc Dennis handed our daughter to my wife and her eyes were slick with tears and she leaned back on the bed in a daze of exhaustion and pain and joy and fireworks lit up the heavens and Doc Dennis smiled and cut the umbilical cord and said, "I'm gonna go have a smoke. Think I tweaked my back in that fall." He left the nurses to get things squared away and went out into the hallway and then out into the parking lot and stood there in the humidity and the dark—when had it gotten dark?—and stared off at the cityscape horizon and finally lit up his cigarette and took a draw and thought he saw the beginnings of a sunrise peeking up from behind the craggy buildings and then, out of nowhere, he noticed that his back wasn't quite as uncomfortable as it normally should have been.

He didn't know it as he stood there watching the sunrise that morning, but he'd never have problems with his back again. That fall onto the floor as he caught my daughter must have shoved that bad disc of his right into line. Right back where it was supposed to be and where it would always stay until he shut his eyes and pointed his toes to the sky for the last time, decades and decades later. He was fixed. Him and my wife both. She slept all through that first night and every night thereafter for the rest of her life. All on account of our daughter.

That was her. That was my Mia: a born fixer.

And that was the problem of her whole entire existence. That's why she died. And I couldn't stop it. And I never will. And life will go on. And so will I. And so will you.

I relive it, now and again. Sometimes it'll lessen, but it'll never go away. And it'll happen again, to someone else, at another school, during another police stop, at another nightclub. And we'll all get angry. And we'll weep. And we'll scream for change. And we'll march. And we'll protest. And we'll move forward.

And then we'll get tired and we'll take our foot off the gas and we'll slide right back here, to this moment. Over and over again.

It's a type of time travel that all of us, each and every one, on this campus, in this country, are all caught in.

There should be a word for the ability to stop crying about a past pain even though it's still in you. There should be a word for living.

Yes, that's it. There should be a word for continuing to live when a part of you has died. There should be a word that sums that up. And the longer you live, the more that word should become a part of you. Because the thing of it is, every day that the person is missed feels longer and there's nothing you can do about it. Nothing you can do to share the long, beautiful days that they are not a part of.

There should be a word in the English language for admitting that the person you love is not here and, yet, you have had a good day.

There should be a word for admitting to yourself that some of the good things in life did not die with them.

There should be a word for admitting to yourself that, somehow, perhaps, you have thrived in this world even though they were not with you. There should be a word for admitting that, in spite of all tears, life does keep moving.

There should be a word for the newly bereaved and the veterans of longing. There should be a word to separate those who have not come to terms with the fact that the world has kept spinning for all these years, sunrise upon sunrise upon sunrise, and their grief has not stopped anything but themselves. There should be a word for the fact that, in the end, life is impatient and will not wait. There should be a word for raging at time.

There should be a word for hating the future. There should be a word for smiles that are taken away.

There should be a word for laughter that you will never hear again. There should be a word for the laughter that people who never met them will never hear. There should be a word for your full heart beating even when your mother is dead and your father is dead and you have gone on and laughed the night away with friends or made love unto bliss or lifted your child into the air in laughter without them ever seeing or hearing your mother or father. There should be a word for loving a child. There should be a word for grieving over decades. There should be a word for surviving.

Then it was all over and people clapped and then there was the book-signing phase and people came up and they got their books signed and then there was this Black kid—an anomaly at a school like this—and he was in line and Soot could tell that he was the type of kid who walked against the wind. He had that look about him. Something about the wardrobe, something about the gait of his step, something about the way he seemed to be trying to make himself smaller with each and every step did the job of letting Soot know that, more than anything, he didn't fit in many places in this world and, shit, that's definitely something that Soot can relate to.

"Do you really see invisible people?" the fans ask.

"Maybe," he says with a grin. Then he hands them their signed books and keeps the line moving.

So, this kid comes up to him and he hands him his book to sign, because that's his job now, and he wants to say something that'll leave a memory for this kid. Wants to say something to make up for everything that he just said a moment ago. But he's tired and all that talk brought up the vision of his dead daughter and the reminder that she will never again be with him and the thought that the land he loves doesn't love him back and the reality that, in the end, this kid grieving over the deaths of his classmates is just the way it goes now and the way it will always be—that's the hardest part, but that's the truth—and so

Soot just signs the book and offers the kid a smile and he hopes it's enough.

The kid takes the book and he offers Soot a handshake and when they're shaking hands the kid just says four little words: "Thanks for being weird."

And Soot breaks right there in front of everyone. He falls apart.

Dylan's back from the dead and, sister, you ain't never seen a good time like we had. Celebrations that rocked that little piece of Paris to the core. The night he came out of it, we ran around singing and dancing and drinking—mocktails for me!—until we were all just about as far out of the world as Dylan had been. And it didn't stop there. Just nothing but good times and high fives all around.

When we asked Dylan about what happened, all he said was that he didn't remember much of anything. We all decided to let it lie at that.

"Sorry," he kept saying.

"Nothing to apologize for" is what we all said to him in our own way.

And we left it at that. We left it at that for a whole week. I mean, whatever he ran into when he was out there in the world of his mind, that's his business. All that really mattered was that he was back and that the good times could start rolling off the assembly line again. So that's what we did: we rebuilt the Good Times Assembly Line.

Thanks to Frenchie's unlimited breadsticks of cash, we never had to leave the estate. There was nothing in this world that we couldn't get for our own. And, yeah, maybe, in the beginning, we blamed our inability to leave on the fact that Dylan was still on the mend and we were all still worried about him. We talked about the doctors and we made phone calls and we told Dylan that, above all else, what he needed to do was lie around and rest. "You gotta take your time getting back."

So that's what he did.

He took his time getting back. He spent the first couple days just lying in bed with the three of us coming and sitting in his room all day. The room had a tall pair of windows on the far eastern wall with these long velvet curtains that, each morning, the serving staff would come in when nobody was looking and open and then, all of sudden, there would just be this wall of dawn shining across the room and it would wake all of us up. We had taken to sleeping in The Kid's room even though he was back from the underground and didn't really need us there. It was a decision that we all made for ourselves. He was going to have us around him whether he wanted it or not. That's how far down the rabbit hole we were and we didn't even know it. Kelly, The Goon, and I, we'd adopted him. He was ours now. Whatever parents he'd left behind back in the ol' U.S. of A., well, they were a product of the past. Nothing to look forward to. Just something to occasionally look back on and, if we had our way, we'd be able to get him out of looking back at anything. There was only us now. We were whatever he needed.

And he took to us just like we all hoped he would. Never kicked us out. We were all together. Every minute of every day. I think that the three of us were just all so happy to have him back that we were terrified that if one of us broke the spell, if somebody dared to go in another direction and leave him alone, then it would all fall apart. We were afraid that he'd go back into wherever he'd been for all this time and never come back to us. And we couldn't let that happen.

We had a life there for that week. A real and true life. Just all of us, together, singing "Kumbaya" every night and drinking in the good times every morning. Somewhere along the way the phones started to be put down a bit more—those who still had one, anyway. Even Dylan, who was always on his phone, always on that computer of his watching

Roland Emmerich blow up the world, even he started to put down the destruction of the planet and pick up the things we were putting down. And, of course, not to be outdone, Kelly and The Goon got in on the action. It started out with them only checking their phones a handful of times throughout the day. They kept them, in separate rooms so that they had to leave the group to get them, and nobody wanted to leave the group, so the longer things went on the less and less the phones came into play.

As for me, well, my phone was nothing but a memory ever since I got here to Euroland—what with all those bad cell towers and the miscommunications not letting me call home for anything. After the phones went away, the computers went next. I mean, you gotta understand, the thing about Frenchie's mansion is that, well, it pretty much has everything you could ever want. And with me and most of the gang being book addicts of a particular sort, Frenchie's library started to become the center of our world.

Somewhere around the fourth day after Dylan's return to the world, we got stuck in the library. Not really stuck, you understand, but we decided, without ever saying the words out loud, that we'd just sorta set up shop in the middle of it and never come out again.

So that's what we did.

When the serving staff came around looking to bring us our meals, they found us on the coast of France, in some far-flung future, in the histories, and deep in science. They found us at Hogwarts and on a small, unknown island with a bunch of kids and no parents and one of the kids was named Piggy and, well, things didn't end particularly well for him. They found us in the future where books were being burned and they found us in the past where monsters had voices and wept when the sky went dark and begged to be a part of the society they both loved and hated. They found us in Troy and on Mars and in other dimensions. They found us everywhere.

They brought us blankets and pillows and meals on those same silver platters they'd set before us when we ate in the dining room proper. And then, somewhere around the fifth day, we woke up in the library and found tables had been brought in and there was breakfast waiting for us and the middle of the room had been turned into a bedroom of sorts and so, when we woke up, we all saw it and just sorta smiled and sat and ate breakfast and talked about the books we'd read the day before and the books we were planning to read today and then we did just that.

Yes ma'am, there was sugar on everything during that time. And The Kid? Well, he was only better and better with each day. When he'd first come out of the time away, he kinda had this nervousness about him. Like he was worried about something or ashamed of how he had gone down so hard and so far. But then, eventually, it went away and he was all smiles and he didn't even talk about Roland Emmerich anymore and that felt like the beginning of something that had to be pretty good. I smiled and went along with it.

The Goon blew through all the Lovecraft books the library had to offer and even the Lovecraft analysis books that were on hand and he never brought up talk of Rhode Island or America or of anything like that again. He would only say, occasionally, "I like this." And we never asked him exactly what the "this" was that he was talking about because we all knew it already and there's no need to say out loud the thing that you all know sometimes.

Kelly had a similar type of ride at Frenchie's place. She dug into the books on Egypt and the dead and on how we used to take care of the dead back in the day. Turns out Frenchie's library was just full of books that almost nobody else in the world had ever read before. Books made in the "dark ages" and kept in a part of the library that nobody outside of Frenchie's staff ever got to see. But Kelly made them all her own. She set up shop there in the middle of a bunch of books that were so old they were on rolled parchment and she wanted to hold her breath when she read them out of fear of her breathing destroying them and, sometimes, the sound of her sobbing could be heard all across the library and we never really asked her what she was crying about on account of the fact that we all knew what she was crying about without her ever having to say it.

That's just how close we all were.

Yeah, sister, it was nothing but gravy during that first week. And I drank down my fair share of it, don't you worry. I rolled in the sun every morning and bathed in the moonlight. Some days I set up shop by the window and read and looked out it and, because of how the estate was situated—with its walls surrounding the whole place—it was hard to tell there was anything or anyone out there beyond the line of sight. The only time you ever got wind of the rest of the world was when you opened the window and the sound of the Parisian traffic would come wafting in. Whirrs and chugs and beeps and screeches and a low-grade Euro clamor that just sorta hung out there and made you want to close the windows and pretend that it was never there to begin with. So that's what I did most days. I shut the windows and there was only the sound of Dylan, The Goon, and Kelly breathing and living and being happy and it was pretty good days.

The peacock came around during that time too. Came and sat out in the branches of one of Frenchie's trees on the far side of the property and it stared at me like it was trying to figure something out. And that was going along just fine until, one day, I started to see that it was losing something. Started to see that things didn't seem to be going all that well for it. It started off with just a few clumps of onyx feathers found on the ground one morning. Then, the next day, there were a few more feathers that I could make out from my window in the library.

Now, I'm no bird doctor, but I was pretty sure that whatever was causing the feathers to come out of the ol' bird wasn't a good thing for it. Not good at all. But I tried to think nothing of it. And it kept creeping in.

After we'd all been living the good life for weeks and weeks, we finally get around to having a full and proper celebration dinner. Now, if we'd been so inclined, all we had to do was pass the word to the staff here at Frenchie Estates. All we had to do was tap someone on their well-bred shoulder and give a nod and they would have read our minds better than we even could and put on the greatest party in the world. But where's the fun in that?

So we plan it ourselves. Dylan and The Goon are put in charge of all the fixin's since they're more used to Euroland and they go all in. There're meats brought in and fancy cheeses I can't pronounce and breads that I can't identify and, all the while, Kelly and I are hip deep in making the place look like a place where a party can really grow into its own. We set up shop in the back wing of the library, surrounded by all those books that we've got a lifetime to read, and we run streamers from bookcase to bookcase and up across the ceiling and over the front of paintings worth more than any of us will ever make in all our lifetimes combined. Now, I gotta say, we made it clear to the staff that this wasn't just our party, it was a party for everyone. But I don't think they knew what to do with that. When we asked to fill the library with Nic Cage votive candles—for just the one night, mind you—they gave us a look like we'd just slapped the Queen of England square on the ass. Maybe that's when they made the call . . .

All I know for sure is that, less than a day later, as I was out walking the grounds, trying to find the right place to set up the bouncy castle, I caught the scent of jasmine and exhaust wafting in the air. Then I heard a car door close and turned to find that, somehow, a small Italian car had pulled up behind me and there, standing beside the car, flanked by what looked like he might have been a carbon copy of The Goon, was none other than ▮▮▮ fucking ▮▮▮▮! . . . Ol' Frenchie himself!

"Frenchie!" I shout. "Long time no hug!" I open both my arms and slap a big hug on him while his hired goon watches—probably to make sure I don't suddenly go rogue. I wonder what it's like to live like that: to have so much money and power that you can't even trust a hug. But, someone in a movie once said: "Never feel sorry for a man who owns a plane."

Frenchie, of course, looks like a few billion bucks. He's dressed in a creamy white sweater that's somehow both softer and fluffier than any marshmallow I've ever put my hands on. His pants are some shade of green that tricks the eye into thinking it's black one second and then green the next until it makes you feel like Frenchie is some sort of forest spirit that's come to visit you. His shoes are Italian, of course, shiny enough to be seen from orbit. His hair is cropped a little shorter since the last time I saw him. I'd go into detail but I doubt any of it will make it past the boys in legal who are afraid of getting sued by Frenchie's lawyers if this story ever sees the light of day. But just take my word for it when I say that Frenchie is doing fine, just fine!

Frenchie chuckles as our hug concludes and places one hand on my face like a father staring into the eyes of a long-lost child. "You are still calling me Frenchie!" he laughs. "And I am still letting you do this."

"It's good to see you again! Did you hear about The Kid?"

"The kid?"

"Dylan."

"Ah, yes," Frenchie says. "I have heard that he is all better and that you all are having a celebration."

"Hell yeah!" I shout. For reasons I can't quite explain, it feels really good to see Frenchie again. Feels like maybe things are settling into something more expected. Feels like things are finally working out, for good, and that's a hard feeling to come by.

"I am excited for you all," Frenchie says. He starts walking in the direction of the middle of the grounds and, without him having to say a word, I jump into lockstep with him. I figure Frenchie is used to having people understand that whatever direction he's heading in, the rest of the world should go the same way. So that's what I do: I go the same way.

"So how's the world treating you these days, Frenchie?" I ask.

"I am rich," he says. "The world can only be so bad for me." He gives another little chuckle and I join in on it. "How has the world been treating you?" he asks.

I raise my hand to indicate this grand place of his where I've been staying. "It's doing me pretty square," I say with a smile.

"Good," he says. "So you're staying?"

"Staying?"

"Yes. It seems that you have taken me up on my offer. You are going to live here now, yes?"

I stop walking and, thankfully, Frenchie does too. Somehow, I'd forgotten about his offer, if only for a moment.

"This is your life now," Frenchie says. "Here."

"You mean I can have this mansion?"

"Perhaps," he says, as if thinking over loaning out his lawn mower. "You can stay here if you would like. And if you would like to stay somewhere else, I will arrange that as well. It is totally up to you."

I think about the last few weeks. I think about Kelly and The Goon and Dylan. I think about the place we've made here. I think about how far away the world feels. I think about the way, for maybe the first time in my life, the pit of my gut ain't locked up in its usual worries: worries about money, worries about crowds, worries about saying the wrong thing to someone, worries about gunshots ringing out when all I want to do is dance, worries about Remus, worries about the things I might be leaving behind for whoever it was that might come next in this world. It's all been gone since I've been here.

It turns out peace can be just as enticing as any bourbon bottle.

"But I can't go back home . . . right, Frenchie?"

"I was worried you had forgotten that."

"Nah," I say. "Can't forget a punch line like that."

We stand there, Frenchie and I—and his backup goon by the car, still waiting—and the wind blows and the sky rolls over and, off in the distance, I think I hear Dylan speaking in Foreign to somebody and I hear what sounds like laughter and, also off in the distance, all of Paris goes quiet and, with it, the whole world. It all just fades away and it reminds me of standing on that rooftop with Sharon back in the ol' Big Apple, staring out together, with her telling me everything was waiting for me, with her telling me everything was going to be different, and me feeling that sense that there was something grand and timeless on the horizon, turning over, awakening from its slumber.

That feeling comes back to me just now. Of being where I'm not wanted and where things never are right. And all of a sudden, I know what that feeling is and I know how to get away from it. All I have to do is walk away . . . walk away by saying "Yes."

"Sure thing," I say softly.

"Yes?" Frenchie asks. "You are saying yes to my offer?"

"Yeah," I say, and I offer a handshake and he grabs it and squeezes with both hands and smiles as wide as a sunrise and he claps me on the back and, all the while, I'm just standing there, repeating the word over and over and over again: "Yeah . . . yeah . . . yeah . . . yeah . . ."

When the handshaking and hugging all ends, Frenchie claps me on the back one last time and promises to get all the paperwork drawn up by tomorrow. His backup goon opens the car door and ushers him in and Frenchie says a bunch of other stuff about how happy he is to have someone like me to tell him about all the things that America once was and never will be again and how I'd just made a decision that would change my whole world forever . . . but all I hear is my own voice inside my head, still repeating: ". . . yeah . . . yeah . . . yeah . . ."

Even though I'm a writer, even I forget that sometimes, all it takes is a single word to change a life. And, sometimes, that life might even be your own.

The rest of the night is a blur. The party goes off as planned. Just the four of us blowing off steam. I don't have it in me to tell them that I agreed to Frenchie's deal. I hold that for myself for just a little while longer. I simply eat, drink, and be merry for tomorrow The Big Score finally shows up. It's glorious and I think I can feel the rest of all of our lives hanging out right here in front of us as we dance and shout and scream in the bowels of that library, among all those books and all those self-made worlds and all the glory we never have to leave again and all the horror we never have to go out and meet again.

"This has been great," The Goon says at one point.

"Purely the tops," I say. I raise a nonalcoholic glass. They all join in and we clink and drink.

"Thanks for staying around," Dylan says.

"You don't know the half," I say, coy with laughter.

Somewhere along the way, sometime after dinner, when the world is quiet enough that we can all step outside and take a walk under the moonlight and not be particularly worried about the rest of the world, somewhere out there we all come to the decision that this is going to be the place where we decide to stay. Or, rather, it's not that we all decide to stay, it's just that we all decide to not leave. I think that's kinda how most of us wind up in places. We don't wake up every morning and say to ourselves, "This is where I'm going to stay for the rest of my life." No ma'am. I think what happens is that we just wake up one day and we stay there. We live out our lives and we go to work and we visit the people that we know and we just stay there that whole day until sundown and then the next morning we do it all again. You do that enough and, before long, a whole life has come and gone and there you are, still where you were.

But maybe this time it ain't all bad.

And I guess that's probably why Remus has to come along the way he does.

The sun had just set—all lights and bedazzlement—and dinner was on the stove—pots bubbling and burping, walls of whitish-gray steam making an inverted waterfall as they climbed the sloped ceiling of the small house while the chilly autumn air came in through the cracked window over the sink and ruffled the curtain and brought with it the scent of the fallen sycamore leaves from the backyard—and, since last night he'd been the one on cooking duty, tonight he got to play the game with their daughter.

He walked slowly through the house, his socked feet muffling the sound of his footfalls but doing nothing to cover the sound of his wife singing Alicia Keys in the kitchen with more of the Alicia than of the keys. "Beautiful, honey," he called back over his shoulder.

"You've never heard a voice this beautiful," she sang.

"Double-check that adjective."

"You know an adjective I like? Jerk."

He ignored her to keep from laughing and returned to the task at hand, moving toward their daughter's bedroom. "I have a question for you," he said in an even voice, listening between each syllable. Laughter was her natural state of being. It was just a matter of time before he heard her. "Where do fruits go on vacation?" he said.

He waited.

"Pear-is."

Then he chuckled because, thanks to fatherhood, he was starting to like his own jokes. But, still, he didn't hear her. "Tough crowd."

He rolled up his sleeves as if he were about to change the spark plugs on an old Ford and moved from the hallway into her bedroom. Standing just inside the doorway, he crouched, looking around the room. Posters hung on the walls and there were a five-year-old's toys strewn about and an unfinished castle of Legos waiting for an invading army to come and capture the queen. "Did I ever tell you about how I don't trust trees? . . . They seem kinda shady."

Again he waited for laughter. Again nothing.

"Okay," he said. "You're getting better."

He got down on his knees and looked under the bed and then he stuck his hand under and waved it about in the empty air beneath the bed. Still nothing.

"You want to know why invisible children can never put one over on their parents?" he called out.

"Why?" Tasha answered from the kitchen.

"You can see right through them."

As Tasha laughed, he heard a light snicker not far away.

"Aha!" he shouted. "I heard you that time!"

He stood and bolted out of her bedroom, making a big show of sliding on the hardwood floor in his socked feet. When he got to his bedroom he headed straight for the closet. It was always a preferred hiding place of children.

"Did you find her?" his wife asked, suddenly standing behind him, which made him scream louder than he expected.

"Jesus!"

And now, finally, their daughter's laughter was clear and crisp on the air. They turned. There she was, sitting in the center of their bed, a small, giggling ball, her arms wrapped around her knees, her hair a dark hourglass atop her head held in place with a red hair band, skin as dark as her father's, with his disarmingly bright smile to boot.

They'd both walked right past her, somehow.

"That was the loudest scream I've ever heard, Dad," Mia said.

"Don't laugh at your old man." He bent forward with his hand on his knees, hamming up the scare, not unlike how his father would do sometimes when he'd played this same game as a child. "My heart can't take this kind of stuff! Watch, one day you'll be a ripe old codger of thirty like myself. Then you'll know my pain!" He shook his fist in the air, like accusing the heavens of cutting him off in traffic.

"Let's go eat," Tasha said. She kissed each of them on the cheek, then took their daughter in her arms. "Dinner's ready."

"Hell yes!" he said.

"Hell yes!" their daughter repeated.

"Just remember," Tasha said to their daughter, "That's an 'inside the house' word. I don't want the school calling here because you're out there dropping the hell-bomb in front of your classmates."

"Hell no!" Mia said. Then: "So you really couldn't see me? Neither of you?"

"Nope," he said. "You fooled us all."

"It never works at school."

"No?"

"Hell no."

"Okay, let's throttle back on the language, you two," Tasha said.

They were in the kitchen now. They took their seats at the table and started eating. Everything was as good as it always had been and always would be in this moment.

"Can I ask you something?" Soot asks.

"Sure," Mia replies.

"Do you get sad some days? Really, really sad?"

She thinks. "Yeah," she says.

"Is it because you're afraid?"

"Maybe."

"What can I do differently? What can I do to fix it?"

"I don't know that you can."

All of a sudden, she's not a little kid anymore. She's sixteen. Dressed in that beautiful dress that he found her dead in. And she's looking at him with those eyes that he will not see anymore.

"I don't think I can save you," he says.

"If it's already happened, then you can't."

"I don't know how to live with that."

"You don't get to choose."

"Can't we just stay here? Now? In this time?"

She's a child again. Years and years away from the gun.

"No," she says. She's sixteen again. Dressed in that dress again. "You can't fix the world," she says. "You can't fix time. People like us, we feel it too much. We want to fix too much. And, sometimes, it just swallows us up."

"People like us?" he says. He is in Minnesota. He is in Bolton. In France, in Italy, in Toronto. He is everywhere he's been and will be.

"Of course. Why else do you think you're writing this?"

Once we got started, we danced for days. Partying in every corner of the mansion with Dylan apologizing every step of the way like it was somehow his fault. Two and a half months. That's how long it turns out he'd been under. And in all that time, the world kept spinning, kept abusing itself, and none of us knew anything about it. We really and truly were away from it all. So that's when we decided we could just stay here, just like The Goon said. Never leave. Just hang here on this Other Continent of our own creation. Turns out that, somewhere along the way, we'd created our own Shangri-La for the melanin-rich. Yeah, it took a billionaire to bankroll it, but ain't that always the way it goes?

Either way, there's nothing but good things on the horizon for us. Nothing but life with a real soft touch. Nothing to do with life but crack open the milk and dig out the honey.

I'm on cloud ten!

I go off into my room, getting away from everyone because I've got the best story idea I ever had buzzing around in my head. The story of a group of people who finally made it. A group that made a world all their own, and lived there happily ever after. This is it. And at what cost?

Just to write something for a billionaire every now and then? Not a bad price to pay, I suppose.

I'm just about back to my room to dive into the page and bang out that story, taking a shortcut through one of the small, almost-kitchen areas, when I hear that whistle. Loud and reverberating. But I already know whose lips put that note out there.

"That you?" I ask.

"It is," a voice says, deep and hard. And then, just like that, there's Remus. In the flesh.

"You had to know that this was coming," Remus says, taking a seat at the far side of the table. "You had to know I'd keep good on my promise."

"Which promise was that?" I ask. I'd ask how he got in here, but I don't think it matters.

He chuckles. "Listen, there's no need to make this any more sinister than it has to be. I've got a job to do. That's all. That's the only reason I'm here."

"To kill me?"

"Yeah," he says brightly. "But don't go thinking about it like it's all that bad. Happens to the best of us, you know? It's one of the few things in the world that we can all depend on."

"That's fair enough," I ask. "But do I get an explanation?"

"An explanation?" he says, and rubs his chin with that dark, scarred hand of his. "You mean why you, or why am I doing this?"

"Why not both?" I ask, and offer a chuckle of my own.

I'm playing it cooler than I thought I would. I've still got the heater tucked inside my coat, nice and quiet. I can feel it now. Feel it more than I ever could before. I feel every ounce of it and you know what? It feels like safety. Feels like maybe these things came along at the right time for the right moment. Like maybe they're not all bad.

"I don't really do explanations," he says. "At least, not on the regular. Did I ever tell you about the college girl I once loved?"

"I don't think you did, but I'm not sure now is the ti—"

He holds up one finger and quiets me. He reaches behind his back and brings out that knife of his—the one I got so familiar with back in Italy. "Let me tell you a story," he says. "Promise it'll be a good one and promise it won't take a second longer than it needs to."

Because I'm a sucker for a good story, and because I know I've got the trump card tucked into my jacket, well, I just let him get on with his story. Hell, what can it hurt?

"Somebody told me one time: 'Don't try to make simple that which was never meant to be simplified.' Ha! Somebody told me that once and I swear to god I thought they were a goddamned poet. Figured they was one of those big-brained thinkers come down from one of those fat Ivy Leagues to mingle with the slum trash like myself. But, nope, turns out she was just a college student who sometimes sang on the weekends. She'd come up from Georgia—I was in Toronto on this particular adventure—and she did summers in Georgia and winters in Toronto. I told her she had that ass-backwards. Who the hell chooses to spend a winter in Toronto?

"If you ain't never been, it's a hell of a city. Don't ever mistake that. But it just ain't the type of latitude you want to be in once the winter months come knocking. The wind comes 'round up there like something you can't believe. It's got big yellow teeth and claws that'll slice you in half if you so much as step foot outside your door from October to March. You take to living underground like a mole. And they got the whole city set up for it. Big underground tunnels and whatnot. Aboveground tunnels that look like veins tying everything together. All of this just so you don't have to step out into that hell that is winter.

"Yessir, it's a scurrying type of life that I never could get used to. And, at this particular time, I'd just come up from Phoenix. About as far opposite as a body can get and my blood was still as thin as nun's lie. Hadn't yet got glued together into that molasses that those Toronto folks got.

"On another note, while I'm taking this long way of defending myself here, I just want it to be said that being a nigger in Toronto ain't so bad. I been a nigger in all kinds of places at all kinds of times. And, pound for pound, being a nigger in Toronto wasn't too far from easy street. For the most part, you just go along with your life.

"But, okay, I'm getting too far from where I want to be and this knife of mine, well, I don't like to keep it out here in the open like this. Got locked up one time before for brandishing a knife and I never forgot it. It's like there's a timer on how long you carry a knife out in the open and what you do with it before you get qualified as 'brandishing.' Ain't that something? It's like a secret code that takes it from 'having' to 'brandishing.'

"Haha! I'm sorry. Back to the college girl.

"Now don't you worry! We didn't do nothing untoward. I ain't that kind of man and this ain't that kind of story. In spite of what you might have heard, every man in this world ain't trying to get inside the jeans of every woman. Just most men, if I'm honest about it.

"So all winter long I froze my ass off working construction during the day and by night I made my way out through those tunnels like the mole person I was and every single night I went to that bar and I sat there and I listened to that college girl from Georgia sing. She wasn't half bad, but the truth is that I never came for the singing. No sir. I came for what followed after the singing.

"As soon as she would get done she would come off that stage and everybody would shake her hand and tell her how good she sung and then they'd ask to buy her a drink or they'd ask her to dance or they'd ask her to come back to their apartment with them or whatever, but every time she just said no and she came over to the back corner of the joint where I was sitting in anticipation and sipping the cheapest whiskey I could get.

"Then the real fun would begin.

"'Remus,' she'd say, 'I wait all day to talk to you. You're a riot. You're a force of nature. An ontological riddle.' That's what she'd say. Every single time. Each and every time like it was programmed into her and she couldn't not say it. It became this kind of magical spell between her and me. Like my brain just started working different when she came around and said those things. I'd try to sound about a thousand points smarter than I was and, sometimes, just for a moment or two, I'd do it.

"A big part of our talks was me telling stories. She couldn't get enough of them. Hell, I'm sure you noticed by now that I like nothing better than the sound of my own voice. I figured out a long time ago that my brain didn't have thoughts. It had whole, goddamned paragraphs or else it didn't have anything at all. And she liked that about me, that college girl, she'd sit there and I'd tell her all these stories about where I'd been and where I'd lived and what I'd been arrested for and what it was like being a nigger in Memphis or a nigger in Brazil or a nigger in Toledo. Like I said, I done been a nigger just about everywhere. I know all the flavors and spices of it.

"I'd tell her all my stories and she would kick back in her chair and laugh and say 'Remus! You're the living dream of Modernism!' And even though I didn't have no idea what the hell it meant I'd laugh with her because, hell, everybody likes being called a dream, even if the dream is something unknown.

"It went this way all winter and it was about to come to an end and we had our one last night where she sang her songs and came over like always and she told me those words she always told me and then, for no reason at all, we had nothing to say to one another. We both just sat there and I swear I could hear her heart beating—even over the gibberish and noise of the rest of the bar—the same way you can hear a river in the distance even over the clamor of a whole goddamned city. That's what she was to me: she was a whole goddamned city and now I was about to leave that city and the two of us just sat there and I wanted to tell her stories about my father, because she always liked those, and I wanted to tell her stories about my mother, because I always liked those, and I wanted to hear her talk about Kant and Schopenhauer—or whatever his name was—and all those other dead White men who I didn't really know nothing about but I knew they were big just because she knew all about them.

"We just sat there. And I heard her for the final time and I kept wishing that something would change the world from the way it was. And it never did. And time didn't stop neither. And just when I thought nothing in the whole world was going to change, then she decided to change everything.

"She reached into her purse—same one she had carried with her every single day since I met her—and she pulls out a knife. Nothing big. Nothing fancy. Nothing scary. Just a regular old jackknife like a thousand granddaddies done give away to a thousand grandkids when he ain't have nothing else to give 'em. Seems like that's all them old men ever gave anybody: a fistful of knives to carry, over and over again, like that was the way to make it in the world. My granddaddy gave me one back when I was a boy. Then he got killed in a gambling fight in Mississippi. I hear they never found the body. Mama used to say that even though he never got buried and prayed over the right way, we ain't have nothing to worry about because she'd prayed him into heaven. If you believe that sort of thing.

"There I am sitting with this college girl and there's that knife on the table between us and she starts telling me how she'd been carrying it with her every day since she was seven. Every single day. Never went anywhere without that old lump of steel on her. Said it was a part of her, like a third hand. Said she didn't feel right if it wasn't on her. And when I asked her why she said because that's just the way the world was. Said the world had always been like that—full of knives or the consequences—and there wasn't nothing anybody could do about it.

"I told her I never carried a knife a day in my life. I showed her my fists and I said there wasn't nothing in this world that couldn't be put down with a good pair of hands, and she said, 'Of course you'd think that, Remus.' She laughed the laugh that she always held back special for when she'd just called me 'a holdover of Modernism.' To this day I still don't know what she meant. But I started carrying this here knife on me because she was the type of person who, I knew, knew things about the world and how it worked that I could never know because my mind couldn't never work like hers even if I wanted it to.

"Then she was gone and I never heard her sing again and I haven't been a Toronto nigger again ever since.

"I know this ain't making much sense. But it's the way I am. I take the long way 'round.

"Now, you're probably wondering about what comes next. Probably still got a few questions about this knife in my hand and what I'm going to do with it. The way I figure it, you got two options, the only two options any of us ever have at moments like this, when somebody's about to get both barrels of what the universe has coming for them: look away, or turn your chin toward the fist." Then he leans back in his chair and sighs, long and heavy. "Okay," he says then. "You can go ahead and pull that piece you got tucked under your shoulder."

"And you still came here?"

"I couldn't not come," he says. "Now go ahead and pull it."

Finally, just like in the movies, I reach for the gun. But, maybe it was because the moment had finally come, the quick draw turns into a fumble and, for an instant, the gun is both in the air and in my hand and neither. An instant later it clatters to the floor.

Remus chuckles. "Pick it up," he says. "Let's get this over with."

I pick up the heater. But it feels cold now.

"Loaded?" he asks.

I blink, suddenly not sure. And because I can tell that he'll wait, I check the chamber.

"Loaded," I say.

"Now," he says. "Are you gonna squeeze one off with me sitting here or are you gonna make me come for you?"

"Wha—"

Before the syllables hit the air he's halfway across the table, eyes wide and filled with rage, those scarred, black hands coming for me just like in all the dreams I've had of him.

Then the gun goes off.

It's the loudest sound I've ever heard.

Like the whole room exploded.

Then his hand is on the gun and the gun is out of my hands and he's got one of those big arms of his around my shoulder and that's when I see the bullet hole in the delicate French glass of the windowpane in the door behind him. And that's when I see Dylan on the other side of it. He's standing on the other side of the door, his eyes wide with surprise.

And that's when he falls.

"I'm sorry," Remus breathes in my ear. His voice shakes, like he might be crying. I can't see because I can't take my eyes off of the kid. "This was always going to happen," Remus continues. "But, lordy lord, I'm sorry. Running away wasn't never gonna fix it. You know that much, don't you? We brought it with us, don't you see? You. Me. Even him. You can't unbake the cake. None of us can. We brought it all with us—people like us, I mean."

Then he places the gun on the table and turns and heads for the door.

Then comes the screaming and the crying. Then The Goon is there, on his phone, calling for the Frenchie paramedics. Then Kelly is there, begging to know what happened, crying, holding Dylan's hand as his body dances this somber dance on the marble floor—his feet writhe, the heels of his shoes squeaking with each involuntary two-step. His eyes are still wide, staring up at the ceiling, blinking, hard and fast as his lungs push and pull, making one of the most horrible sounds I've ever heard. And since I don't know what to do to make any of it stop, I just stand there, flat-footed, staring down at it, trying to understand where it all went wrong, trying to retrace all the steps, trying to figure out the fix, and all I can think to do is run. All I can think to do is escape, just like in the movies, just like in the old black-and-whites where the gun goes off and the body falls and there's nothing left to do but disappear for the sake of survival.

So I give it a shot. I snatch up the gun and bolt through the door—with Kelly and The Goon screaming after me. I don't stop. I run—with all that Pennsylvania steel and death clutched in my fist—through two-thousand-year-old Parisian streets. I run away from now. I run through history. And all the while the kid is still dying. All the while Dylan's little macabre mambo gets a little slower and his lungs fill up with just a little more blood and I know, above all else, he's looking for me. I know he's calling for me. I know he's begging for me to do something, to change time and history, to rewrite it all. He's saying to me: "Tell it all a different way. Make it all turn out better. Write away the blood. Write away the bullet. Write away the death." He's saying to me: "That's what people like you do." He's saying to me: "I don't want to die."

He's calling for that mama and papa of his. He's thinking about all the others who have caught the bad end of a barrel. He's thinking about all the days he won't get to have anymore. But above all else, he's thinking about how some things just can't be undone.

I run. I run. I run.

I run until my breath gives up. I'm somewhere in the European night—the only American on the planet, it seems—and I'm standing atop a cobblestone bridge heaving and wiping my tears and there, right below me, is the Seine. Its surface glimmers with reflected starlight.

Constellations pinpricked into the inky surface of the water. As I look down, losing myself in it, I see the gun, still in my hand.

It would have all been different if the gun had never come along.

But it did come along, and it's like Remus said: You can't unbake the cake. You can't be un-American. You can't wash it away . . . But maybe you can let it go.

I step up onto the edge of the bridge. In the distance, there's the low din of Paris traffic. Car tires slide over the pavement in light applause. There's laughter somewhere. Music. I'd lay out even money that, right now, some people are kissing, making love, a child is being born. The sound of it rises in my ears and I struggle to keep my balance against the railing of the bridge, as I stare down into that inky black water.

I hold the gun out in front of me.

. . . You can't wash it away, but maybe you can let it go.

So I do just that.

I close my eyes.

I open my hand.

I let the gun go.

I exhale. Finally, after all these years, maybe even after a lifetime, I exhale. The day I knew would come finally has. The ideation, the wait . . . they're both over.

And when I open my eyes . . . the gun is still there, floating, hung in midair like a steel question mark, not falling into the river, not sinking into the murky depths. No. The gun is only there, waiting. Even after I've let it go, everything is still there.

At least now I know. At least now I can stop wondering, I can stop waiting. Finally, after all these years, the gun—which was always there, always in the stitches of my red, white, and blue life—now hangs in the chilly Parisian air, floating impossibly, in defiance of all the laws of the universe.

. . .

. . .

. . .

. . . And, still, the gun hangs in the air, and no amount of letting go or running away will make it fall.

Meanwhile, elsewhere in Euroland . . .

The biggest thing I've never told anyone is about the time when I was fourteen that I almost killed myself. Snuck into my parents' bedroom one evening while they were hanging out at my uncle's. Grabbed my daddy's quail shotgun—heavy bastard—and took a seat on the edge of my bed. I loaded it. Placed it across my lap—the blue-black steel pressing down like a whole mountain on my thighs. Then I just sorta stared at it for what felt like hours. Just stared and thought. Stared and thought and waited for . . . something, until I heard the rumble of my father's pickup truck turning off the highway and onto our dirt road.

Out where I lived—back then, in that place and time that doesn't exist anymore—it was so quiet at night that, if you paid attention, you could hear your daddy's truck at a half mile. You could separate it from every other vehicle on the road. The low growl. The rhythmic lope of the motor that wouldn't start some days in winter and wouldn't start some days in summer. You could hear it over the cicadas buzzing, the crickets trilling, the owls hooting, the grapes growing, the lone hunting dog running rogue off in the woods, chasing deer long after his owner had given up calling for him to come back home.

A half mile of dirt road is plenty of time to pop the shell out of the shotgun, put everything back where it came from, and pretend to be asleep when your parents come into the house.

A handful of years later—what was I? Twenty-two? Twenty-four?— I'm sitting on the edge of my bed staring up in the direction of the top of my closet where I keep my brand-new Heckler & Koch. Forty-five caliber. First handgun I ever owned. I lusted after it for a full three years before I ever bought it. Did years of research. Stared at pictures. Argued over AOL message boards about whether or not it was worth the price. Read stories about how a pricier version of it was the one the Navy SEALs carried.

Good enough for SEALs? Good enough for my Black ass.

Like I said, it went this way for years before I finally pulled the trigger—metaphorically speaking. And literally speaking too, I guess. Every time I got the money up for it, I let something else get in the way. I told myself I was waiting for it to go on sale—which I knew it never would. I told myself I was waiting for ammunition to come down in price—which I knew it often did. I told myself I was waiting until I had more in my savings. Just in case my car's engine finally blew or I was sued by someone at Walmart for ringing up their groceries wrong. I kept putting it off and pretending I didn't know the real reason, until I finally stopped putting it off.

"What do you want a handgun for?" my girlfriend at the time asked me on the day I brought it home.

"Just in case," I told her.

"Just in case what?"

Even though she never said so, I think she knew, better than I did, why I wanted the gun.

Fast-forward two decades or so and I'm at the height of my career. Less than two days off a plane from Paris. Nearly three whole weeks zipping around Europe on somebody else's dime. Finally, and for the first time in my life: The star of the show. No longer the one waiting and hoping and doubting, but finally anointed. Finally bona fide. Got the bronze hardware to prove it.

A goddamned National Book Award.

Finally wrote something that, one evening in Minnesota, after reading to a crowd full of professors and lecturers still mourning the deaths of their students—students who died so recently that they haven't even been buried yet—a dark-skinned sophomore comes up to me and shakes my hand and says, "Thanks for being weird, my nigga" and I nearly fall apart crying right there in front of everyone.

Finally *said* something.

Finally got my hands on all the things that I've spent my life chasing.

This time the gun is in the bedside table. First my parents' closet. Then the top of my closet. Now bedside. Just an arm's length away.

It's still that same German-made .45 from twenty years ago.

The clinical term for it is ideation.

It's some fancy job I bought online—the table, not the ideation. Paid more for it than I did for my first couch. Money's easier to come by these days than it once was. Still not effortless—let's just say Stephen King and I do not travel in the same circles—but definitely easier.

The nightstand came from some boutique furniture builder in Switzerland. They had a website full of old, gray-haired European men standing in a valley of reclaimed wood—the eco-friendliness was part of the sales pitch. The website showed the men crafting tables and desks by hand. Their brows lightly baptized by sweat. Specs of sawdust dancing in midair in color-corrected snapshots. The website promised "generational craftsmen."

I'm not even sure what that means, but I know it adds to the price.

There's a six-month waiting list when I finally decide to pull the trigger and make the order. Nine months later, it shows up at my door.

Looks just as good in person as it did in HD. There's a note inside—handwritten, no less—from a man named Jans who says that he personally built this little nightstand for me. He says he hopes I enjoy it. He says, "I appreciate you."

It's the kind of thing that sounds like a translation error. But who knows? Maybe he actually does appreciate me. Either way, it's this overpriced nightstand that now holds that same Heckler & Koch from all those years ago. It's still loaded. It's still waiting. Patient as ever.

It's strange how international a suicide can be if you give it enough effort. Nightstand from Switzerland. Gun from Germany. Bullets from Kentucky.

All my girlfriend knows is that I've just come back from Europe and I keep bringing up the idea of moving there. I talk about the croissants. I talk about the pasta. I talk about hearing cars backfire and realizing that ". . . over there, it's just a car!" I talk about the beauty, the Velvet Bubble, of not knowing what anyone is saying. I talk about not having to decipher niceties. I talk about not having subtext. I talk about not having to read between the lines because you literally can't read. I talk about words as nothing more than sounds hung on pins in the air.

I tell her we should pack up our friends and move. I call it the Other Continent. When she asks me what that means I say, "I don't know, but it's accurate." I tell her that, with enough planning, we could all make it happen. Each of us. Everyone we care about. Her family. My family. All our friends. I tell her we should just get everyone together one night—invite them all down to my little double-wide trailer at the back end of this dirt road where all my family's graves are—and lay out a five-year plan. "We'd only have to live through one more election. Maybe two. We can get out before it all blows up." I talk about Republicans and Democrats. I talk about cops. I talk about abortion bans. I talk about book bans. I talk about the Statue of Liberty. I talk about the Constitution. I talk about Columbine. I talk about Selma, Alabama. I talk about Trayvon Martin. I talk about George Floyd. I talk about cycles. I talk about the next time it happens. I talk about temporary outrage. I talk about student loans. I talk about medical debt. I talk about presidents who "Grab 'em by the pussy." I talk about truck nuts. I talk about all the things I've already talked about.

She sleeps through it all.

I speak softly so that I don't wake her.

I speak so softly, that I never actually say any of this aloud to her. I only imagine, like usual.

Ideation.

As she sleeps, maybe I tell her about my uncle who killed himself when I was twelve. Not a blood uncle, but a chosen uncle. My father's best friend. We used to play horseshoes in his driveway next to a cornfield and eat blue crabs steeped in Old Bay that he cooked under the overhang of his tractor shed. He would promise to drink my first beer with me when I was old enough and, if my father was there, he would hand me his beer just so my father could swat it away and the three of us would laugh at how well we'd all played our parts yet again. On those horseshoe-throwing evenings, babe, when the sun got low enough my uncle and my father and all of their friends would park their pickup trucks on opposite ends of the horseshoe stakes and turn on their headlights and those U-shaped chunks of metal would fly through the air and *clank* against the stakes until the moon rose and the night got too long for the kids and my cousins and I fell asleep in the beds of our fathers' trucks.

It was the best time of my life. I wish you could have been there with me, somehow. Just to see it. Just to see who *I* was back then. That version of me, he hadn't gotten the news yet. Rodney King hadn't taken that drive yet. Bill Cosby was still Bill Cosby. It was truly *A Different World*.

That version of me, he hadn't come home yet and found his daddy sobbing in front of his CB radio because his best friend in this whole world—his son's favorite uncle—went out to the garage, where he kept those beers he always promised to one day drink with me, took out his hunting rifle and put the butt of it on the concrete floor and aimed the barrel at his head and reached down and pulled the trigger.

"Why did he do it?" I asked my daddy.

"I don't know," he sobbed.

That version of me from back then, he'd never seen his daddy cry. Never knew that, once he saw it, he'd never be able to forget it.

Looking back on it now, I still don't know why my uncle did it. Maybe he saw Columbine coming. Maybe he'd seen the way niggas were being put into jail. Maybe he knew the sea levels were on the way up. Maybe he, with his high school education and a little bit of imagining, saw AI coming for us all. Maybe he was already on social media before it was ever invented. Maybe he doomscrolled before any of us and felt the same way we did. Maybe he stared at his iPhone—all the way back in 1990—and read about Standing Rock and the Dakota Access Pipeline and the Pulse nightclub and January 6. Maybe he'd seen it all coming from the time when he was a boy—decades and decades and decades before it ever showed up. A time traveler. Maybe the whole world had been haunting him for as far back as he could remember. Maybe his therapist diagnosed him with "hyperempathy." Maybe she told him, "You can't fix everyone. And you damned sure can't fix the world." And maybe every day of his life he lived with that. He lived with the need to fix the world churning in his belly, weighing him down, keeping him tethered to this earth when, in some other life, if that ball of grief wasn't there, he'd literally be able to fly. Maybe each day he struggled with wishing the world was one way, but waking up, again and again, to see it be a different way. Maybe he thought about leaving this place. Going to some Other Continent where he'd be surrounded by all the friends who understood. All the people who felt too much or who were afraid, every day. All the people who loved, and suffered for loving. All the people who just wanted to love who they loved in public the same way they loved in private.

Maybe that old uncle of mine saw it all but never saw the way out. Maybe he never found a way to reconcile his place in America with his place in the universe. Maybe he never saw a student try to explain, through a poem, how afraid they are of living under the gun. Maybe he never found his art. Maybe he never found the words. Maybe he told all his stories to no one.

Maybe he was just like that girl, out there in the middle of that verdant field, among those grape trellises. Maybe, somewhere, he is a she and that's okay. Maybe, somewhere, she doesn't pull the trigger. Maybe, one day, months after I'd won The Big One and done the whole tour thing again, I was in Paris at Festival America and it was my last day and, in a hotel elevator, I ran into this dark-skinned American girl, barely sixteen, and she said to me, nervously: "Are you American? And . . . are you ▮▮▮▮ ▮▮▮▮ ?"

And maybe I answered straight for once. Maybe I didn't claim I was Coates or Whitehead or Laymon or Kendi or Jones Jr. or all those others who I am not now and who I will never be, no matter how much people like us get mistaken for one another. Maybe I was a version of me that didn't go to bookstores and sign my name on the title page of other authors' books for kicks. Maybe I wasn't just some face that hides my own name because, deep down inside, I've always been afraid of people and, at the same time, always worried about people. Maybe deep down inside I've always been afraid of America and, at the same time, always worried about America. Always African. Always American. Always neither. And, somehow, even at two hundred pounds and a fistful of accolades and a bank account that's happy enough and a pistol in my bedside nightstand and a purple belt in jiujitsu and staring down the barrel of fifty, I still feel safest when I'm completely invisible. Unseen by anyone. Alone, so that I don't have to fit anywhere because I'm always terrified that, one day, I'll realize again that I don't fit anywhere. And I never have. Maybe I've always felt most like myself when I'm wearing someone else's name. Or, better yet, wearing no name at all.

Maybe, this time, I stopped hiding.

Maybe I turned off the invisibility switch.

Maybe, for once, I just said, terrified, but willing: "Um . . . yeah. I'm Jason Mott."

And maybe, a little while later, as we sat under the sun at this croissant bar on the Seine, after she finished telling me how much she liked my books and how she hoped, one day, to be a writer and tell stories of her own, maybe her face went dark and sad and she told me, completely unprovoked: "My parents and I are going back to America soon and I don't want to go. I'm terrified. I'm going to die at school one day. I know it. I dream about it every night. I'm scared all the time. I think about killing myself. It would take away the fear. The dreams. But I'm scared of that too." And then she cried. And then maybe, just maybe, I patted her on the shoulder. Maybe, for reasons I couldn't understand, I wept with her. And maybe I did understand why I cried with her. Maybe the reason was because I know those dreams of hers. I've lived my whole life running from them.

So maybe then we both sobbed on the edge of the Seine for almost an hour, all the while being stared at by worried and confused Frenchies who asked, in Foreign, questions we couldn't understand. Maybe, for once, we were both afraid together—both finally willing to admit it out loud—and that made us feel a little less afraid. And then maybe she and I started laughing all of a sudden because, somehow, even though we couldn't put it to words, we knew we weren't alone. Right there in the middle of a country where we fit but didn't fit, where we were just the loud Americans, where we went or were even invited, but nobody understood us and maybe even didn't want us, we'd found it.

We'd touched our toes on the shore of that Other Continent.

And then maybe we both cried again, but it had a different lilt to it. There was joy underneath it. And then maybe we both laughed and laughed and laughed without explanation, standing outside long into the Euroland night. When it was over, I said to her, this poor girl who reminded me of someone I used to know, "Sister, let me tell you: I've seen the back side of hurricanes. I've seen birds fight off bears and I've seen the northern lights dance a soft-shoe over Tuscaloosa. Seen a man get tossed into the air by an eighteen-wheeler and walk off laughing. I've seen an alpaca riding shotgun in a Toyota Camry in the middle of Atlanta. I've seen forty-year-old bare breasts dangled out of a Burger King drive-through window and given over to the dappled sunlight on an Easter Sunday. I knew a woman who sneezed every time she orgasmed. I've shook hands with a Black president and watched *Fury Road* in the same afternoon.

"I've seen rockets break orbit! . . . So let me tell you a story, kid. A story about a family, a story about a gun, because that's what all American stories are and, in spite of ourselves, that's what we'll always be. A story with sea monsters and snail cars. A story with just enough lies to make sense of the truth. It won't fix things, this story of mine. No story ever has. But, sometimes, the right fistful of words can be a help to people like us."

"'People like us'?" she asked.

ACKNOWLEDGMENTS

As always, a special thanks to the family and friends—shoutout to The Cage Match Crew—who have been helping me find the words for more years than I probably deserve. Sincere thanks to all the new people who have entered and impacted my life over the course of this novel, particularly Kate (for understanding and love), Victor (my profiterole hookup and Euroland informant), Mateo (for use of his name and permission to remix facts), and Robert Jones Jr. (who scratched parts of this out my head when I was ailing).

Some research for this novel was made possible thanks to a grant from the National Endowment for the Arts, for which I am incredibly grateful.

Thanks to my wonderful agent, Michelle, who has believed in me for more than a decade and to whom I am perpetually grateful. Thanks to my editor, John, for cleaning up all the strange, misshapen objects I bring him after years of digging around in the mud.

An embarrassingly deep thanks to my readers—with a special shoutout to that one woman who called me her Taylor Swift. I have no idea how to repay any of you for the gift of your readership. I hope this book helps in any and every way that it might.